The Christmas Tree of Doom!, The Tannenbaum Terror, Jolly with a Pistol, The Final Gift, Vault of the Dark Burgeoning God, The Teeth of Winter, and Dillon and the Night of the Krampus are Copyright © 2014 by their respective authors.

ISBN-13: 978-0692332054
ISBN: 0692332057

PulpWork Press, New York.

PulpWork
Christmas Special

2014

A Word from the Publisher:

The fact that you're reading this annual effort from PulpWork Press indicates that you have survived yet another year of turmoil and hardship. However, before you get too terribly excited about this accomplishment, you might take some time to ponder all the poor souls that succumb to the holiday pressure and stresses, and suffer sad demises during the Christmas season.

Herein, you'll find a septet of holiday tales in which the poor characters come to grisly, gory, and sometimes gruesome ends. Pay close attention, and learn from their fates, so that you might not make the same mistakes as they.

You may find it safer to eschew the holiday tradition of the Christmas tree, for at least two stories in the coming pages warn of coniferous killers of the most sinister variety.

Just when you're getting comfortable with the idea of deadly flora, Josh Reynolds and Joel Jenkins turn things topsy turvy by swapping characters. Jenkins tries his hand at a tale of the British Royal Occultist, Charles St. Cyprian and his intrepid and sometimes bloodthirsty apprentice Ebe Gallowglass—both characters created by Reynolds.

Not to be outdone, Josh Reynolds borrows Jenkins' Native American gunfighter, Lone Crow, and teams him up with St. Cyprian and Gallowglass as they hunt down a wendigo in the Canadian wilds.

You'll also find masterful and unnerving Christmas tales by Robert Mancebo and Thomas Deja. Then Derrick Ferguson treats us to a full-blown novella, in which the global instigator, known only as Dillon, takes on the evil entity called the Krampus. Don't know what the Krampus is? Why the Krampus is drawn from one of the most malign Christmas legends ever recited to frightened, shivering children. I suggest you read on!

Trebor Drahow
PulpWork Press, Editor in Chief
PulpWork.com

The Christmas Tree of Doom!

By Russ Anderson, Jr.

To start with, the Christmas tree was nearly eight feet tall.

By the time Tommy's dad had finished propping it up in the also-massive tree stand, it scraped the living room ceiling. Huffing and puffing, Dad asked for the pitcher of water Tommy had been holding, and then he got down on his knees and reached beneath the pine to pour the water into the base. The pine's branches were tied up, lashed tightly to its trunk, and for a moment, Tommy had a vision of the tree toppling and smashing his father against the hardwood like a falling redwood squishing an unwary lumberjack.

But it didn't happen. "You want to stand back for this part," Dad said, standing up and handing the pitcher back to Tommy. He drew a pocket-knife out of the front of his shirt and cut the twine. The branches sprang free like they'd been on springs. Dad laughed, ignoring the pummeling he was receiving, and pulled the loose twine out of the liberated branches.

"What do you think?" he said, turning to Tommy with a grin.

The tree looked monstrous to Tommy. It was like a giant, looming creature with dozens of prickly arms, squatting in the corner and swallowing the light in their spacious living room. It almost completely blocked the picture window that looked out across the front lawn.

"I like our old one better," Tommy finally said.

Dad's face fell a little bit at that. "Well, you'll get used to it," he said, shrugging. He took a deep breath through his nose. "Smell that pine! Isn't that better than that dusty old thing we've been using?"

The 'dusty old thing' in question was a six foot artificial tree that Tommy's parents had been pulling out every winter since some time before he was born. It was currently taken apart and folded up and shoved into a box in the hall closet, destined for the local Goodwill.

Tommy's mom entered the room, carrying a tray loaded with egg nogs for the three of them, and pulled up short. "Oh my!" she said. "It's bigger than it looked on top of the car."

"We used to have real trees like this every year when I was a kid," Dad said, taking his drink off the tray. "The whole family would go out and pick one, and then we'd cut it down, tie it up, throw it on top of the station wagon, and bring it home."

Tommy didn't like the wistful tone in his father's voice, suggesting that all that unnecessary labor was about to become part of their own family's annual Christmas traditions. He'd successfully dodged the bullet this year, since dad had just decided that he wanted a real tree a couple of days ago. Tommy's Boy Scout troop had their final campout of the year this weekend, and Tommy had only returned from that trip half an hour ago—dropped off in front of his house just in time to see Dad's Volvo struggling into the driveway with this monster on its back.

Mom had gone along with it, but now that she was seeing the behemoth in her living room, she seemed to be having second thoughts. "Isn't it a fire hazard?"

Dad waved that off. "As long as we keep the stand full of water and don't decorate it with lit candles, it'll be fine," he insisted. He took another deep breath. "Man, I never realized how much I missed that smell! It really feels like Christmas now."

Tommy didn't agree. He'd been a Scout for two years, and he'd been going fishing with his dad since he was four years old, so it wasn't like he was averse to the outdoors or anything. But he thought the pine was overpowering, filling his nostrils, completely overwhelming every other scent in the house (including his own, which was not inconsiderable after a weekend in the woods).

Dad took a drink of his egg nog and wrinkled his nose. "Whoops, I got yours, Tommy. Sorry, buddy." He handed the paper cup over to his son and took one of the remaining cups. These were the grown-up nogs, the ones with a healthy splash of rum in them. Mom set the tray down and took up her own cup, tapping it against Dad's before drinking.

"I hope we have enough decorations for it," she said.

Tommy's cat, Priscilla, sauntered into the room from the hallway. Tommy crouched to pet her, but the cat noticed the tree first, and literally leapt away from it. She slipped on the hardwood, scrabbling until she found purchase on the rug that sat between the couch and the television. When she was steady again, she glared at the tree, her tail puffed out like the world's biggest pipe cleaner and her back arched. She darted past them into the kitchen.

Mom and Dad were laughing, but Tommy just stared after Priscilla. He'd had that cat as long as he could remember, and he knew that hadn't been surprise at something new being in her space, as his parents apparently thought. That had been sheer feline terror.

Tommy looked at his parents. He wanted to say something, wanted to tell them that he didn't want this monster tree, that he wanted their old tree back. But he couldn't explain why he felt this way. Was it because it was big? Was it because it smelled? He couldn't explain, and he knew he would have to if his parents were going to take him seriously. So he just kept his mouth shut instead.

"Come on, buddy," Dad said, handing his cup to Mom and turning Tommy toward the hallway. "Let's go dig out the decorations and see how much tree we can cover."

***

As it turned out, they had enough to cover quite a bit. It meant they had to hang some ornaments that hadn't seen any action in quite a few seasons, but that was actually sort of nice. There was the little teddy bear in a wagon, holding a sign that said "Tommy's 1st Christmas"; there was the clear, crystal White House ornament Tommy's grandparents had sent them when they'd spent a few weeks in Washington, D.C. almost a decade ago; there was the tiny piano that had once played recorded music, but now was silent—just another pretty plastic bauble to hang from the branches.

Tommy didn't like getting too close to the tree, preferring to stand at arm's length as much as possible as he hung his share of the ornaments. His parents, on the other hand, waded in with abandon, even Mom. His parents had to first lean over the tree and then shimmy into it in order to reach the higher branches. Each of them had one or two more spiked egg nogs, and they were both clumsy and giggly by the end of it.

"We're gonna need the ladder to put the star on," Dad said, his hands on his hips as he eyed the distant peak of the tree.

"Tomorrow," Mom said with a sigh. "I think that's a good night's work."

She took Dad's hand and leaned against him, nuzzling his shoulder with her cheek. She always got affectionate when she'd been drinking, and Tommy realized that it was time for him to go. Romance was in the air.

"Good night," he said without preamble, and moved past them into the kitchen. His parents were too busy staring into each other's eyes to reply.

He hadn't seen Priscilla leave the kitchen while they'd been decorating, and sure enough, she was still in there, lounging drowsily on top of the kitchen island.

"Bad kitty," Tommy admonished, scooping the cat up. "Mom would kill you if she found you up there. Then where would I be? Huh? Huh?"

Priscilla purred and rubbed her head against his chest… but tensed when she realized Tommy was taking her back toward the living room. As the huge Christmas tree came into view, her claws extended, sinking through the thin material of Tommy's shirt and into his forearms. She wasn't hurting him, but he gave the tree a wide berth for her sake anyway, muttering another good night to his oblivious parents as he passed. Priscilla relaxed as soon as they were on their way up the stairs.

Tommy was tired from his camping trip, and the egg nog had made him feel bloated and too heavy. He knew he was dirty and probably smelly, and that he definitely needed a shower, but he just couldn't bring himself to expend the energy tonight. He dropped Priscilla on the top step, leaving her to find her way to his room, while he paused in the bathroom long enough to brush his teeth. That single allowance to hygiene taken care of, he went to his room, changed, and collapsed face-first onto his bed. A moment later, Priscilla curled up beside him and started purring contentedly.

Tommy's bedroom was directly above the living room. As he lay in bed, he heard his parents' voices softly from below. Then he heard them turn on the stereo. Christmas music drifted up softly through the floorboards, singing Tommy to sleep.

***

He woke up in the middle of the night to the sound of scratching. His first thought was that Priscilla was sharpening her claws on his bed frame again, but as he came more awake, he realized that the sound was wrong for that. It was coming from underneath his bed.

Tommy clicked on the bedside lamp and looked down at the floor. His room was on the second story and at the front of the house, directly above the living room. And the scratching… it wasn't just beneath the bed, it was beneath the floor itself.

It sounded like something was scratching at the living room ceiling below his room.

Tommy's mouth went dry, his heart raced. He looked around and found Priscilla staring sleepily at him. She didn't seem bothered by the scratching, only by the fact that he was moving so much.

Tommy flopped back into bed and pulled the covers up to his chin, staring wide-eyed at the ceiling and wishing the noise would stop. It didn't though. His eyes flicked to Priscilla, and amazingly, the cat was sound asleep again.

Looking at her like that, he was suddenly mad at himself. He was twelve years old—he wasn't some little kid. And he was a Scout! Was he really this terrified of a tree? He flipped the blankets off, eliciting a startled yowl from Priscilla, and got out of bed.

The hallway was black as pitch as Tommy crept out of his room. The door to his parents' room was cracked, and he poked his head in to make sure they were in there. They were, both of them snoring soundly.

Some of Tommy's bravado evaporated at the sight of his sleeping parents—he'd hoped the scratching he'd heard had been his dad trying to get the star on top of that stupid tree in the middle of the night—but at least he couldn't hear it anymore, and that left him with enough courage to reach the switch at the top of the stairs. He flipped it on, dousing the stairs and the house's entry foyer in light.

Staying on the top step, he leaned over and craned his neck. From here, he could just see the entryway to the living room. The lights were out in there, of course, but he could sort of make out the silhouette of the Christmas tree against the window it was blocking. It didn't appear to be moving.

"Hello?" he said into the silence. Nothing replied. There was no more scratching, no telltale movement or sound from the living room.

He wasn't going down there. Nothing could have made him do so. But maybe if he went back to his room and got his flashlight, he could shine it into the living room from the stairs, get a better look at what was—

His parents' bedroom door creaked open, and Tommy very nearly screamed.

It was just Mom though, standing there in her pajamas with bleary eyes and an unhappy expression on her face.

"Tommy," she said. "What are you doing?"

"I thought I..." He started to say heard a noise, but stopped himself. Something was scratching at the living room ceiling? Seriously? Is that what he was going to say to her?

It occurred to Tommy, standing there in the reason-enhancing glare of his mother's displeasure, that he might have dreamed it. He was beat from the camping trip, and a little wigged out by the tree. Wasn't it possible, that when he thought he was awake and hearing that scratching, he might have actually been asleep? Wasn't that more likely than the alternative?

"Bathroom," he said finally. "Just going to the bathroom."

"And you need to turn on all the lights and shout down the stairs for that?" Before he could answer, she shook her head and waved a hand. "Forget it. I don't care. Please just go to bed, honey."

He nodded. "Okay, sorry mom. I love you."

"Love you too, kiddo," she said sleepily, and disappeared back into her room. This time she shut the door all the way.

Tommy turned and ducked into the bathroom. He didn't have to pee at all, but he waited about thirty seconds, and then flushed the toilet. He crept back out onto the landing and took one more look down the stairs. When he'd convinced himself (sort of) that nothing was going to come rushing out of that darkness at him, he flipped off the light and hurried back to his room.

Priscilla had rearranged herself on the blanket. Tommy slipped beneath the covers again and lay there for a moment. Then, with a sigh, he reached over and flipped off his bedside light.

Immediately, the scratching started again.

Tommy lay in bed, eyes wide, too terrified to go investigate again or even to move. Beside him, Priscilla was already asleep.

***

Eventually, the scratching must have stopped, or Tommy must have grown too exhausted to be terrified by it, because the next thing he knew, he was waking up to an explosion of sunlight across his face. It had snowed last night, and the glare of the sun across the newly fallen powder made the light coming through his window excruciating. He groaned and put his hand up to protect his eyes. He could just make out Mom standing at his window, pushing the drapes the rest of the way open.

"School," she said, patting his feet through the blankets as she walked past his bed. "And you need to take a shower, kiddo. Up and at 'em."

Tommy rubbed his eyes and got out of bed. Priscilla wasn't in the room, but that wasn't unusual. She usually woke up before the sun and wandered the house for awhile before the humans got up.

Tommy took his shower and got dressed without entirely waking up. He remembered the sounds he'd heard last night, but that all seemed dream-like now, and it faded in clarity and importance the more he woke up.

The tree was just as enormous as he remembered, and its top branch was indeed scraping the ceiling—Dad would need to cut it if he wanted to mount the star there—but with bright sunlight framing it through the picture window, it no longer seemed dangerous. It just looked like the world's most unnecessarily large Christmas tree.

Tommy thought it did look different this morning, though, and it wasn't just the fact that the sun was pouring through its branches now. He stood in front of it, munching thoughtfully on a bowl of cereal, while in the kitchen, his parents spoke in low voices in deference to their hangovers.

School was uneventful. Things were winding down for the year, and Tommy spent most of the day reminiscing with his Scout buddies about the camping trip they'd taken that weekend and trading stories about what they were going to do over Christmas break. He got through his day without giving the tree much thought at all. That was, until the bus dropped him off and the first thing he saw was the monstrosity filling the front window.

Inside, he tossed his backpack into the corner of the foyer and shucked his winter coat. He walked right past the tree, noting that a few wrapped presents had materialized beneath it while he'd been at school, and went into the kitchen, where he helped himself to a banana. After some careful consideration of the vast array of options available to him, he decided to spend his afternoon sitting in front of the television, and he was heading back out to the living room to make that happen when he paused.

Priscilla's food and water bowls were in their usual spot at one end of the kitchen island. And they didn't look like they'd been touched since he left that morning.

It was possible that Mom had fed the cat while Tommy was at school, but the amount of food and water wasn't what had drawn his attention. He was pretty sure the food piled in Priscilla's bowl had looked exactly the same this morning, the hills and valleys of tiny dry nuggets in that exact configuration. He couldn't be totally sure, of course—he hadn't been expecting a test—but he was pretty sure.

Even at her age, Priscilla ate like a mountain lion. She should have finished that bowl before Tommy got home.

Tommy crossed the living room, calling for his cat. She didn't respond, and a feeling of dread began to creep up his throat from his stomach as he searched first the ground floor, and then the second floor. She wasn't in any of her usual haunts, nor in any of her unusual haunts. Tommy went and got the key for the basement out of the garage and searched down there too, but the cat was nowhere to be found.

By the time Mom got home half an hour later, Tommy was frantic. Together, they went through the entire house again, and then put their coats back on and went outside to search the yard. But there was no sign of her.

"There aren't even any tracks in the snow," Mom said. "She must still be inside."

They searched the entire house a third time, but the result was no different. Dad got home as they were finishing, and he did yet another circuit, even going so far as to check the crawlspace above the second floor.

"She didn't get out," Mom said. "I'm sure of it."

"She's probably just hiding for some reason," Dad said. "I'll bet she shows up in your bed tonight, buddy."

Tommy might have believed them if it wasn't for Priscilla's food and water bowls. Tommy spent the remainder of the day and evening looking for her, retracing his steps, pulling out furniture and appliances, pressing his ears to the walls. But the cat was simply gone.

He didn't have much of an appetite that night as he sat at the table, picking at his dinner. He tried to smile and nod at his parents' encouragements, and their progressively less likely theories about what could have happened to Priscilla. But even Mom and Dad didn't believe the things they were saying, judging by the despairing looks they shared when they thought Tommy wasn't looking. The thing that nobody had said aloud yet, but that they all knew, was that Priscilla was ten years old. On the off-chance that she had gone off looking for an adventure, she wouldn't have stayed gone so long if she could have helped it. She was too used to being fed and cuddled and kept warm at night.

When Tommy couldn't bear it anymore, he pushed away from the table and got up. "I'm gonna go lay down," he said. "She always sleeps with me. Maybe she'll show up if she knows I'm in bed."

Dad nodded and patted his shoulder. Mom put out her arms, and he went around the table to give her a half-hearted hug. Neither of his parents had any further words of encouragement for him as he left the kitchen.

As he was passing through the living room, his eyes fell on the Christmas tree again—it was hard to not look at it, since it took up so much of the room—and he stopped to consider it. The presents he'd noticed that afternoon were still there, and they were probably all for him, but he had absolutely zero interest in them at that moment. There was something about the tree, something he'd sort of noticed this morning, but now…

Was it bigger?

That wasn't possible. Of course it wasn't possible. But… it seemed to be covering more of the window, it looked like its tippity-top was pressing more firmly against the living room ceiling. There was more tree visible between the ornaments, he was sure of it, as if the tree had subtly expanded.

Tommy leaned closer, being very careful not to actually touch the tree, but studying it. There were new ornaments on it that he didn't recognize. Had they been there all day? It was hard to say—he'd been sort of preoccupied since he got home from school—but he didn't think they had been. They were plain red balls, about the size of his fist, unusually dark and dull against the sparkly plastic and glass of the rest of the ornaments. He counted and found there were three of them, scattered randomly across the tree.

They looked funny—strange somehow—and he couldn't investigate without getting a lot closer than he wanted to.

He found a ballpoint pen on the table beside the couch. Then, returning to the tree, he leaned over and poked at the nearest of the new ornaments.

The red color sloshed, and Tommy realized with horror that the ornament wasn't red at all. It was filled with something red, something liquid and thick.

He dropped the pen, and it was swallowed by the lower branches of the tree. He stepped back, and the step turned into a stumble. He fell back against the back of the couch.

Priscilla always got up in the early hours and came downstairs to get something to eat. It was why Tommy hadn't worried about her when she hadn't been in bed with him that morning. She would have had to cross the living room to get to her bowls, when everyone else in the house was asleep. She might have tried to give the tree a wide berth, but it was so big...

And now she was gone, but the tree was still here, and bigger—he was sure of that now. And how much blood would a housecat have anyway? Enough to fill three ball ornaments on a Christmas tree, maybe?

Tommy heard screaming. He thought the sound was coming from the tree, the hateful tree, but then his parents came running into the room, panicked looks on their faces, and he realized that the sound was coming out of him.

***

Later, Tommy lay in his room, the covers drawn up to his neck and his eyes on the ceiling. He was concentrating on remaining very still. He could hear his heart thumping in his chest and feel the gentle pulse of it inside his throat and ears. Occasionally, he would hear his parents talking in hushed voices and the rustle of movement downstairs.

He heard Mom coming up the stairs and across the landing long before she got there. She knocked, pushed the door open, and peered in.

"Hey," she said.

"Hey," Tommy replied.

"Feeling better?"

He shrugged. Mom stepped into the room and sat down beside him on the bed, touching the back of her hand to his forehead. It was something she always did when he wasn't feeling well or he was upset. She probably didn't even realize she was doing it, but it infuriated Tommy. He wasn't sick!

"Do you want to talk about it?" she asked.

Tommy looked away from her. Earlier, in the midst of terror and confusion, he had told his parents exactly what he was thinking: "The Christmas tree ate Priscilla!" But it was clear that they didn't believe him by the fact that they had been more concerned with calming him down than removing the killer tree from their living room.

"I heard it scratching against the ceiling last night," he said.

"Heard what? The tree?" She looked down at his floor. "Is that why you got up and turned the light on?"

Tommy nodded. Mom sighed.

"Just… think about what you're saying, kiddo. You're saying the Christmas tree ate Priscilla, and that it's moving on its own."

He looked away from her and she brushed some hair out of his face. "Your dad really loves that tree, kiddo. It reminds him of when he was your age. If we get rid of it, that's going to kind of ruin Christmas for him, I think."

"What about the red balls?" Tommy asked. "There are three new balls on that tree, mom, and they're full of blood!"

Mom clucked her tongue. "You think they're new because you haven't seen them in years. And they're not full of blood, Tommy. For Pete's sake…"

"I don't expect you to believe me," he said. "But I'm not going near the thing. It's dangerous."

"You're not going near the Christmas tree that's going to sit in our living room for the next six weeks." She smiled gently. "You do realize the Xbox is in the living room too, right?"

He was already turned away from her, so to further illustrate that the conversation was over, Tommy squeezed his eyes shut. Mom sighed, then she leaned over and kissed his forehead.

"Sleep on it," she said. "This will all seem silly to you in the morning, and maybe Priscilla will be back by then."

Tommy wanted to scoff at that, but he was afraid it would invite further discussion, so he clamped his jaw tight and kept his eyes shut. After a moment, he heard Mom get up and leave the room, shutting the door softly behind her.

He opened his eyes. Below, he heard his father put on some Christmas music and, if he listened really carefully, he could hear both parents talking in low voices, probably about him. He wasn't quite brave enough to turn off the light, so he lay there like that, looking at the wall and feeling the absence of his cat beside him.

***

Tommy woke up, and was momentarily confused by the bedside light being on and the darkness at his window. It wasn't morning. It was the middle of the night.

He could still hear Christmas music playing from the living room. Some overdone version of Silent Night. He looked at his clock and saw that it was almost one in the morning. He got out of bed and went to his door.

The upstairs hall light was off, but he could see that all the lights downstairs were still on. Tommy went down the hall and peeked in his parents' room, the thought occurring to him that maybe, free of their child for the night, they'd gotten drunk and gone to bed without turning anything off. It had happened before… but it hadn't happened this time. Their bed was empty and unrumpled.

Tommy went to the top of the stairs and looked down. "Mom? Dad?"

Nothing. Silent Night was finished, and was immediately replaced by a jaunty rendition of O Come, Ye Merry Gentlemen. Tommy descended the stairs.

Slowly, the tree came into view, overpowering and shading from sight everything else in the room. Tommy stopped halfway down and called for his parents again, but still they didn't answer. Fear rumbled in the pit of his stomach, but he continued moving downward.

The tree was bigger again. It nearly filled the entryway between the vestibule and the living room, its limbs extending across the opening like the bristly legs of a giant spider. When Tommy had almost reached the bottom of the stairs, he saw his dad's old metal stepladder, the one he kept in the garage, set up next to the tree.

The Christmas star that went on the top of the tree every year, plastic frame adorned with colored foil and tiny bulbs, lay loose and upside down in the tree's upper branches, as if it had been dropped there.

Tommy called for his parents again, but he was becoming more and more certain that they weren't going to answer. He edged toward the entryway to the living room, straining to see around the tree without getting any closer than necessary. No one moved in the living room, and the music kept right on playing as if there was nothing wrong. Tommy could see a scattering of Christmas ornaments on the floor, as if the tree had shaken them off. Some of the more delicate ones had broken into pieces.

Tommy froze.

One side of the tree, the side that he hadn't been able to see from the stairs, was covered in the dark red ornaments he'd seen earlier. There had to be forty of them, hanging from nearly every inch of available space.

The tree twitched, the branches stretching across the entryway actually seemed to reach into the foyer at him. Tommy leapt back, slamming his back hard against the wall beneath the stairs and staring in horror.

He could see it. He knew what had happened as surely as if he'd been there. His dad had brought the ladder out of the basement with the intent of finally mounting the star. Maybe he was spurred on by his son's wild accusations, trying to illustrate that the tree was staying whether Tommy liked it or not. But the base of the tree was so wide that he wouldn't be anywhere near that top branch when he reached the top of the ladder—he would have had to lean way over to get the star up there. And then?

Maybe he'd fallen on his own. Maybe he'd been grabbed and pulled in by one of those questing branches. In any event, Dad had gone into the tree. And Tommy's mom, seeing that something was wrong, would have waded into the branches to save her husband.

When it was over, the tree would have sprouted those dull red bulbs like fruit, knocking the real ornaments to the floor in the process. But not the star. No, that stayed where Tommy's father had dropped it. The tree had no use for it, after all—it wasn't made of meat.

Tommy wanted to run. But the tree—the bloody Christmas tree. It had eaten his family. And the only thing keeping it from eating him was that Tommy had gotten wise to it a little earlier than everybody else.

He couldn't let the tree get away with it.

Keeping his back pressed to the wall that was farthest away from the living room, Tommy sidled to the front door. There was a hook on the wall there, with his father's keys hanging from it. He got them, unlocked the front door, and stepped out into the night.

It was bitterly cold, and a thin sheet of ice covered the sidewalk Tommy's mother had shoveled that afternoon. Tommy was wearing only flannel pajamas and no shoes. He used the fob on his dad's keychain to open the garage door, and then hurried across the front yard, trudging barefoot through three inches of snow. He made sure to give the big living room window a wide berth as he went. He could see the tree looming in there, its branches waving angrily and scratching at the window.

His feet were aching and starting to go numb by the time he reached the garage, but he didn't let that slow him down. There was a big plastic bucket in the corner of the garage, holding a squeegee and some wax and the other things Dad kept on hand for washing the cars. Tommy dumped everything out of it except for some old rags, then let himself through the side door of the garage and directly into the kitchen.

It sounded like a wrecking crew was working in the living room. From where he stood, Tommy could see furniture toppling and lamps knocked over as the tree flailed blindly. There was no more subtlety, no more pretending to be something it wasn't.

Tommy put it out of his mind and went to the cabinet over the sink where Mom and Dad kept the liquor. His parents liked to drink, and they kept a wide selection in the house. Tommy went through the cabinet quickly, pulling down everything that was at least 80 proof. Most of it he uncapped and dumped into the bucket, except for one almost-full bottle of Vodka, which he held in reserve. The empty bottles he tossed into the sink.

When the bucket was full, he got one more thing out of the cabinet. Then he took the bucket by the handle and very carefully carried it to the entryway between the kitchen and the living room.

The tree had stopped its flailing. The furniture next to it had been flung all around the room, some of it shattered to pieces against the walls. The ladder was laying across the floor at Tommy's feet, as if left there in a vain attempt to block Tommy's way. The picture window was cracked and the drywall next to the tree was scratched and gouged.

More of the red bulbs seemed to have bloomed across the green face of the tree, as if it was still ingesting its last meal. Though it clearly didn't have eyes, Tommy felt like he was being watched anyway. He took a step into the room, lifting the bucket in both hands, and the tree quivered, its needles rustling in… what? Warning? Fear? Tommy hoped it was fear.

"You killed my mom and dad," he said. Then, as an afterthought, "And my cat."

He waited to see if the tree would respond in any way, offer some sort of defense. It didn't, so he flung the bucket's contents across the room.

The tree spasmed as the alcohol doused it from top to bottom, its branches twisting and slapping whatever they could reach. The window at its back finished breaking, and frigid air rushed into the living room. The remaining ornaments—the real ones, anyway—were flung from its branches. Tommy took a step back, worried for just a second that the thing was actually going to topple over onto the floor.

When it didn't, he tossed the bucket aside and unscrewed the cap on the bottle of vodka he'd held in reserve. He jammed one of the car wash rags into the top, and drew the other thing he'd gotten out of the kitchen cabinet—a box of wooden matches—from the front pocket of his pajamas.

The tree continued to thrash, and then Tommy's heart stopped as it actually hopped toward him, the heavy tree stand scraping across the hardwood. It managed one more hop while Tommy stood there, frozen in equal measures of terror and wonder, but then it drew up short as the strings of Christmas lights encircling it drew tight.

That wouldn't hold the tree for long, though. Tommy struck one of the matches and held it to the rag in the vodka bottle until it caught.

"Merry Christmas," he snarled, and rolled the bottle across the living room floor.

It slipped right underneath the tree's flailing branches and jammed up against the base. The flame leapt from the rag onto the lower branches and from there the tree ignited like a torch. The branches continued to flail and the heavy stand slammed up and down until it shattered the vodka bottle, spreading even more flames across the living room floor.

It might have been wishful thinking, but as Tommy backed toward the garage door, he was sure he could hear the tree screaming—a high, animal cry pitched right at the upper limit of human hearing.

Imagined or not, the sound filled him with a cheer that was downright Christmas-y.

***

A couple of minutes later, Tommy had appropriated his dad's boots and a hunting jacket from the garage and was standing outside, watching the house burn.

He could see through the front window that the living room was completely engulfed, the hated tree a blackened skeleton in the middle of the yellow and orange flames. It tilted at an odd angle as it collapsed under its own weight. He hoped it would be awhile yet before the firetrucks showed up, and he thought there was a good chance that would be the case. Nobody was awake in their sleepy little neighborhood at this hour, and the houses were far enough apart that the fire would have to burn for some time before the light or the smell woke somebody up. The fire alarms his dad had diligently maintained throughout the house were sounding, but that was little more than a low buzz from outside.

Tommy turned and looked down his street. He didn't see anybody coming out to investigate, no bedroom lights snapping on.

He saw something else though. Something much worse. He saw a dozen houses with large picture windows in the front, just like the one on the front of his house.

And in nearly all of those windows, there was a Christmas tree.

Some of them were probably artificial, and of the ones that weren't, some of those were probably regular trees. But Tommy knew from all his years in the Scouts that, when faced with a wild carnivore, it was best to play it safe.

The wood matches were still in his pocket. He pulled them out as he started moving toward the nearest house.

About Russ Anderson, Jr.:

Russ Anderson can usually be found in the suburbs of Baltimore, where he lives with his wife and his daughters, Jasmine and Laurel. He is the editor of the HOW THE WEST WAS WEIRD series of anthologies and the author of MYTHWORLD. He really, really likes pie.

Books by Russ Anderson, Jr.

How the West was Weird 1
How the West was Weird 2
How the West was Weird 3
How the West was Weird: Campfire Tales

Mythworld
The Origin of Flight

The Tannenbaum Terror

by Dale W. Glaser

It's when the terrified screams of the crowds thronging the concourses of the Deerpoint Mall rise enough to drown out the omnipresent holiday Muzak that I know things are getting completely out of hand. Once the all-synthesizer instrumental version of Silver Bells is completely swallowed by panicked shouts and high-pitched shrieks, the thunder of feet running for the door, the chaotic crashes of storefront displays knocked to the floor and thudding of temporary kiosks overturned by the fleeing mob, it's probably too late for me to salvage much of anything. That goes not just for the mall, but for the city, the surrounding area, maybe even the world and life as we know it.

The towering Christmas tree in the center of the mall atrium is still growing. Its regenerated roots are digging deeper and deeper into the ground, forcing foundation concrete aside as they quest blindly for the underlying soil, churning the faux-marble tiles into pulverized ruin. The trunk is expanding and the branches are lengthening, having long since shaken off their decorations, which shatter against the floor below. The fiberglass props and cotton-batting snow of Santa's workshop are burning merrily thanks to errant sparks spitting from the remains of photo processing computers that were smashed to the floor. The tree grows and grows, heedless of the flames. The top branches reach the massive skylights doming the atrium, and push through with a series of smart cracks as panes of glass separate. A couple seconds later a new sound breaks through the din, a chorus of off-key chimes as all of the dislodged glass smashes against the floor.

I'm just far enough away from the Christmas tree that I'm only sprinkled with a few small flying shards of the broken skylights, and I'm the only person anywhere near the atrium. Rent-a-Santa and his seasonal helpers, moms and dads and their kids, gift-wrappers raising money for charity, mall security, and everyone else in their right mind chose the better part of valor shortly after the Christmas tree started to expand, weaving back and forth and looking as if it were about to fall over in some sensationally newsworthy accident. If only it were that simple.

The tree isn't conscious, not really, not following any agenda of its own that involves trying to hurt people. But it's being controlled, almost possessed, by something that isn't at all averse to hurting people to get what it wants. Right now the only likely candidate for getting hurt is me, one guy who didn't get much sleep last night, has maybe three or four rounds left in his gun, and is all out of ideas, naughty or nice or otherwise.

On the bright side, I have a great excuse for not finishing my gift shopping. Although if no one's left alive on Earth when Christmas dawns, it's probably a moot point.

***

The morning hadn't given me any indications of how the day would wind up, no harbingers of doom to speak of. It was a pretty typical Monday; the alarm went off, I listened to the news on the radio long enough to learn it had snowed overnight again, and I went back to sleep for a couple more hours so that by the time I walked to the office the sidewalks would be shoveled clear. Sleeping late was more typical than snow, honestly. What's the point of being a self employed PI if you can't make your own hours? I've been working as a private investigator for as long as I've known that I wasn't temperamentally well-suited for any other line of work, and that realization came to me easily and early.

At mid-morning, I hoofed it through the restored old town district toward the office with my head down. The overnight storm was long gone, the sun was bright in a half-blue sky and the thinnest spots of snow were already melting, but my eyes were on the cobblestone sidewalk because I was avoiding the holiday window displays in all the shoppes and galleries lining the street. Nothing against Christmas in all its many forms, not really, but each and every presentation of wares reminded me that I had three days until Christmas and no clue what I should buy for my mother, who was notoriously hard to shop for and just martyrish enough to tell me it was fine if I didn't get her anything, which of course meant I had to get her something heartfelt and perfect.

I scuffed my shoes free of slush on the mat outside the building's front door, crossed the lobby and hustled up the stairs to the door with the gilt painted letters spelling out KELLAN OAKES - INVESTIGATIONS across a frosted pane of glass. I let myself in and immediately made an offer to my secretary Phoebe: "I will give you double your usual Christmas bonus if you come up with the perfect gift idea for my mother by the end of the day."

"Does that mean you'd get me two separate bouquets of remaindered flowers, or just one bigger one?" she asked.

"If you want to negotiate, you better be prepared to deliver," I shot back. "Besides, I thought you liked flowers."

"Be that as it may," Phoebe said. "You have someone waiting to see you." She pointed across the reception area at a woman, whom I hadn't even noticed when I walked in, sitting quietly in the corner.

In all my time as a PI, I've never been approached by a classic femme fatale. Not once, not even close. The foot traffic through my office has been split about evenly between men and women, but when those feet happen to be wearing high heels they're never of the stiletto variety. I got overprotective mothers concerned that their sons were wasting their lives, which they usually were; distraught wives convinced that their husbands were cheating on them, which they only sometimes were—probably less than you'd think; doddering old ladies arrived at the inescapable conclusion that some shadowy cabal had poisoned their cat, which is extremely rare; women of all stripes, young and old, morbidly obese and neurotically underweight, well-off and barely-scraping-by, and one and all were the kind of women you would pass in the street and never give a second glance. No knockouts, none of them a tall stack of hotcakes slathered in sexy syrup, none of them all big bedroom eyes and pouty lips, heaving bosoms and come-hither hips. More's the pity.

Sometimes, particularly in the lean stretches between clients when the cashflow was at its lowest ebb and I was hoping for a new case to walk through the door anyway, I'd wish specifically for a voluptuous Venus in a spot of trouble, or a young widow with no one else to turn to. But the truth is, women like that always have someone else to turn to—can't turn around without bumping into someone only too happy to help turn that pout into a smile. A private dick is always a last resort, and that was something I wasn't likely to let myself forget.

Those thoughts and a few others not worth repeating floated through my mind when the woman sitting in the corner stood up and walked through my private office door, embodying the exact opposite of the pulchritudinous pin-ups of my idle fantasies. Short, for one thing, really exceptionally short, maybe four foot ten at most. Petite build, too, with no curves to speak of, only angles where her tailored blazer cut in and flared back out again at her waist. The jacket and matching skirt were holly green, with a lighter green camisole underneath. Her dark heels, sensibly chunky, brought her up to a grand total of four eleven and a half. She wore gold jewelry, earrings, a necklace, a broach on her lapel in the shape of a Christmas wreath, and carried a dark red leather purse. Her hair was a lacquered helmet of nut brown, her eyes the same shade behind round wire-rimmed glasses. She looked older, late fifties at least, but almost no wrinkles as of yet—probably stayed out of the sun or used some kind of treatment, or both. All in all she had a prim and proper vibe, like a librarian or a high school English teacher. "Mr. Oakes," she nodded to me as I walked around my desk and sat down in my chair. "Thank you for your time."

I shrugged and shook my head, a combination of 'Think Nothing Of It' and 'Please Don't Think About How Much Unoccupied time I Have To Spare'. I gestured for her to sit opposite me, the ridiculously oversized desk between us. I assumed she'd already had time to collect her thoughts in the waiting room, already had time to accept a coffee if she wanted one, since offering them to prospective clients was what I paid my receptionist for. That let me cut to the chase, "What can I do for you?"

She fixed me with a shrewd look, one that told me she appreciated my no-nonsense approach and wanted to match it in kind. "I want you to investigate an incident involving … sabotage," she began. "Recently, one of the clients of my employer was approached by someone claiming, falsely, to be affiliated with our enterprise. The imposter succeeded in making off with one of our products, intimating that there had been some sort of recall, when in fact nothing could be further from the truth, nor could it ever be true."

Her all-business demeanor was slipping a little, and I could tell she was legitimately angry over the whole business, so I tried to let her down easy. "Ma'am, sounds to me like you need a good lawyer who knows his way around a cease and desist, not a private eye. Or maybe a PR firm, get the word out to your customers that there is no recall but there's a scam being run to that effect."

"I'm afraid it's not so simple, Mr. Oakes," she answered. "At the moment I would be unable to tell an attorney to whom the cease and desist should be sent. Hence the need for your investigative skills. Also, the majority of our customer base would be difficult to reach via standard public relations methods, which are quite honestly out of the question in any case. But I believe you can deliver results quickly enough to minimize any additional fallout."

Something in the way the lady leaned on the word 'you' made me feel like she knew more about me than she was letting on. "Why me?" I tried.

"Because you, Mr. Oakes, are perhaps more likely than most to believe that my employer exists."

"All right, I'll bite," I said. "Who's your employer?"

"If you haven't already deduced that, Mr. Oakes, then perhaps I was wrong to attempt enlisting your services in the first place," she answered.

I stared at this strange little woman in her green outfit and tried to pin down her angle. She was so cultured, so well-mannered, but at the same time she carried on like she had known me for years, like she had some kind of claim on knowing me longer and better than I knew myself. She was like one of those half-crazy old aunts you only see once a year at the holidays…

It hit me like a runaway sleigh. "Santa Claus?" I scoffed. "You're trying to hire me to take a case for Santa Claus? Unreal."

"Santa Claus is very real, Mr. Oakes," she said, unperturbed by my skepticism. "He is simply not entirely human, no more than your secretary."

"Excuse me?"

"I had the pleasure of chatting at some length with Phoebe, while awaiting your arrival," the woman—or elf, I now assumed she would claim to be—informed me. "I must say it's been some time since I had the pleasure of conversation with anyone of any amount of dryad heritage. Tree spirits are scarce at the North Pole, as you can imagine."

I wanted to laugh in her face, and tell her I had no idea what a dryad heritage was supposed to be, and that Phoebe was a girl from a good family in Meeksville. But I held back, because I expected it would be wasted effort. The little woman… elf…

"Ma'am, pardon my manners, I haven't even asked your name."

"Dazbog. Ms. Dazbog," she informed me.

Ms. Dazbog wouldn't change her opinion that Phoebe was some kind of supernatural creature no matter how much I hooted and howled, I could tell by the way she spoke with conviction and held herself with rectitude. Also, she happened to be bang-on correct. Phoebe was the offspring of a human father and a wood nymph mother. For that matter, she was an old family friend, or at least acquaintance. Really, our mothers were the ones who went way back—Phoebe's mother the dryad and my mother the druid priestess.

When I dodged the family business and set myself up as a private investigator, I figured I'd enjoy being my own boss and solving problems that other people could probably handle on their own if they weren't constitutionally non-confrontational. And I did get my share of those overprotective mothers and fathers and distraught husbands and wives and lonely pensioners. But I got other clients, too. The one thing I hadn't counted on was the special recognition that would come when I hung out a shingle, got listed in the phone directories and bought some online ads, all under my real name. That Kellan Oakes would immediately be known as the son of Foltchain of the Oak, and a steady trickle of trolls and fairies and nymphs and gnomes would add to my caseload—maybe one woodland supernatural for every ten run-of-the-mill humans with run-of-the-mill problems. Never an elf until Ms. Dazbog walked through the door, but there's a first time for everything.

"All right, you know who I am, and you assume you know what I think about the things most people choose not to believe in," I said. "You and every other lonely heart catawampus, every redcap with a missing daughter who stepped on a stray sod, and every hobgoblin suspicious of what's going into the treasure-crock next door. But you're going to have to give me more than that if you expect me to believe in Santa Claus, let alone take a case for him."

"Very well," she said. "I mentioned your secretary for good reason, Mr. Oakes. Santa Claus is much like her."

"A dryad?"

"No," she shook her head, a tight back and forth barely more than an involuntary twitch. "He is half human, and half... not. His mother was a mortal daughter of Eve, while his father... to tell the truth, Mr. Oakes, no one knows what his father was, beyond being a powerful immortal. Not even Claus himself."

"That's conveniently ambiguous," I noted.

"Mr. Oakes," she steeled herself, something I could actually sense from where I sat across the desk, "Santa Claus is in many ways a mystery, and if he were not, he would cease to exist. Yet he exists as a lovely metaphor in the minds of adults and an irrefutable fact in the hearts of children, and he lives and breathes in the flesh at the North Pole. He wields potent magic, but only toward the most benevolent ends. However many mysteries comprise his state of being, please understand that I am not asking you to solve them. Nor am I asking you to proclaim them to anyone else. I simply ask you to accept that I am here on behalf of Santa Claus, and that we need your help."

"Go on."

"Santa Claus received a letter in the usual way..."

"Usual?"

"Written by a child, burned in a fireplace, so that the ashes could be carried by the north wind to his enchanted mailbox—all of which is beside the point. The letter writer was one Tommy Bellenger, age seven. Tommy made mention of one of Santa's elves waking him in the middle of the night and asking for the train Santa had given Tommy the Christmas before. Tommy surrendered the toy, and in his letter asked if Santa had determined what was wrong with it, or if he would be bringing Tommy a new one."

"But none of your fellow elves admitted to visiting young Tom," I guessed.

"Certainly not. I promise you, Mr. Oakes, if this were some kind of inside job, Santa Claus would know. No, some other creature impersonated an elf in order to obtain one of Santa's toys."

"Why would they do that?"

"For the magic inside it, of course," Ms. Dazbog snapped. For a second I was annoyed, but then I realized this was all really taking a toll on her. She was distraught over the whole situation, but she had a job to do, and she was determined to do it. She had moxie, and she wasn't done yet. "Are these questions the opening lines of your investigation, Mr. Oakes? Are you agreeing to take the case?"

"You want me to find out who or what went to Tommy Bellenger's house and swiped one of his toys. You want me to find out if it's happened anywhere else—which let's face it, it probably has, and if so, when and where. You want me to figure out what the angle is, why Santa's toys are suddenly in such demand. That's the job?"

"It is. And if you accept, I suggest you begin making investigations of your own immediately, because I have effectively exhausted my own stores of information. You know everything I know on the matter."

"Except one thing," I pointed out. "Why does Santa even need my help? What about that whole sees-you-when-you're-sleeping, knows-when-you're-awake thing? Can't he just look in his... magic snowglobe, or whatever, and see who's scamming the kids?"

Ms. Dazbog shook her head. "Santa Claus's human side is the reason why he devotes himself to the happiness of human children. But it also limits him. He can expand his awareness to encompass the actions of the boys and girls he loves, but no further. And that is how we know... how he knows... that whatever creatures are poaching the toys, they are not human. They are something else, something which occludes Santa Claus's powers of observation."

"Something supernatural."

"Something dangerous."

"Fantastic."

"All that being said, you accept the case?"

"Yeah, I do."

"Excellent. Here is an advance against your usual fee." She reached into her purse and pulled out a stack of bills, laid it on my desk. Each greenback was straight and crisp, like the kind of money you'd find in your stocking on Christmas morning. Of course.

"How do I contact you once I've got the information you're looking for?"

For the first time, she smiled. "Oh, he'll keep an eye on you, Mr. Oakes. And when you've completed your business, I'll be back."

***

Little Tommy Bellenger, age seven, lived out in the burbs. I headed for his neighborhood, knowing I needed to talk to him, to get as much info as possible on the individual who contacted him while impersonating an elf. But strange men approaching young boys often give the wrong impression, and I had no good plan for dealing with that.

I caught a lucky break once I reached the quiet street where the Bellengers lived. School was already out for Christmas break, and Tommy was playing in the front yard, building a snowman as I pulled up and parked the car in front of the neighbor's house. Inspiration struck just as I killed the engine.

I waved to the kid as I climbed out of the car, and he waved back. I popped the trunk and pulled out a box, carried it up the neighbor's driveway, and set it on their front steps. The package, a cardboard box printed to look like Christmas wrapping paper, was an old jelly-of-the-month set a well-meaning client had sent me years ago, and I had never gotten around to getting rid of. Now it made for a reasonable decoy parcel. The Gorman family would no doubt throw it away for me, assuming it was an errant delivery. When I walked back down the driveway, I got Tommy's attention. "Hey, little man, make sure no one takes that box, all right? I'm sure they'd hate for it to go missing, and I would, too. And my boss definitely would."

"Who's your boss?" Tommy asked, free of guile.

I winked at him and smiled. His brow crinkled for a second, then smoothed out in awe as his eyes went wide with understanding.

"Is it?" he stopped himself, clamping his lips shut and looked around, as if afraid that some older bullies from school would overhear us. He took a couple of steps closer to me and asked, "Did he get my letter?"

"He sure did," I said, lowering my own voice conspiratorially. I felt a twinge of guilt for leading the kid on, making him think I was one of Santa's helpers, but then I supposed in a roundabout, temporary, fee-based way, I was at that. "But Tommy? Can I ask you something, for the boss?"

"Sure!"

"When the elf came to your house… remember, what was his name?"

"He… he never told me his name," Tommy said, realizing it for the first time.

Strike one for me, but I pressed on, "That's okay, buddy. But did he say anything about going somewhere else after he left your house with the train, before he'd take it back to the North Pole?"

More confusion on Tommy's face. "He didn't leave with the train."

"Oh?"

"He said to leave it by the edge of the woods along the back of the baseball field at school. He knew about the big hollow stump. So that's where I put the train, the very next morning. Did Sa—did your boss not get it?" he asked, crestfallen.

"No, don't worry, he got it," I lied. "Just a little dinged up, was all, like it had taken a sidetrip or something. That's probably what it was."

"Is it gonna be all right?" Tommy asked. "I mean…" His gaze fell, like he knew what he was doing didn't demonstrate the best values his parents had taught him, but he couldn't help himself. "Is he going to be able to bring me a new one, still?"

"He'll bring you something just as good, or better, don't you worry," I said, hoping that was more or less true. "If you're good, that is, right?"

"Right!" he agreed. "I'm… well, mom says I'm doing my best."

"That's all any of us can do, Tommy," I told him. "Like right now I'm doing my best to figure out what happened to your train, like the boss wants me to. You know how busy the boss must be this time of year! But I forgot which elf came and asked you for it, and that makes it hard for me to track him down, doesn't it?"

"Uh huh."

I was putting on the sunniest disposition I could muster, somewhere between a preschool teacher living out a life's calling and a character from an animated fairy tale. It was mentally exhausting and made my cheeks hurt, but it seemed to be working on Tommy, so I kept it up. "Hey, maybe if you just tell me what he looked like, it'll jog my memory?"

Tommy's face clouded over again, but with something darker than mere confusion. He looked worried. "I don't… it was pretty dark in my room. It was the middle of the night. I couldn't really see him. His eyes were kind of… yellow, I think?"

"Yellow eyes, okay," I said, staying sunny.

"And he was short, I guess… I thought all elfs were short, but…" He looked at me like I should be apologizing for breaking stereotypes.

I patted my chest. "Not an elf. Just a helper. But sure, the elf you met was short. Can you remember anything else?"

"He smelled like a Christmas tree," Tommy said. "I really don't remember anything else."

"That's all right," I told him. "I'll get it sorted out, don't you worry."

But he still looked worried, fundamentally bothered. "He's...not going to come back, is he?"

So there I was, on the cusp of the so-called teachable moment with a little kid who, yeah, probably should know better than to talk to strange non-human creatures that manage to find their way into his bedroom in the dead of night. Hell, maybe he should know better than to talk to strange men who deliver packages on the neighbor's doorstep and then stop to have long chats with little boys. But instructing anyone on the finer points of withholding trust would basically mark the end of innocence, and I wasn't sure it was my place to draw that line with a seven-year-old. "I don't think he's going to come back, little man," I told Tommy. "But if...if you ever feel like anyone or anything's in your room that shouldn't be, you call out to your mom and dad, okay? Scream your head off to wake 'em up and get 'em running. And they will take care of you and protect you, 'cause that's their job. If they ask what made you scream and you can't explain, just tell them you had a bad dream. Got it?"

Tommy seemed cheered by that. I gave him a little salute, he waved and turned back to his snowman. I trudged down the driveway to my car. At its heart, what I had said was true, in that I was relatively sure his parents would take care of him as best they could. No harm in letting Tommy think, a little bit longer, that nothing could touch him under his parents' roof. There were bad things out there in the world, human and non-human, which very few people could scare off, stand up to or survive a meeting with. But Tommy didn't really need to know about those things. It wouldn't do him a hell of a lot of good if he did.

***

I drove across town to Tommy's school, Carver Elementary. I might have been stretching the truth about being Santa's helper, but I didn't need the big guy's all-seeing eyes to tell me where Tommy attended second grade. A smartphone and public records of school district zonings did the trick.

But the internet was less helpful on supernatural bestiaries, so I resorted to mentally running through possible suspects with yellow eyes and the scent of conifers about them. Plenty of creatures were known for glowing yellow eyes, but at the same time lots of supernatural beasties consider white woods, like pine, anathema, so the combination of the two threw me off. Of course there's dryads and half-dryads who don't so much work with trees as descend from and embody them, but by and large they're pretty benign; stealing Santa's magic toys didn't seem like their scene. And on top of everything else, Tommy might have been mixed-up and unreliable. I believed he had told me the truth, as much as a second-grader could grasp it but, in terms of investigative leads, that didn't amount to much. Trying to build a profile of the perp based solely on Tommy's say-so might be skipping ahead a bit.

So I parked the car and crunched across the snow-covered baseball field. I spotted the tree stump Tommy had mentioned and made for it, leaving the only set of footprints visible in the new layer that had fallen the night before. Once I reached the stump, I looked down into its hollowed center, and found it was plenty big enough to hold a good-sized toy. It was empty now, of course, and again that didn't mean much. Maybe the elf-impersonator came by for the pickup after Tommy made the dropoff, or maybe some other kid happened upon an abandoned toy, finders keepers.

I walked around the stump, in and out of the woods, looking for tracks—tracks which the sheltering canopy might have preserved even through multiple snowfalls. But the ground was a mess of rotten dead leaves and needles, scraggly yellow weeds, unmarked patches of bare earth, frozen solid. No visible signs of passage. No good reason for me to have come out this way at all. Dead ends don't get much more dead than empty tree stumps, slowly decomposing on the edge of school grounds. As I walked away from the stump, I gave it a good backwards mulekick, a parting shot of aggravation.

I stumbled over a root and sprawled to the ground, came up spitting snow and snorting ice crystals. I hadn't even seen any exposed roots when I had been walking around the stump, and as I got my feet under me and started brushing snow off my clothes, I looked back. I saw a curve of root sticking up out of the snow like a croquet hoop, which was odd enough, but nothing compared to watching the root move of its own accord, flattening back to the ground and burrowing into the frosty soil.

I went back to the stump, cautiously. I contemplated pulling my gun from its holster but severely doubted how much good shooting a stump would do me. I stepped over the root like it was a poisonous snake, but it seemed inert now. I walked all around the stump again, and didn't see any other moving parts. I looked down into the hollow center again, this time using the beam from the Maglite in my pocket to give the interior a little more scrutiny. Most of the inside was dark, eaten away by insects, the elements, and time. But a couple of spots were brighter, new growth with some pale green shoots.

Regeneration wasn't supposed to happen just like that—not to dead wood and not in the dry, cold, waning daylight at the end of December. But the signs of life were unmistakable, no matter how long I stared at them. And the longer I stared, the more I became aware of a pattern in the resurgent sprouts. They were in two rows, evenly spaced, all along one side of the trunk's interior. If you were to put a toy train inside the stump, and mark where the wheels came in contact with the dead wood, you'd have the same pattern as the growth spots.

I backed away from the stump, onto the snow-blanketed baseball field, keeping an eye out for any stray roots that might trip me up. When I was reasonably sure I was clear, I turned and ran for my car.

***

As I drove, I thought about the reasonable assumptions I could make. Someone, something or some group of things was trying to get hold of toys made in Santa's workshop in order to extract a little of the magic inside those toys. Maybe Tommy Bellenger had been the only one to write a letter to Santa mentioning it, but it was a safe bet he wasn't the only one bothered in the middle of the night by an ersatz elf. A little magic from one toy could bring parts of an old dead stump back to life. Enough magic from a whole lot of toys could… I didn't honestly know what it could do, but it would be big and bad.

I suddenly realized that, with my driving brain on automatic pilot while I went over what I knew and what I didn't, my car had been taking a direct route to my mother's house. It made a lot of sense to consult with a practicing, powerful druid about what kind of creatures would take a shot at hoarding and exploiting the wooden vessels of Santa's brand of magic. Or so I told myself, to gloss over the fact that I was essentially running to my mommy for help.

Mom lived out in the country, in a small house on a big lot with a long, unpaved driveway that connected to a barely maintained road. I eased my car up what was basically a wide hiking path, covered with snow, and killed the engine as soon as the cottage was in sight. Force of habit; Mom never cared for cars, didn't own one herself, said the exhaust fumes were poison. Maybe I could get her an electric car for Christmas, if I happened to find a spare thirty or forty grand lying around.

The house felt quiet as I mounted the front steps, and my knock on the door went unanswered. I let myself in, called out "Mom?" to no response. The air in the cottage was still.

My mother was unavailable for consultation, which limited my potential courses of action. Option one, I could attempt some self-directed research in her private library. Mom had a fair number of obscure titles on her shelves, including a handful of rarities that were worth more than my investigations practice could clear in a year. The drawback was that they were books—not all of them in English, almost none of them indexed in any easily searchable fashion. I had wanted to pick Mom's brain not only because it contained about as much information as the tomes she collected, if not more, but because a conversation with her was significantly faster than flipping through a sheaf of vellum.

Option two, I could turn around and leave and try to track down other leads. I didn't have a clear idea of what that would entail, exactly, other than cruising areas where neighborhoods abutted treelines and the nasties I was trying to ID might have set up other dropoffs for other kids to turn over their toys from Santa, then maybe canvassing areas where I found new growth on dead stumps or other signs of magic and seeing if anybody happened to notice anything out of the ordinary. That also seemed excessively difficult and time consuming, bordering on pointless.

Option three occurred to me as I stood in the entryway, trying to decide what to do. With Mom not at home, I could poke around the whole cottage and see if there was anything broken or used up that needed replacing, or any signs of recent interests Mom had taken up. None of which would get me any further along in the case, but it might give me an idea for a halfway decent Christmas gift.

I started in the kitchen, which looked the same as I remembered it from my last visit. In my opinion, almost everything needed an upgrade, from the potbellied woodburning stove Mom somehow managed to cook with, to the icebox that was literally a big zinc box with a drawer at the top filled with ice. But those fell under the same protocols as a car. Sure, I could get Mom an actual electric refrigerator, if I was also willing to spring for getting the cottage wired, and install solar panels on the roof. Otherwise, I didn't see any evidence in the kitchen that Mom had suddenly taken an interest in artisanal cheesemaking or streaming internet videos on a borrowed Wi-Fi signal or any other hobbies. I moved through the kitchen and into the dining room.

Usually the tabletop was kept clear except for a vase of flowers or an earthenware bowl of fruit, but now it looked like Mom was in the middle of some research of her own. Several books sat on the table, most with scrap paper peeking out from between pages, and a notepad where Mom would have been sitting. It looked extremely orderly, as if whatever had been going on was either unimportant enough to be undertaken in a leisurely fashion, or perhaps had been completed altogether. But I knew my own mother better than that. If she had truly been in no hurry, she would have taken the books down one at a time. If she were finished, all of the books would be back on the built-in shelves where they belonged. More than one closed book on the table was, for my mother, the equivalent of a dozen books splayed open on their spines and overlapping one another. I walked around the table to look at what she had been writing on the notepad.

Half of it was a drawing, as it turned out, a large ring with four differently shaded segments. At the border of each segment Mom had written two four-digit numbers, stacked one atop the other: 1985 and 1863 at the nine o'clock position; 1955 and 1836 at six o'clock; 1924 and 1805 at three.

Above the top of the ring were three numbers rather than two: 2015, 1895, and 17??, with 2015 circled repeatedly. Mom had been trying to track some kind of multi-year cycle and had determined that one was about to start over at the end of this year.

The bottom half of the page had a few random words and phrases jotted down: Donar, Koliada, haustoria, Eiresione, public square, dominant crown. Some of the terms rang distant bells for me, others might as well have been written in secret code. But at the bottom of the page were a few phrases I recognized well enough: Ashby Farms, Pioneer Plaza, and Deerpoint Mall. The last was circled with even more inky orbits than the year at the top of the page.

I went back to my car and started driving back toward the city. Whatever Mom had been researching, she had left in a hurry once she reached a conclusion about Deerpoint Mall, and her haste pushed me into high-speed pursuit. The odd thing was, Mom generally avoided overdeveloped commercial centers like it was her religion. Actually, as a practicing druid, it more or less was her religion. Was she truly on her way to the mall, on one of the busiest shopping days before Christmas? Was she feeling suicidal with seasonal depression?

Ashby Farms I remembered from one of the conversations Mom and I had growing up—yet another teachable moment, because with Mom everything was a teachable moment. The Ashby family ran a tree farm, including stands of Douglas firs and Scots pines with a cut-your-own Christmas tree operation—probably the biggest tree farm for hundreds of miles around. Mom had tried to impress all kinds of ideas on me about sustainable harvests, renewable resources, responsible stewardship—all her usual live-and-let-live-and-love-nature stuff. She was ultimately cool with the Ashbys' livelihood, although we never went and cut down a tree. We decorated a live tree in our backyard every year, and most of my Christmas morning memories involved standing in the cold and the snow, opening one symbolic gift at the tree, and then running back inside the house to warm my frost-bitten fingers.

Pioneer Plaza was a shopping center, older than Deerpoint Mall, but known for the Christmas tree emporium that half of its parking lot turned into every December. The Ashbys sold some trees there, but the Plaza had all kinds of trees shipped in from around the country, probably Canada too. So clearly, Mom was fixating on Christmas trees in large numbers.

Deerpoint Mall didn't track with that, though. Nobody sold trees there. Did it connect to something else Mom had scribbled down? Public square? It was public enough, and there was a central atrium that was kind of square-like, with a 90 foot Norway spruce... OK, so one giant tree, not for sale but definitely visible. Mom thought a single massive Christmas tree was of more interest than massive amounts of regular sized ones. But of interest to whom, for what?

There are very few coincidences in this world, I've learned. Santa had sent an elf to hire me to investigate an unknown supernatural creature up to... something bad. Mom had freaked out and left the cottage in a hurry because of... something bad. It might be something unrelated to the concerns of the North Pole, but in my gut I thought that was unlikely.

Tommy Bellenger had left his train in an old tree stump and the stump had started to sprout new growth. No, not just sprout, more than that, it had come back to life. Or come to a new kind of life—a more animated existence that allowed it to flex its roots right up out of the ground and trip me as I was walking away.

What if the creatures, whatever they were, had more than just Tommy's toy train to work with? What if they had enough magic to infuse something a lot bigger with even more vitality? Something like the colossal Christmas tree at Deerpoint?

Mom could move fast when she wanted to, even without a car. A ten mile hike was nothing to her, especially given the extensive forest lore that allowed her to cover ground in ways that might not be entirely beholden to rational physical laws. I, on the other hand, was limited to driving a car and deciding which traffic laws to ignore. I put the hammer down and tore along the highway towards the mall.

***

Even the handicapped spots were full in the Deerpoint parking lot, so

I simply sidled up to the curb and hopped out and ran in. Maybe, probably, my ride would end up getting towed, but I decided it was worth the risk to get to the Christmas tree as fast as possible.

I pushed through the glass doors fronting one of the anchor department stores, and moved through the tinsel-trimmed displays as quickly as I could without drawing undue attention to myself. I hadn't been to the mall in years, but I was reasonably sure that if I kept dead reckoning straight ahead, I would hit the interior entrance of the store where it met the mall concourse. Even that much proved challenging, with the mobs of people milling around bargain tables looking for last-minute guilt appeasers, and the long lines of shoppers grimly awaiting their turn at the understaffed cash registers. For a brief, terrifyingly disorienting second when the glass doors leading out to the parking lot appeared in front of me, I thought I had been turned around a full 180 degrees, until I realized that the department store had two sets of exterior doors on two different corners of the overall footprint. I got my bearings and realized I only had to work my way around the massive candy-cane colored banners flanking the perfume counter in order to get out of the department store and into the mall proper.

I found myself on the upper concourse and spied the highest boughs of the Christmas tree in the central atrium, partially obscured by the glass elevator shaft maybe a hundred yards ahead. I stared at the tree trying to ascertain if I had gotten here ahead of the bad guys, ahead of Mom, or if things were already playing out according to the agendas I still hadn't quite wrapped my head around. I stopped at the railing near the elevators and looked down into the atrium, where an ersatz winter wonderland had been constructed around the base of the tree, with plastic birches flocked with fake snow and festooned with unnaturally colored toy birds. If Mom were down there, she might be having seizures in an artificial snowbank.

Most people didn't even seem to notice the tree, not really, minding their own business and in too big a hurry for it to even register. Folks waiting in line for Santa were going nowhere fast, talking to the people they were with, or looking at their phones, or staring blankly at the ornaments and lights on the tree. Nobody looked deeply at the tree itself. Nobody but me, that is. Which is probably why, when I noticed movement deep inside the branches, near the trunk, and saw a pair of yellowish flashes that could only be inhuman eyes, nobody else in the mall reacted at all.

I didn't have a lot of time to make up my mind what to do next. I could wait and see what was going to happen, with the bad feeling down in my gut only getting worse. Or I could take preemptive action while I maintained something like the upper hand. I reached under my arm for my gun, thumbed off the safety, drew a bead on the Christmas tree. I spotted movement again, something climbing the trunk, and I squeezed off one shot, two, three.

The sound of gunfire immediately caused a certain amount of alarm in my immediate vicinity. People down in the atrium looked around to see where the noise was coming from, some of them gawking openly and not sure what they heard, others crouching down instinctively, or hugging their kids fearfully. I heard the obligatory bystander scream "Hey that guy's got a gun!" Pretty much the reaction I anticipated. I probably had less than a minute before mall security showed up, considering how they tended to beef up the manpower around the holidays.

The furtive thing hiding among the boughs of the tree managed to put the trunk between itself and my gun, which was another possibility I had expected. I waited, readying myself to aim and shoot in rapid succession as soon as I saw it flinch.

What I wasn't prepared for was the Christmas tree lashing out at the provocation of taking three slugs. Like something out of a time-lapse nature film, a branch about halfway up the tree elongated in a matter of seconds, and then broke from the script entirely. It reared back like a rattlesnake and struck at me, sending dislodged ornaments and a snapped string of lights flying. I didn't even have time to try to shoot it. The branch whipped into my side and wrapped around my waist, lifting me off my feet and slamming me into the exterior of the glass elevator. My vision went white with shooting stars and I came close to biting my tongue in half, but the branch didn't let go right away. It dragged me over the railing first.

I fell, trying awkwardly to orient myself to land on the broadest part of my back, and to keep my gun in my grip but my finger away from the trigger so it wouldn't go off on impact, all with a dizzy ringing in my skull. By the time I hit the atrium floor, knocking the breath out of my lungs and freshening up the pain cocktail in my head, more of the onlookers were screaming. At least people were starting to clear out, common sense prevailing, among even the ones who were next in line to see Santa.

I got to my feet and tried to find my original target, but now the angle was all wrong and, looking up through the tree, it was impossible to see anything along the far reaches of the trunk. And those far reaches were accelerating farther and farther away every moment, because the whole tree was growing, trunk widening, crown surging towards the skylights, more and more tentacle-like branches undulating around the main mass of the tree, shaking off frayed strands of lights like a flexing pro wrestler sheds ripped shirts.

Several of the branches closest to ground level shot out like battering rams, exploding whatever calm remained in the area. The patrons scattered as they cried out in terror, leaving inanimate objects to absorb the brunt of the tree limbs' assault. The cash register stand where photos with Santa were purchased, the computers and photographic equipment, the massive peppermint-striped speakers alternating holiday kiddie tunes with pre-recorded instructions on watching their step when they mounted the stairs to Santa's special seat, the plywood scenery of the toy workshop and reindeer barn, all toppled or trashed by the boughs chopping at them.

I attempted to take a quick inventory of the chaos that had engulfed me: at least twelve dozen shoppers stampeding, eleven mothers wailing, ten children bawling, nine teenagers rubbernecking, eight managers evacuating, seven security guards floundering, six baristas bailing, five smoldering photo computers, four falling light fixtures, three exploding amps, two bruised ribs, and a nasty beastie in a pissed-off gigantic Christmas tree.

I struggled to my feet and noticed, out of the corner of my eye, movement separate from the growing gyrations of the ever-enlarging tree. Someone, instead of sensibly fleeing from the atrium, was approaching. I headed toward the newcomer in what I intended to be a sprint but ended up as a blundering, skewed side-shuffle attempted by the half of my body still up for exertion, and protested by the battered muscles and joints of the other half. The upside was that if I had been bolting full-speed to reach the newcomer and urge them into an about face and hasty retreat, I would have likely been blindsided by the whipping bough that was trying to get to the newcomer first. The downside was that, even seeing the incoming sweep of the needle-studded limb, there wasn't much I could do about it besides tackling the newcomer to the ground. The tree limb still managed to clip me at the base of my skull as we went down to the cracked tile floor.

The woman let out an oof on impact, and suddenly I recognized just who I was rescuing: Ms. Dazbog. "Are you all right?" I asked her.

"More or less," she answered, sounding more irritated than scared or hurt. She was giving the stinkeye to a cardboard stand-up elf with pointy ears and buck teeth, which no doubt struck her as an offensive racial stereotype, but then her focus returned to me. "Are you?"

"Fine, but you really shouldn't be here," I insisted, rising and helping her get upright. I exercised my gift for understatement and elaborated, "It's not safe." Helpfully punctuating that bold claim, the tree tore a section of brass rail and glass wall panels from the walkway over head and sent them crashing to the floor.

"No, it's not," Ms. Dazbog agreed. "But perhaps that means you are the one who should find himself elsewhere as quickly as possible."

"Excuse me?"

"You've done very well, discovering where these creatures would strike," Ms. Dazbog went on, reaching for the small purse on her shoulder. "But, correct me if I'm wrong, you seem to be at a loss as to what to do next."

"As opposed to you?"

She pulled a tiny red velvet satchel out of the purse and untied its silver-thread drawstrings. "As opposed to me," she confirmed, shaking black powder from the satchel into the palm of her hand.

"Is that… gunpowder?" I asked, holding up my gun.

She ignored me and strode purposefully toward the tree. I got the feeling I was supposed to clear out, having been dismissed, or at least stay back, but I followed her. Another branch slashed through the air at Ms. Dazbog, who stood her ground, held up her handful of glittering black, and blew. The dust met the branch and stopped its motion as forcefully as a solid wall, inches from Ms. Dazbog's determined face. The entire fir shuddered from roots to crown and then went still, frozen in an unnaturally contorted twist.

The light bulb went on above my head. "Coal dust?"

"Coal dust," Ms. Dazbog nodded. "Not common anthracite, of course. My employer's coal has its own particular properties which, as I've now demonstrated, are equal and opposite to those of his toys."

"Demonstrated, as in for the first time?" I probed.

She turned to look directly at me, reminding me once again of a school teacher who has mastered the art of the withering glare, because it would be both unseemly and unprofessional to use the word "duh". All the same, I had to admit that my respect for her had gone up considerably, just based on her willingness to go up against the freakish monstrosity of a giant animated tree with nothing but a theoretical magical counter-effect.

Then, a sharp cracking sound rang out. Ms. Dazbog was shot, and crumpled to the atrium floor.

I crouched beside her in a warrior-medic hybrid pose: my gun raised in one hand, my other hand checking her bullet wound, my eyes darting back and forth between her and the giant tree concealing the sniper. No immediate follow up shots came from the weird, ruined hulk, so I managed to take a few seconds to actually check on Ms. Dazbog. What I had thought at first was a sizable bloodstain on her shoulder was actually sticky, dark brown resin. Something like a peach pit jutted out from the seam of her jacket sleeve, fixed in place by the substance, but it hadn't gotten through the sturdy material, let alone broken the skin.

Ms. Dazbog was struggling to stand up. "You shouldn't move," I admonished her, even as the realization that she hadn't actually been shot continued to nag at my brain, as if there were deeper associations and connections I should have been making.

She ignored me, as she discovered that her only difficulty in rising was due to her shoulder being stuck to the floor by the resin. She wriggled out of her jacket, pushed herself to her feet. "I'm all right, Mr. Oakes," she informed me. "But it seems that those responsible for the disturbance here tonight are most displeased."

I was about to ask her if she knew who "those responsible" were, when they saved me the trouble by jumping out of the tree and landing in front of us. Three of them, all more or less identical: inhuman but roughly human-shaped, short and squat, no more than three feet tall and almost as wide. None of them wore any clothing, and their bodies were covered in waxy, scaly yellow-orange sheaths. Instead of feet and hands their limbs ended in chaotic fan-shaped profusions of gnarled rootlike appendages. The tangles at the ends of their arms supported clusters of pale green globes that looked like underripe berries, translucent enough that I could see the seeds inside them which resembled the one glued to Ms. Dazbog's jacket. The creatures studied us with bulging yellow eyes full of malicious resentment, as if we were taking away from them something they needed badly and expected unquestionably.

It hit me then what they were: parasites. And in a rush, all of the forest lore my mother had tried to impart to me throughout my young life came back. Well, maybe not all, but enough to recognize what type of creatures the trio before us were. "Mistletoe dwarfs," I said.

Ms. Dazbog made a small clucking noise in the back of her throat—the kind people make when they're disappointed in themselves for needing something obvious pointed out to them. "Has it been a hundred and twenty years already?" she asked, more of herself than of me.

"You know these creeps?" I pressed her.

"I know their kind," she replied. "Stunted little miscreants."

"Bulletproof?"

"Hardly."

That was good enough for me, as I aimed at the closest one and pulled the trigger, blowing apart the lump of fibrous plant tissue that passed for the dwarf's head. The other two were charging me before their compatriot hit the floor, and both were shooting seeds sticky with resin from the twisted tubules they had in place of fingers. I sighted the dwarf on my left, hit the deck while squeezing off shots, and managed to score two hits to the parasite's right shoulder that separated its arm most of the way from its body. Murky sap oozed from the wound, and the limb dangled uselessly against the dwarf's body. It was probably only a temporary distraction, but

I took the opportunity to shift my attention to the last member of the trio.

Unfortunately, it was already on top of me. The mistletoe dwarf lacked the momentum of an animated bough swung by a hundred-foot tall fir, but still landed on me hard enough to make my every roughed-up part flare with brand new pain. I tried to twist around enough to get my gun in the dwarf's face, but that was easier said than done. And the dwarf might be nasty, but it wasn't stupid; it hacked at my wrist until I dropped the gun.

I rolled hard, getting myself on top of the dwarf, then rolled again, under and over and under and over. The dwarf held on tight, probably assuming I was trying to disentangle myself. I sold that idea myself with some squirming and twisting, but mostly I was trying to reposition both of us. After a half a dozen tumbles across the wreckage of Santa's workshop, I finally put the dwarf's feet to the fire, literally; I rolled until the tangle of mycelium that made up its lower extremities were on top of a pile of snowy batting that had been set ablaze by shorting wires. The waxy hyphae went up in flames that greedily ran up the dwarf's legs and back. I pushed the dwarf away as it let go of me, jumped up, and grabbed the dwarf by its shoulders to toss it into its one-armed buddy. The sap drenching the other dwarf caught fire readily, and in a heartbeat both were burning like deformed Yule logs.

"Mr. Oakes!" Ms. Dazbog called out, and I turned around just in time to see the first mistletoe dwarf lunging for me, headless but apparently still very much able to move and act and want me dead. There's really no good reason to assume that any of the plant-based forest folk will suffer as many adverse effects from a headshot as your average living thing with a nice meaty brain in its skull, but I had hoped things might go my way for once. Those hopes died as eighty percent of a mistletoe dwarf tackled me hard.

The mall's sprinkler system kicked in, dousing the two burning mistletoe dwarfs as well as all of the smaller fires crackling around Santa's workshop. The headless dwarf throttled me with its tendril fan hands, and smashed my skull against the floor. I couldn't use the immolation trick again, I was out of other ideas, and if my head took much more damage, I might never have another idea again.

I felt something sharp scratching against my sternum, something that felt too coolly metallic to be part of the mistletoe dwarf's vegetative body. It was in fact the business end of a pike that Ms. Dazbog had driven through the parasite's back and out the front of its chest. I wriggled out from under the dwarf and pulled myself upright. The dwarf didn't have a heart any more than it had a brain, but the spear through its chest had momentarily stunned it, at least. It also kept the dwarf on the floor, so long as Ms. Dazbog held the other end. I reached to take it from her, finally identifying it as a fragment of an aluminum tripod that had been holding up the lights for Santa's photo ops. Ms. Dazbog relinquished the improvised pike, and I pushed the insensate dwarf across the floor, looking around the atrium at the closest stores: a jewelry shop, a cell phone retailer specializing in cheap disposables, a manicurist's…

I headed for the nail salon, skidding the dwarf along in front of my feet like a weird pushbroom. I hoisted the mistletoe dwarf up and positioned it against the wall, then shoved all my weight against the length of tripod leg, driving it into the wall and pinning the dwarf. I crossed the salon to a supply closet, opened it, found an empty bucket and mop and several industrial-sized bottles of acetone nail polish remover. I filled the bucket with acetone, carried it to the dwarf and dunked its feet in the solvent. My eyes were stinging from the fumes, and I figured odds were good the last dwarf would be as dead as its torched friends by morning.

I went back out to find Ms. Dazbog, but she was already gone. I had the atrium all to myself, in all its devastated glory, scorched and drenched in equal measure. The mall was weirdly quiet except for the patter of water falling from the sprinklers and the buzzing and bleeping of assorted fire alarms, with a Muzak rendition of I'll Be Home For Christmas echoing in the background. I hustled out of the mall, relieved to find that my car was still right where I had left it. I took off in it just as the first fire engines and police cars were arriving.

***

I opened the door to my office and started talking immediately. I had seen the glow of a desk lamp through a window from the street below and I knew my receptionist was working late yet again. "Phoebe, I need…"

was all I managed to get out before I heard a menacing hiss like dead branches scraping against each other, and saw Phoebe behind her desk, not sitting, but standing with her back arched gracelessly. A mistletoe dwarf hid behind her, peeking around the side of her arm, one of its tendril fans wrapped tightly around her throat.

Given time to think it through, I probably could have come up with "malevolent tree parasites" as a hamadryad's worst fear, and the look in Phoebe's eyes left no room for doubt on that score. Her lips were pressed together tight, maybe to hold herself back from screaming, maybe to keep any of the dwarf's haustoria shoots from slithering into her mouth. Probably both.

I held my hands up in the universal gesture that we should all just relax and not do anything unreasonable. I wasn't sure how much further the dwarf's communication skills extended, or what it really wanted or expected to get out of this stand-off. If it wanted me, and was willing to let Phoebe go, I could live with that. If it tried to leave with Phoebe, I needed a good plan to stop that from happening. But I was exhausted, and still in no small amount of pain, and I had yet to come up with any really good plans in this entire scrape.

"Kellan?" My mother's voice resonated from the hallway, just before the office door, still ajar from my interrupted entrance, swung open wide at her touch. In all the excitement at the mall I had forgotten that she had never turned up there, and now it seemed she had been on her way to me all along.

The mistletoe dwarf snarled and took its yellow eyes off me to look at my mother, who stopped dead in her tracks as she realized what she had stumbled into. On pure instinct I reached into my jacket for my gun, drew and sighted and squeezed the trigger. One bullet blew a chunk out of the dwarf's right shoulder; the next tore off the rightmost third of its scaly face. The dwarf let go of Phoebe's neck to aim its uninjured arm at me and fire back, and Phoebe had the presence of mind to run as soon as the mycelium relaxed. Her movement threw off the dwarf's aim, and a viscid seed hit the ceiling.

Now I had a clear shot and fired again and again into the squat torso of the mistletoe dwarf. Waxy splinters and gobbets of sap flew everywhere, but when my action snapped back empty, the dwarf was still standing. Then it was mounting Phoebe's desk and jumping across the office at me.

The dwarf's weight pounded me to the floor and I figured if it got in one good hit I'd probably lose consciousness. But there was no follow-through, as the dwarf went stiff and teetered off me. I looked up to see my mother standing over both of us, holding a small vial, the kind she always used for her homemade herbal draughts. "Fungicide?" I asked her.

"Elixir of mistletoe," she answered.

"Lucky me."

She shrugged gently. "I always make extra around the holidays."

***

I woke up the next morning in the office waiting area, sprawled across the battered old sofa, with clean sharp white winter light streaming through the windows, my eyes, and directly into my brain. My body felt sore as I sat up, but the pain wasn't nearly as excruciating as it had every right to be. I had some dim recollections of Phoebe and my mother helping me settle on the couch and administering some druidic balm or other before I passed out fully and deeply. Not a miracle cure, but pretty close.

I started a fresh pot of coffee and stood at my window, looking out at the morning and listening to the rhythmic percolation. The door of the office opened and the delicate click of high heels sounded on the floorboards. I turned around slowly and nodded at Ms. Dazbog, who looked just as primly polished as she had the day before, if not moreso. She was wearing a different blazer and skirt, but her hair and makeup were composed in a perfect copy of their previous arrangement. I might have felt a little self-conscious about my wrinkled pants and untucked shirt and stubbled jawline if not for the number of vicious parasitic woodland spirits I had personally thrown down with the night before, and the fact that Ms. Dazbog was well aware of those exploits.

"Good morning, Mr. Oakes," she nodded. "I understand you had another encounter after the mall incident last night. I'm glad no one was seriously hurt."

"No permanent damage," I agreed, although serious hurt and permanent damage don't always amount to the same thing. I've come back from serious hurt, and I will again.

"More to the point," Ms. Dazbog went on, "I'm very glad that this matter has been successfully resolved."

"Has it?" I asked.

Ms. Dazbog considered the question. "I believe it has, in its most troublesome aspects. Yes, there may be other mistletoe dwarfs lurking and plotting similar invasions, scheming to leverage my employer's magics as obtained by underhanded means. But now that we know who, or what, we are facing, we can deal with them far more efficiently and proactively. That was the gap in knowledge that needed to be bridged, and that was what you were hired to do." She reached into her purse, pulled out a stack of cash just as crisp as my advance but about five times as thick, set it on the desk. "That means our business is concluded."

I shrugged a little. For a moment, Ms. Dazbog looked a bit lost, as if she were about to venture into uncertain territory, but there was too much resolve in her elvish spine for anything to hold her back for long. "I... I hope that you might accept a small bonus in addition to your fees for the case, Mr. Oakes. A token, really." Her ageless brown eyes met mine again.

"Well, I wouldn't say no to it," I answered, which satisfied her enough to send her looking through her purse once again. She pulled out a small box, long and thin, white with a red ribbon tied in a bow. She set it on the desk. "Should I open it now?" I asked.

"By all means."

I slid off the ribbon and removed the lid. Inside was a sharpened pencil. The shaft was painted a twinkling red, with a high gloss that gave it the illusion of scintillating depth, but a pencil all the same. "Thanks ...?" I tried not to sound like a little kid finding socks inside a package he was sure was a remote controlled racecar.

Ms. Dazbog favored me with a slight smile. "It's a special order, direct from the workshop."

I realized the pencil was primarily made of wood, and plucked it from its case, half-expecting it to thrum with power in my fingers. It felt like pretty much any other No. 2. "Magic?" I asked anyway.

"Has there been anything troubling your mind lately?" she asked me in return. "Questions in need of answers?"

"Doesn't that pretty much describe every human being all the time?" I countered.

Ms. Dazbog sniffed. "Perhaps. And this implement is no cure-all for every dilemma. It has a more specific, seasonal application. Excellent for list-making. Gift lists," she added meaningfully.

I pulled a notepad to the center of the desk and set the pencil to it, thinking almost unwillingly about my continued lack of ideas for what to get my mother for Christmas. At which point the pencil started twitching on its own and, as my fingers tightened on it, I found myself scribbling down the words "blown glass" and "cold frame" on the paper. My mother had been talking for years about installing a microclimate enclosure out-side her kitchen window, where she could tend some more exotic plant life than our local weather generally supported. I hadn't thought about it in a while, which was probably why when a new boutique of blown glass art had opened a month earlier on the same street as my office, even with a sign in the window advertising custom commissions, I hadn't thought about inquiring after a special order top pane. But seeing the two ideas written together, I suddenly had a gift idea that was unique and thoughtful and perfect for my mother, not to mention realistically obtainable with a modicum of effort. "That's a neat trick," I admitted, as the pencil start-ed twitching again, jotting down ideas for specific flowers and birds that might decorate the lid of the cold frame.

"It seemed appropriate, given the timing," Ms. Dazbog demurred. "I hope you have a merry Christmas, Mr. Oakes."

"Thanks. You too." She adjusted her purse strap and walked out of the office, back straight and head high; for a moment she seemed much taller than five feet. Off to the North Pole she went, I imagined, back to whatever her normal duties would be during the busiest time of year. I dropped the magic pencil and picked up my case fee, flipped the edges of the bills and stuffed the wad into my pocket, deciding to step out myself. I could squeeze in some shopping for my mother, right after I bought myself a proper cup of coffee. I'd leave the pot I had started for Phoebe, due in for regular office hours in about half hour. On the heels of that thought I picked up the magic pencil again and jotted down a few new gift ideas for Phoebe, as well. What the heck, I figured, it's Christmas.

☠❄☠❄☠❄

DALE W. GLASER once played Santa Claus in a third-grade play, but felt the narrative lacked a certain something in the way of external conflict with giant monsters. He was relegated to non-speaking background elf roles thereafter. Since then he has realized that if he wants a good earth-shattering epic told right, he'd best tell it himself, and has done so in collections such as PulpWork's own How the West Was Weird anthology series. He currently lives in Virginia with his wife, their three children, and five pets. Only some of the children and absolutely none of the pets can be trusted around Christmas trees.

Stories by Dale W. Glaser

The Demon Wrestler　　　　　　　　How the West Was Weird 2
Ellie Froggett and the Charnel Pit　　How the West Was Weird 3
My Name is Melise　　　　　　　　　Twice Upon a Time

Jolly with a Pistol

A Dreamcatcher Story by Thomas Deja

…we dwelt on the thundra, rejoiced in the magic in our veins. We hunted for the foxkin and avoided the cold drakes. At night we gathered around the fire and listened as the storyteller told us of how we came into being through a union of the moon and sun, and how a disagreement led to the schism between the Chill and the Warm. We slept in the nooks and crannies of the world, our mates wrapped around us to stave off The White Death. It was a simple life, but it was a satisfying one.

And then the change came…

Maybelle Tremens put her hands deep within her long black 'battle coat.' Her face was curiously immobile.

"Outside of some of the accouterments, Wynoski, I don't see anything out of the ordinary."

The detective smirked, displaying deep laugh lines. He stood up from the crouching position in the middle of the elegant hotel room and shrugged. "Come on…'tis the season. Given the time of year…well, at the very least, it's creative."

What Maybelle and her friend were discussing was the cooling corpse slumped against the grimy, now bloodstained bed in front of them. An older man with a shock of white hair and a hawkish nose lay there. His body was irregularly festooned with silver and gold tinsel. Blood dried from a bullet wound in the center of the man's forehead. The expression on his face was one of shock, but that was natural given that very few people expected to be shot in the head. In his cold hands, someone—presumably the killer—had placed a sheet of oaktag paper upon which was scrawled one word:

Naughty.

Maybelle's right hand slid out of the long black coat with a multitude of hidden pockets and moved toward the body. A few random dots of lumi-nescence rose from her fingers like the embers of a dying fire. "There is some magic residue," she told the white-haired man, "but it's so faint it could be just ambient mana. Given that Nocturne is soaking in manna, I'd bet on it."

"But there's still a possibility there's something nutty going on with this mug's slaying?"

"It could very well be the killer is the one who's nutty. I would not bet on this crime being magic based." She moved away from the body and start-ed wandering the room. It was not the sort of place she expected someone as well dressed as the victim would be found. The dirty walls were cracked, and a dark stain spread from one corner. The desk and nightstand were chipped at the edges, and there was a faint hint of mildew. For a moment the two friends were silent before Maybelle said, "You're still going to ask me to help you on this case, aren't you?"

"You and your Shadow Legion buddies don't have that consultant status with the NPD for nothing."

Maybelle smiled softly. Ever since the older man helped her stop an underaged magician from destroying his neighborhood, a strong bond had developed. She had come to look upon Wynoski as something of a surrogate father. "Ever the flatterer. I assume you know who the victim is?"

Wynoski flipped open the long, thin pad all detectives used to make notes. "I'd be a pretty poor detective if I didn't."

Maybelle waited for a moment. She raised her eyebrow expectantly un-til her friend rolled his eyes.

"Fine. That bag of inert skin and bones used to belong to Benedict Clay."

Her expression went from expectation to surprise. She moved closer to the macabre display, stepping over an overturned lamp. "As in Clay Toys?"

"Yeah. Someone disagreed with his assessment of how nice his product was."

Maybelle ran her fingers over the surface of the cheap particleboard desk. It was dusty from disuse. "So a leading light in Nocturne's business world is found dead in a cheap hotel room. He is decorated, shot and de-clared 'naughty.' Surely someone must have come in with him."

"I'll have one of my men look in on that," Wynoski replied. "Shouldn't take too long. I find if you lean on hotel dicks, they get real talky. What are you gonna do?"

"There's something at turns sadistic and personal going on here. If we are to take your assumption that magic was involved, we have to assume it was a person or persons who wanted to see Clay suffer for some preceived slight; why else use something as mundane as a gun when the killer may have known magic? So I'm thinking I'm going to look in on our victim's life leading up to his being displayed like some—"

"Christmas tree?"

Maybelle made a face. "I used to love this holiday so much."

"I'll call you when I get something from the hotel."

***

…we did not notice when the magic began to change, become something darker and more predatory. What we noticed was how the animals we fed on died off and disappeared, how our bodies strained when usually they did not, how we found ourselves aging and dying.

In the space of three generations, the Tribe Of The Chill had fractured, a whole nation shattered into little splinters that skulked in caves and crevices in search of warmth. We began to accept that our time had passed, that it was time for The Chill to cede this world to what will follow.

That was when he came…

***

The truth was Maybelle *did* love Christmas, but ever since moving to Nocturne her holiday spirit had been muted. Existing, as it did. in one of the southernmost portion of the country, any precipitation came in rains—quite torrential ones at times, as December was the heart of hurricane season. She was used to Chimera Falls winters, with gentle snows transforming the city into something magical. Here, being frequently damp only emphasized how much she missed her home town.

Clay Toys had its headquarters on Orange Street near where Jubilee bordered on La Rouse. Maybelle was amused by how you could see the ritzy, high class shops to her left, then turn around to see more eclectic shops just a short walk away. She was familiar with both sides—one as the common law wife of one of Nocturne's wealthiest citizens and the other as the city's premiere occult adventurer.

She could tell word had gotten out of their founder's death at the company's offices. The various employees from the lowliest mailroom worker to the most powerful executive had a stunned look on their face, moving through the day like zombies. The somber mood amongst the people provided a stark contrast to the lobby festooned with Christmas decorations and the twenty foot tall tree near the far window. She walked to the pretty redheaded receptionist who seemed to struggle with the simple tasks her job entailed. Under her battle coat Maybelle was dressed respectably in a tasteful pale pink blouse and a grey wool skirt that reached to mid-calf. Sensible flats of soft leather—the sort of thing that would not invite tripping or stumbling when she needed to be in action—allowed her to tread quietly. She displayed the badge given her as an official full time consultant to the NPD. A quick conversation led to her being directed to the fourth floor, and Mr. Kenneth Giamatto.

Giamatto was a broad shouldered man with an olive complexion and heavily lidded eyes, dressed sensibly in a simple navy suit. His pale blue eyes seemed to have a great deal of emotion in them; right now the emotion depicted was sadness and distress.

"Thank you for seeing me," Maybelle said as they shook hands.

"I'm just happy the police are putting all their resources on finding out who killed Benny," Giamatto replied.

"I'm friends with the detective in charge of the investigation. I can assure you he's one of the best."

"They suspect magic?"

Maybelle groaned inwardly. She hated being known as an occult investigator, if only because it inhibited her ability to actually investigate discreetly. But the combination of her unwillingness to conceal her identity as Dreamcatcher and the reputation of her sister in Chimera Falls made it clear where her interest lay. "We are not certain, Mr. Giamatto, but the detective is not ruling it out."

"Well, the resources of Clay Toys is at your disposal."

"Thank you for that," Maybelle said, smiling blandly. "Actually, given the nature of Mr. Clay's death, I was wondering if you had an idea why the killer—"

"Thought he was naughty?" The executive chuckled mirthlessly.

"Yes."

Giamotto's demeanor changed. He seemed to become awkward, making a show of adjusting the blotter on his desk. "Please understand, Ms. Tremens, that I considered Benny my friend. He insisted I acted as a partner even when I resisted. He was great to his employees, kind to his wife, and generous with the charities who approached us. More importantly, he loved children, and devoted his life to make them happy."

"And then there's a but," Maybelle said.

"Benny did have certain…predilections. He liked women of a certain age, and was not discriminatory as to where he found them. If you ask me— and I trust that you'll tell people you did not—the reason he was in that hotel was to indulge in his passions."

"Did he have…regular women he indulged in?" Maybelle asked.

The man looked pained, as if he hated telling these stories about his friend. "No. Believe it or not, he loved his wife…and he felt only seeing a woman once or twice prevented him from violating his, well, emotional bond with her."

"How nice of him," Maybelle sarcastically commented. She ran her fingers along Giamotto's desk. "These girls…were they…paid for their services?"

"No. Mr. Clay didn't want to bring home a disease. He felt dealing with prostitutes increase his chances of being infected."

"Fair enough. Do you know of any of the women he indulged with?"

"I'll make a list for you. Just be prepared. The list could be quite long."

Maybelle smirked. "Forward the list to Detective Wynoski of the NPD. Thank you for your time, Mr. Giamotto. If you can, I'd like to call on you again if circumstances indicate I need to."

"Certainly," Giamotto said. "As I said, Clay Toys—"

"Is at my disposal, yes. Take care."

***

...he wore crimson and white and melted out of the angry swirl of the cold winds. He had the stink of the mammalian on him, and spoke in the tongue of the new beings we had glimpsed out of the corner of our eyes as we searched for shelter, for food.

He told us he knew of our plight and wished to help us. He needed people to help him work wonders, people who could survive in the extreme cold of his homeland. If we would ally ourselves with him, we would never want for a home or sustenance or a purpose.

We had no choice. We agreed...

***

Wynoski called her an hour later. She asked to meet him at the hotel. Before leaving, Maybelle slipped the ingredients for the spell she had in mind into her battle coat. With the appropriate spell, the woman who may have killed Benedict Clay could be found quite easily, and if she could be found her complicity in the man's murder could be solved even easier.

The artist's rendition showed that the woman had very delicate features and long, straight blonde hair. Her eyes had a very slight almond shape, and her pupils seemed unnaturally large. The strangest thing about the depiction was her head proper. There was a decidedly male cast to the shape and planes of her head. It was as if someone had put a woman's features onto a male skull.

"How androgynous," she said.

"There's something real crazy about that picture," Wynoski added. "So you going to spit in something and find this woman like when we were looking for that crazy kid?"

"That spell was for when we knew who we were looking for. This situation is a little different." The two of them reached the hotel room door. The detective tore the police tape and gave her entrance into the murder scene. Maybelle nodded her thanks. "We have a vague idea of our perpetrator—we know her sex, her face, but little else. Without a solid image of the quarry, a sense of who she is, I have to approach searching for her in a different way."

Once more her fingers worked over the notched edges of her battle coat. Nimbly she pulled out a mandrake root. She placed the brownish tuber, its form vaguely mimicking a human shape, on a nightstand. Wynoski's eyes were upon her as she produced a fine greyish-white powder. She sprinkled a handful on the drawing and brought it to her lips. Ancient words were spoken, and she blew the fine grains of material onto the root. There was a strange musical noise as the root contorted and contracted until it became a replica of the woman in the drawing. Maybelle's eyes darted sideways; if her detective friend was surprised, it did not show on his face.

Another pocket produced what appeared to be a long, thin string. This one sparkled and gleamed in the light. Slowly, Maybelle wrapped the string around the altered mandrake, then bound it to her left hand. The sparking quickly gained a pattern, a strange mobius strip of glitter. She raised her hand.

"The mandrake has always had an affinity with humanity due to its shape," she explained to her friend. She waved her bound hand before her, the moving band of infinity illuminating her face and chest in a way that made her seem inhuman. "I created a stronger bond with our suspect with a mixture of…that's odd."

Wynoski frowned. "Odd? I don't like odd."

"You shouldn't," the magician replied. She spun in a circle. Her face slowly contorted into an expression of consternation. "The facsimile mandrake should have picked up the temporal residue of its original, allowing me to follow her trail to where she might be…but there's a lot of, well, static preventing me from synchronizing the replica with the real thing."

"Static? What in Sam Hill would cause magical static?"

"One thing I can think of," Maybelle replied.

She looked directly at her friend. "Whoever our murderer is, she isn't human."

***

...he took us deeper into the Chill than any of us had ever been, so deep we could only see in shades of white. We traveled so long that we became blind with the snow and ice around us. After an endless march, he brought us to our new home.

It looked like a simple shack with a thatched roof. The place was clean of snow—none gathered anywhere on its structure, and it radiated a strange but pleasant warmth. He laughed as he welcomed us. Another figure as corpulent as him, but female in its shape, opened the door. She added her own musical voice to his in greeting.

As she stepped aside to let us in, a sick feeling crept into my stomach. There was something wrong here, and I could not verbalize what it was in time to save my tribe...

***

Maybelle was reasonably certain that her assumption was true. Whoever killed Benedict Clay—maybe due to his serial infidelity with younger women—was not human.

Which was why she was venturing off the well-trod paths of Madeline Walk to find Beaumont Place. The crooked street, barely more than three blocks in La Rouse, was reportedly one of the first roads built when Nocturne was founded over a century ago. On the northernmost end was The O'Brion Cafe, and that was where Maybelle was headed.

On the outside, the Cafe looked like any other greasy spoon. The neon sign was partially broken and buzzed like a horde of flies. The windows were caked with dust. If she squinted hard enough, she could see a string of Christmas lights lopsidedly hung with what appeared to be duct tape. A sad, broken Santa stood on the counter, bent backwards at the waist. There were specks that moved around the cake case that could be roaches. It was one of the most unappetizing restaurants a tourist could ever see.

Once Maybelle walked through the doors, it was anything but. Inside the Cafe the glamour—or, as the case may be, anti-glamour—ceased to affect her perceptions. The interiors were elegant and dignified. Instead of tarnished chrome there was natural wood. There was plant life everywhere, which was understandable given who was in charge of the place.

To her right, little balls of light flew past her calling her name in soft tones. Some of the plants turned towards her, verdant leaves quivering in what could be greeting. She moved deeper into the comfortable environment and took in the denizens of the place, looking for the owner.

This was what made The O'Brion Cafe unique; the patrons were exclusively of the supernatural variety. To her right, a crimson-skinned, horned thing bragged of being an Archduke of Hell to a downy-furred woman. To her left, a woman in a black suit glared at her with ophidian eyes. Off in one of the many booths, two fashionably thin women with long whitish-blonde hair obscuring their naked forms gossiped between themselves, their gossamer wings unfurled. She maneuvered her way through the demons, fairies and varieties of the undead, focused on finding the man who knew everything that happened in Nocturne's otherworldly community.

The man in question sat in the back, sipping champagne. He was tall and powerfully built, muscles straining against the fabric of his grey plaid suit. His skin was so translucent it shone in the dim lights. As he turned his narrow head to contemplate Maybelle, his golden eyes seemed to shift as if they were liquid.

"Well, Tremens," he said, rising and indicating the opposite side of the booth. "A friendly visit, I hope."

Maybelle slid into the booth. "You should know better than that by now, Oberon."

The man snorted and smiled slightly, displaying impossibly straight, impossibly white teeth. "I should have known given that damnable coat of yours. What do you want?"

"There's been a murder—"

"Of course there has," Oberon said with a yawn, "and there's a supernatural element to it."

"No. But the murderer is not human."

"Well that *is* a new one, Tremens." Oberon adjusted his cuff. His golden eyes sparkled darkly. "Do I need to remind you of the first rule I instituted as duly elected head of the extranatural community?"

"You know what they say about rules."

"You know what they say about being bitten."

"Regardless," Maybelle continued, "I need to know if you've had any new arrivals who might have a fondness for Christmas."

The man laughed with the sound of a church bell being rung repeatedly. "This keeps getting richer and richer."

"Will you stop being the high and mighty Fae Noble and listen to me?"

After a moment, Oberon's laughter stopped. Imperceptibly to anyone but Maybelle, he nodded. She took a breath and began to tell her story, watching his face all the time. Throughout her story, Oberon's eyes seemed to shift and change like molten gold.

When she was done, he said, "This cannot stand. We've existed in this city by being smart and keeping to ourselves. Having someone running around executing—"

"Exactly!" Maybelle exclaimed with a smile. "So now I will ask you again…have there been any new arrivals with an obsession with Christmas?"

Oberon thought for a moment. "No," he said finally, "but I will ask my subjects—"

"They're not subjects, they're peers."

Oberon's mouth compressed into a tight, mirthless smirk. "…my peers to search for such a personage."

Maybelle rose from her seat. "Thank you."

"Thank you for bringing this to my attention."

"And Merry Solstice, Lord Oberon."

***

...the bulk of us were brought to a darkened room, an endless crypt filled with benches and parts. At the man's direction, we began to fashion the toys the young ones of his world needed.

But a small gathering of us was brought to another room. This place was positioned at the top of our new home. It was sunny and bright, a large skylight reaching from wall to wall. Here, the man explained, The Holy List was built. We, the smartest of the tribe, were brought here to peer through the Universal Mirror to observe his children. We were to take note of their actions and judge them. Once judgment was made, we were to add their names to one of two lists.

Naughty. Or Nice...

***

Maybelle didn't even notice that Colin had come into her library until he spoke.

"You have a three year old daughter—and incidentally a husband—who are presently decorating a tree, drinking cider and wondering where you are."

She closed the grimoire on the table before her. "Well, technically," Maybelle replied, "he's not my husband, and he's not downstairs."

Colin Palmersdale grinned, exposing white teeth—some of which were sharp like an animal's. "So you're saying you're unattached and fancy free?"

Maybelle rose, leaving the copious notes she was making behind. "Oh, I do have my eye on a certain man," she murmured as she stepped into his arms. "Even if he is a stubborn mule who won't leave well enough alone."

She bit her lip, waiting for the protests from her lover that his legacy to fight injustice was more important than his life, but he said nothing. She felt his lips on the top of her head. For a moment, the feel of his strong arms soothed her even as the subtle sound of the reptilian scales on his tricep rubbing against the fabric of his shirt dismayed her. "You need time off," he told her quietly. "Augusta needs her mother."

"I know. I just keep thinking about this poor creature. She has to be lashing out for some reason."

"Is that why you've locked yourself in here?"

Slowly his embrace loosened. She looked up at the man she loved. "I've had to try and devise something new. Given my lack of knowledge about our culprit and her supernatural nature, most tracking spells won't work or are unreliable."

Colin broke away from her, still keeping hold of Maybelle's hand. She felt his thumb gently rubbing the back of her hand. "Can't it wait? Just for a few hours?"

"It could be scared…or compelled by some geas. I can't leave it out there."

Mismatched eyes studied her softly. "An hour?"

Maybelle bit her lip. She thought of Wynoski; he was a good man, but if the culprit was frightened and lashed out, he'd react with his gun. But the thought of drinking cider next to this gorgeous, unusual man while watching her daughter play…

"An hour," she replied. "Nothing more."

It took forty three minutes for the phone to ring, and for her heart to sink.

***

…I sat before the mirror every day, tribemates to either side of me. Unlike the place where the bulk of my tribe toiled, this place was brightly lit so I and my fellows could pass judgment.

The pictures revealed by the mirror changed rapidly, giving me split second glimpses of every human child on Earth. I observed their every moment, those of joy and those of malice. I did as instructed by the man who saved our tribe from extinction, evaluating their behavior utilizing strict rules he provided.

And as the big midwinter celebration neared, I made a notation on the seemingly endless list before me.

Naughty. Or Nice…

***

The corpse, this time, was a woman, but the method was the same. Her dark skin had turned grey from lack of blood. Maybelle didn't bother to do the inspection she did with Clay. She knew that the magic residue, as slight as it was, came from the shooter and not the ritual. The woman was assaulted in her kitchen, bakery ingredients scattered all along the shiny chrome of the cooking space. As she moved about the room, flour clotted the soles of her shoes.

"And this is…?"

"Jessilyn Wardlow, a.k.a 'Mother' Wardlow—noted figurehead for several orphanages." answered Wynoski as he rubbed his temples.

Maybelle bent down to examine the grey-haired, harmless looking woman. "And her vice is…?"

"We never had any proof, but there were the reports of her skimming money off the operating budget of her sites and cutting corners to the detriment of the kids."

"Well, you must admit that is naughty."

Wynoski visibly sighed. "I'm going to release that artist's rendition if you can't find that vigilante—"

"So she's a vigilante now?"

"You're a smart girl, Tremens. One of the reasons I like you. Surely you know this dame is passing judgment on some people who hurt kids," grumbled Wynoski.

"Clay with his predilection for younger girls—maybe too young—and Wardlow stealing money earmarked for kids," Maybelle muttered. She turned away from the macabre corpse. "An argument could be made for a pattern."

"I'd rather we find this palooka before she strikes again."

"I'm working on it," Maybelle said as she moved back toward her police ally. "Magic is not like science; it's a touch imprecise."

"Yeah, yeah, I figured that out some time ago," the detective grumbled as he fumbled through his overcoat. In a moment, Wynoski produced a cigarette. "You got a light?"

With her eyes still on the handiwork of the mysterious murderer, Maybelle motioned toward her friend with an elegant hand, eldritch words subvocalized. There was a quiet sizzle before the tip of the cigarette flared with flame briefly. "Will that do?"

"Yeah, thanks." Wynoski took a drag and exhaled. "You better get to that solution quickly, Tremens. If another one of these murders takes place—"

"We'll have a spree killer on our hands, and all the panic that comes along with that," she finished. "We can't have that."

"The commissioner is putting a lot of pressure to get this thing solved before Christmas. We've been able to keep a lid on the details, but that's only going to be for so long."

"I just need a little more time, detective."

"That's all you're going to get, Tremens," Wynoski said as he blew a plume of smoke. "A little more time."

***

...Naughty. Nice. Naughty. Naughty. Nice. Nice.

They continued to unroll before my eyes, sudden glimpses of young lives. I surveyed each of the tiny portraits before me, striving to get the most information out of them. I did not rest. I did not pull away. The man who saved my tribe would not allow me a moment's respite.

And while I struggled to focus on these children, and these children only, I saw other things. In the background I witnessed the actions of adults. I began to understand how some of the naughty children became that way. They were taught how to be that way by the adults around them.

It was not naughty children who were the problem. It was naughty adults.

***

"What are you two doing?"

Maybelle looked up from where she and her daughter knelt on the floor. Between them was a paper model of what looked like Nocturne itself. Augusta was busy cutting out a building with extreme concentration. Her long black hair was tied up in a barrette with Maybelle's signature symbol in golden wire woven in amongst the teeth. Both mother and daughter were sparking gently with magic energy.

"I'm helping," Augusta told her father before handing the latest paper construct to her mother.

Colin's gaze fell on his lover. "Is this a spell?"

Maybelle nodded before placing Augusta's latest handiwork in what would be Tyson's Quad. "It would be foolish if I denied it."

Her daughter continued cutting out paper buildings. Colin took in the sight with his mismatched eyes. His face became stony. "I thought we discussed keeping her out of our unfortunate business."

"Considering her parents are a metamorph doomed to end his life as a patchwork monster and a woman who absorbs the manna around her whether she wants to or not, I would think that was an impossible task. She's just making paper cut-outs, not following me into battle."

Colin's mouth became a grim, thin line. "Does she know what she's doing it for?"

"She knows it's for mommy's work. She doesn't know how it's for mommy's work."

"It's Christmas Eve, May," her lover said, his voice softening. "I understand we need to continue our obligations, and I agree that this murder case is important. But bringing her into this…"

"You have to trust me," Maybelle replied.

"Look, Mommy!" Augusta exclaimed, her smile lighting up her face. She held up a squat, carefully cut out strip of paper designed to resemble the Bartholomew Museum. Maybelle turned from her lover and knelt down besides her daughter.

"That's wonderful, sweetie! Do you think you can make me one of the statue outside?"

Augusta nodded with the seriousness only a child could muster and went to work. Maybelle remained on her knees. She reached out and stroked her daughter's hair. "This is our heritage, love. She'll take over the Tremens obligations once I'm gone. Best she start learning now."

Colin stared at her. For a moment she was positive he was going to continue his press for leaving their daughter out of this.

Instead, he said, "Just this once," and walked away.

***

I watched as adults hurt the children, corrupted them, enslaved them. I saw them take advantage of their innocence, and of adults who genuinely cared about them.

It angered me.

Just as being a slave to the bearded man in red did.

It took me months to figure out a way to escape. There was still a pit of fear as I enacted my plan, fleeing that accursed place in middle of the night as he and his wife slept and my fellow tribesmen toiled. If my fellow compilers of the list were aware of my leave taking, they did not acknowledge it. They simply continued their task…naughty. nice. naughty. nice.

I took my mirror with me.

***

Maybelle stood in the mock Nocturne she and her daughter had made, feeling like a giant with the world at her feet. It was near midnight on Christmas Eve. She needed to finish this tonight so she could spend time with her family as expected.

In her hands was a mixture of herbs, painstakingly measured out to get the exact compound she needed. She tamped down the anxiety and frustration she felt since the mandrake spell did not work. Once more her eyes surveyed the rows and rows of paper cutouts, knowing how powerful a child's innocent hands were when casting spells like this. Maybelle hoped that Colin never found out how calculated her involving Augusta was.

With words derived from ancient Atlantean on her lips, she began sifting the mixture over the model city. As the grains left the spaces between her fingers, they sparkled like snow and descended. As they reached what would be ground level if this was the actual city, hazy forms began to gain substance, pale simulcra of the citizens within the City That Lived By Night's border right at this minute.

Once every granule was distributed, Maybelle contemplated the tableau. Before her was a miniature version of her city as it was right now, complete with representations of every being within it. These glowing homunculi moved and slept and stirred in the same exact way their originals did.

And then she went to work.

She removed the males with the right words, dissipating them into the air around her. Another set of words, and all the human beings disappeared. The glowing simulations disappeared in number. She scanned what was left and tried to pick out the culprit. When she could not, Maybelle started dismissing classes of non-humans she was aware of.

What had started as a million had become thousands, then hundreds. When she got down to tens, she found who she was looking for.

And who she was looking for was approaching the Argo Tower.

***

...Nocturne provided me with a place I could disappear into, given all those similar to my kind that dwelled within it. I sought out an unassuming place, a place of squalor an despair; after being a prisoner for so long, being free in a hovel like this was nourishing enough. The mirror was hung on the wall. I sat down before it and watched the quick flickers of children's lives. But my eyes were not on the children.

When I found the right adults, I grabbed the weapon of the humans and went forward.

***

Maybelle was able to teleport between her quarry and the magnificent tower that served as Argo Industries' headquarters. The culprit wore a long crimson coat and a green dress. In her left hand was a valise, a pistol in her right. Maybelle's body shimmered with magical energy, which confirmed what she suspected. As the culprit stepped back, Maybelle took in the delicate features, the pointed ears, the thinness of the form inside the coat and realized something.

"You're elven."

The woman's voice was soft and musical, but firm. "Let me pass."

Maybelle raised her hand, third and fourth fingers extended. "I cannot do that. Who are you looking for within?"

Her opponent stood there, the statue of the Horae in the shadows throwing her form into sharper relief. Rain began to fall, random drops landing on their bodies. "Why should I tell you, human?"

"Because if the person you're hunting deserves it, I will bring her to justice—but in accordance with the laws of humankind."

The elvish woman cocked an accusatory finger in the direction of the building. Her narrow face flushed with the color of roses. "Within that building is a mortal man who does horrific things to his issue. He forces them to serve him in ways they should not!"

Maybelle's hand began to shine, the radiance shifting into a number of colors. "This is not your concern! You have no authority here."

"THE CLAUS GAVE ME AUTHORITY!" the elf roared. The rain was coming down harder, beating a tattoo on the cobblestones surrounding the statue. Maybelle felt a pang of need as she imagined how this would be snow in her hometown. She thought about what this curious being was saying.

Slowly, she lowered her arm. Her hand lost its shine so that only the ambient glow remained. Maybelle carefully stepped forward. She felt the desperation and insanity from the elf's body language.

"Tell me your story," she said. "Maybe then I will stand aside."

***

Maybelle listened to the elven woman's tale with an extreme sadness. She felt for this strange, demented creature, and realized the isolation she must have endured. In a way, it wasn't the elf's fault she had degenerated in this way.

She had moved close enough to face her. "What is your name, my lady?"

The elf told her, the sound coming off as chimes on a sunny day.

"And what is the name of the man you came to punish?"

The elf gave the name to her.

Maybelle knew what she should do. She knew Wynoski would insist that this ancient being be arrested and made to stand for her crimes. But the season, the testimony, the passion with which the elf spoke affected her.

She could not arrest her. So she did what she could.

Maybelle subvocalized a new spell. She gently placed her hand to the female creature's temple as thin tendrils of greyish green energy snaked up her arms, slid between her fingers and sank in the elf's skull. She could feel her magic working in the elven woman's brain, reworking it, fashioning it to her wishes.

There would be no more madness. No more rage. No memories of slavery. No more naughty or nice.

Maybelle watched this beautiful, magical being's face as her spell worked its way through her mind. The anger smoothed away. A beatific smile burst on her face. The woman's eyes sparkled like jewels on silk as memories washed away to be replaced by newer, happier recollections.

Without the pain and anger, without the memories of being forced into slavery, of being made to pass judgment on young humanity.

Maybelle did not know if the elf's story was true, or if it was some fabrication brought on by dementia. But she knew the being had suffered enough. She deserved to live her life free and in oblivious bliss.

Her hands drew away from the being's head. "Go on. Find your way in this world. You are free."

The elven woman hesitated at first. Her eyes searched Maybelle's as if looking for trickery.

After a moment, she dropped the pistol and the valise and walked away.

Maybelle put on her gloves and picked up the gun. She placed it in the valise and closed it. She already was working on the story she would give Wynoski to convince him these murders were over.

A quick cantrip marked the man who, unbeknownst to him, almost died. He would find it difficult to hurt his children with that spell inhibiting him. And before long, she would come for him and bring him to justice in the court of human law.

Off in the distance, the church bells chimed midnight. Maybelle stood up, stretched and yawned. It was Christmas Day. There were presents to be opened, egg nog to drink and familial love to be shared. There was a husband to comfort, and a daughter to shower affection on.

Her role as a protector of Nocturne could wait.

Now it was time to go home.

☠❅☠❅☠❅

About Thomas Deja:

Thomas Deja has been writing professionally for almost twenty five years. Starting with a column and random horror serials in the seminal Brooklyn 'zinei, Thomas began placing stories in such independent magazines as After Hours and Not One of Us before becoming one of the contributing book reviewers and feature writers for Fangoria magazine, a position he kept for over fifteen years.

He found himself authoring stories in the 90's featuring classic Marvel Super-heroes for The Ultimate Hulk, X-Men Legends and Five Decades of The X-Men. Recently, he had become known for writing stories in what he calls The Chimera Falls Universe, including tales in all three editions of How The West Was Weird, The Shadow Legion series, starting with New Roads To Hell and short stories featuring paranormal detective Maybelle 'Dreamcatcher' Tremens in various anthologies, including A Grimoire of Eldgritch Inquests.

Thomas co-hosts the podcasts Better In The Dark with best friend Derrick Ferguson and Mollyfog The Music with rapper Kelen 'B Hyphen' Conley. Thomas' passion for film has extended to maintaining Damn Your Ears! Damn Your Eyes!, a blog where he publishes his notorious '10 Statements About' kinda, sorta movie reviews. Thomas lives in New York City, where he struggles with his lifelong devotion to the Jets and strives to improve himself every day.

People who are interested in learning more about the Chimera Falls Universe are invited to visit The Nocturne Travel Agency at http://welcome-tonocturne.blogspot.com/

Books by Thomas Deja

Shadow Legion: New Roads to Hell
How the West was Weird 1
How the West was Weird 2
How the West was Weird 3

A Final Gift

by Rob Mancebo

Part One

World of Winter

Ten-year-old Tammy Burke didn't feel tired. She took in a monster breath that made her lungs burn and let out a bellow of laughter that echoed through unseen hills surrounding her.

She was completely enraptured in the joyful, physical sensation of being away from the stiff sheets and antiseptic smell of a hospital room for the first time in months.

Tammy threw herself down and made an angel in the smooth, untouched surface of the snow. Then she made a half a dozen snowballs and threw them, one after another, at the trunk of a pine tree she could just make out in the icy fog. The balls hit and smashed nobly, and a curtain of snow sloughed off the branches at each strike falling to the ground with a muffled thud.

Tammy laughed, as much to feel the joy of the act as to hear the sound in the quiet winter world she found herself in. It had been a long time since she had the strength to give a good, hearty laugh and she made up for its lack.

When she caught her breath, she walked to the tree and ran her fingers along its rough bark. She would've climbed nimbly into its branches to get a better view, but she expected she would've just seen more fog. Instead, she began to walk.

She walked uphill at first but changed her direction toward the shadow of a forest when it loomed off to her right. She didn't know why she chose that way to go. Possibly because the trees seemed like some sort of company in the wide winter world she had stumbled into.

It was not a thick, dark forest. It was cheerful and open to the indirect light of the fog-dimmed sun. She was dressed in normal jeans, sneakers, and the old winter jacket that was a little too small, and she walked rapidly to keep warm. There was no path or trail to be seen but she went boldly forward guessing that she would come upon some road or dwelling eventually.

After a while, she began to hear the faint sound of disquieting noises following her. Looking back, she saw that the fog was thicker and darker, as though night was closing in behind her as she moved.

She walked on. The snow-covered forest of tall trees seemed to stretch on forever. She began to get hungry and wondered how wide the wilderness could be. Turning and pulling back her coat's hood, she saw that the darkness behind her was creeping closer. Tammy wasn't afraid of the dark, but the approaching wall of darkness gave her a bad feeling. There was nothing else to do but continue to walk.

She was beginning to become frustrated by the complete lack of roads or houses, when she glimpsed the first shadow move in the forest. Tammy comforted herself with the thought that it was only her imagination, but then she saw another. It was definite the second time. A low, slinking sort of shadow, little more than a dim blotch in the fog. She looked around but didn't see any others. Tammy continued walking. Eerie darkness was still closing in behind her and walking forward was all she could do to keep ahead of it.

Off to her left, from the corner of her eye, she caught another shadow of movement. When she whirled to look, it disappeared, but she had glimpses of shadows on both sides of her this time. There were definitely things out in the woods, things that were pacing her as she moved.

Tammy's parents had taken her camping many times when she was younger and she looked around quickly for a big stick to use as a weapon, but the ground was too deeply covered with snow.

So she continued walking and watching, trying to remain calm.

She recognized that there were more figures closing in around her and they were circling closer. She could almost make out their shadowy shapes, skulking through the trees. She tried to count them but they were too furtive.

They moved in and out of the trees in the fog. There might've been five or a full dozen.

"Hello!" She finally gathered up her courage to yell. "Hello!" her voice sounded scared and thin as it echoed through the trees. But the sound gave her courage and she shouted again, "Hello! Who's out there?"

There was no answer and the figures melted away into the snow and gloom. The world was silent around her except for the gentle sighing of the breeze and the creaking of the forest branches.

There was a slope to her left, and Tammy turned that way and began to move faster. Her heart, so feeble for so long, now thundered in her ears and she ran through the snow. Whatever the silent shapes were, she didn't want to meet them in that lonesome forest.

The ground grew steadily steeper as she trudged on. Soon it was a snowy hill and her panting breath left long steamy clouds trailing behind her. A halo of light silhouetted the top of the hill before her and she began to run upwards toward it.

As she crested the hill, a huge gray wolf stepped out in front of her.

Chapter Two

The Great Hall

Tammy leaped back and fell down in the snow. The wolf raised its head and let out an echoing howl and the hunting pack closed in around her. More than half a dozen wolves had been closer than she could imagine. They appeared from behind every tree and snow-dusted bush, and added their voices to their leader's mournful call.

Surrounded and terrified, Tammy shut her eyes and held her hands over her ears to block out the eerie chorus. Curled up like a ball in the snow, she tried not to breath. Her heart was roaring like an express train. Mountain lions you should try and scare away, for bears you were supposed to play dead, but what did you do when surrounded by a pack of wolves?

She didn't know. Wolves didn't attack people! At least that's what she'd read. She wondered what the people who'd written those books would say in her situation!

Tammy realized suddenly that there was no sound around her. Ever so cautiously, she opened one eye, no more than a tentative crack. She had a very close, sideways view of unmoving wolf feet. The pack wasn't even smelling at her to see if she was alive.

She closed the eye again, but still nothing happened. Finally she could stand it no longer. She took a long, slow breath and sat up abruptly screaming, "Well are you going to eat me or what?"

The wolf in front of her jumped back but the rest of them simply sat, as though waiting.

The wolf she had frightened into movement came back to his position in the circle surrounding her and sat down once again.

"What, you're not going to eat me?" she demanded in a much harsher tone than she meant.

At that the wolves simply laid their heads down with their noses resting upon their paws. The pack leader walked cautiously forward and looked into her eyes. She could see that he wanted something. He was asking something of her, she could tell even though she could not hear him speak.

"What do you want?" she asked.

The wolf looked to the wall of black shadow following her then turned and walked several steps the other direction and looked back expectantly.

"You want me to follow you?"

At that, the wolf began to walk. When she followed, the other wolves stood and scattered into the forest once more.

The creature did not try to communicate to her in any other way. He simply walked onward and she followed along. She caught the flicker of a shadow now and then to tell her that the rest of the pack was still with them, filtering along through the trees. Tammy didn't know if she were a guest or a prisoner. Only that things were very strange and she really couldn't think of anything else to do.

The wolf walked on for a long time. Bored with the silence of the trip, she began to talk.

"My name is Tammy Burke, do you have a name, Mister wolf?" The wolf glanced back, but didn't answer. "Well you seem to be a very great and important wolf to me, the sort of wolf that all the other wolves look up to. So, since you don't seem to have a name of your own, I shall give you one—ummmmm. How about Constantine? That seems a proud and pompous name. Constantine Ambrosias Maximilian von Wolf. Now that sounds lordly enough to be the leader of a wolfpack, doesn't it?"

The wolf looked back and lowered its ears.

"No-no-no—Constantine, don't argue," she scolded. "Those who don't introduce themselves are fated to be named by others."

"I could probably change it to something simpler and less pompous," she offered, "if you were to tell me where we're going."

The wolf looked back her disdainfully and continued to walk.

"All right, Constantine," she said.

The wolf suddenly broke into a trot and she was forced to run to keep up.

"Hey wait!" she called after him. "I'm sorry, Mister wolf. I was only teasing—" her puffing breath caught suddenly in her throat.

The mist opened before her to reveal a great, dark mansion that reared up out of the snow.

It was a fairytale wonder brought to life. The structure was built of peeled logs whose edges were trimmed into a puzzle of sweeping curves and axe-hewn archways. Its glowing, diamond-paned windows were surrounded by wooden sills of carved, brightly painted flowers, and its many-peaked roof exhausted plumes of smoke through crafted holes rather than chimneys.

The wolves came out of the woods, ran under the arching eaves, and sat upon the porch to wait for her.

Tammy's approach was slowed by wonder. It was the most marvelous structure she had beheld. Its construction was of humble materials, hand-hewn timbers and fieldstone, but so cunning was the work that it seemed as magnificent as any palace.

She found that the entire face of the massive door was carved with a scene of epic battle.

"It's Saint George killing a dragon, see?" she whispered to the lounging wolves as her fingertips brushed the carven oak delicately.

"Should I knock?" she asked. "There's no bell."

The wolf leader simply stood up and pushed the door with his nose. It had neither lock nor latch and swung open at his touch.

The wolf led her inside where blackened iron lanterns gave off an eerie, yellowish light. The floor was of polished wooden planks that sent echoes dancing through the room from both the wolf's toenails and her wet shoes. It took several long moments for her eyes to adjust to the lighting. She simply blinked and followed the wolf through the gloom.

So it was that she found herself standing in front of a blazing fireplace. She warmed her chilly hands at the fire and rubbed her cold nose before she threw back her jacket's hood to look around the rustic hall.

A gasp escaped her when she realized that she and the wolf were not alone.

The wolf had lain down at the left hand of a great carven chair, almost like a throne. A man sat in the chair and looked at her with a knowing smile upon his face. He was dressed in heavy trousers and his white hair and beard swept down to brush a flowing robe of forest green trimmed with supple ermine. He was thick and powerful, and the fingers of his right hand loosely encircled the ivory hilt of a long sword, the tip of which rested by the toe of one tall, black boot. A woven crown of holly encircled his head.

"I know you," she said with a quiet confusion in her voice. It was as though a dream had sprung to life before her, recognizable, but not at all what she had expected or envisioned.

"Yes, Tammy." The man's voice was deep and calm. "I think you do."

"You're not—?" she whispered.

"Names mean little in this place. Most of us are known by many of them. So then, Grandfather Winter, Father Christmas, Saint Nicolas or Santa Claus, I don't suppose it makes any difference what you wish to call me."

Tammy rubbed her eyes and tried to take in the rustic opulence of the dim hall. With the fire as its greatest source of light, it was dusky and shrouded.

"No," she said to herself as she looked around the hall. "This isn't the North Pole. I don't even believe in Santa Claus anymore!"

The man gave forth a bellowing laugh that was nothing at all like 'Ho-Ho-Ho'.

"No, this is not the North Pole, this is my hall." He stood up and rested the sword against his chair. "I am Nicholas, once the Bishop of Myra, now a protector of hope."

She was startled when he stood up and she stepped backward and fell into a chair that was waiting to receive her.

Nicholas waved a hand and the walls flared with the cheerful flames of many candles so that their light flickered and twinkled off every polished surface in the hall. There were lush spruce boughs draped above the windows and twisting garlands of holly ran about the walls. Clusters of pinecones dangled and bright berries peeked through the greenery.

"Up Rill," he beckoned at the wolf that lolled by his throne. "Cast off your cloak and collect your kin. We must see to our guest."

The wolf stretched and stood. Then it did a strange thing. It reared up upon its hind legs and cast off its furry skin. It was suddenly a little man holding a wolf skin in his hand. He was short with a smooth, ageless face. Broad and powerful but perfectly formed in his own size.

With a smile and a bow to Tammy, the little man skittered to the entrance to bring in the others.

"Is that an—elf?" Tammy couldn't help herself from asking.

"Rill is one of the small-souls, one of the lesser people of the earth," Nicholas told her. "The Northern folk called them dwarves, but if you choose to call him an elf, I think he will not mind."

"Can he talk?"

"They have always had the power of speech, but the small-souls speak softly. You must listen very carefully."

Tammy looked around at the merry hall once again and shook her head as though it might vanish. The weirdness of the entire scene was finally sinking in and her curiosity was awakening.

"But where am I? How did I get here? What's going on?"

"You are in my home. You were led here by Rill and his brethren for my protection. You have been given a very special gift. You have paused in your journey to spend some time with me."

Her questions were interrupted as a group of little men burst in through the front door with wide eyes. Rill was first among them and ran to Nicholas. The Saint lowered his head to allow the small man to whisper into his ear. Then he nodded grimly.

"What's wrong?" Tammy asked.

"They've tracked you down," Nicholas told her as he picked up his sword and proceeded to a wall whereupon was hung a great shield painted with a wreath of holly surrounding an evergreen.

Chapter Three

A Feast for the Soul

"I don't understand—"

"Stay here with the lads," he ordered her. "You, of all people, should not see them."

Then he strode boldly across the long hall and outside. Despite his warning, Tammy began to follow but the entire group of little men blocked her passage, with spreading arms and shaking heads.

Through the open door she could see little. An evil black mist, like some poisoned shadow given physical form, seeped in through the portal but it burned off from the merry light of the hall. She could hear the sound of many blows, frightening voices, the rumble of thunder, and see flashing like lightning.

Then Nicholas came back. He was puffing only slightly and he hung his shield back upon the wall before he turned to look at Tammy.

"You had many, very powerful fears, child."

"My fears?" she asked.

"Yes. They were following you. They would've overwhelmed you if they had caught up." One of the little men brought him a tremendous golden goblet from the table. The Saint nodded his thanks and took several deep gulps from the vessel before handing it back. This being done, he seemed so full of power and vigor that he fairly glowed.

"I don't understand," Tammy shook her head. "This is all getting weirder and weirder! I feel like my head is going to explode!"

"Come," he invited her. "Sit at my table and I will tell you my story. Perhaps then you will understand."

He led her to a long table where many plates were set. Nicholas indicated that she should sit upon his right. When she sat down the little men brought in heaping platters of food before sitting down themselves.

At the smell of the food, Tammy realized she was mortally hungry. It felt like years since she had eaten and for a long while she concerned herself with stuffing her face.

The little men were hungry too and their manners were horrendous. They ate with their greasy fingers mostly. They tossed bones to the floor or at each other with gleeful laughs. They wolfed down meat like starving dogs and drained their drinks with splashing gusto.

The food was the best Tammy had ever tasted and the mysterious sweet drink in her cup never emptied, but refilled itself whenever she drained it.

"What is this?" she finally asked when wonder overpowered her hunger.

"That? That is the best drink ever, child," Nicholas replied with a smile. "That is the prayers and good wishes of people who care about you. So long as that cup is full, you shall remain as my guest."

Two of the little men had begun wrestling and Nicholas snapped, "Rill, Wythe!" and let fly with a bone from his own plate that bounced off a little man's head. "Fighting is to be done outside. Leave each other's food alone or you'll leave the table!" The two little men let go of each other's ears and sat back down scowling.

"Now," Saint Nicholas returned to talking to Tammy, "to my story. I survived the persecution of the Christians by Pagan Rome, saw the Emperor make Christianity the official religion of Rome itself. I became a Bishop in the Church. I was good to the poor and needy, as all men should be. I led a full life and in due time, I died.

"That was more than sixteen hundred years ago, as it is measured in the world of men. Though, to speak truly, it seems a mere moment to me here where there is no time."

Tammy looked around the wounderous hall. "But what happened?" she asked. "You're still here."

The man looked at her for several seconds as though considering his next words with the utmost care. "Mark you the size and weight of this cup?" He slid his own drinking cup over to her. "The vessel is formed by the wishes, prayers, and pleadings of humanity's hearts. It is to me, like the anchor of a great ship. It binds me to the world of men so that I cannot leave."

"Binds you?"

"Yes, the clinging thoughts of the living can bind those who have passed on. So it was with me. My faithful flock held my memory so closely that they unwittingly bound me to the lower realm of the heavens. Then they proclaimed me as a Saint and added the prayers of many other men to hold me here. After a time, they spread my fame to other nations. My name became an icon of the great celebration of the birth of our Lord, and my own fame was multiplied many times. Now I have a score of names throughout the nations and each time a child focuses a sleepy thought upon me in wistful longing or joyous blessing, I am bound all the tighter to the physical world."

"How terrible!" Tammy whispered.

"No, not at all, child," Nicholas said with a laugh. "For whilst I am bound, so too I am given power within the domain of humanity. A greater power than when I was a poor Bishop of a simple people.

"You see, the depths of winter used to be a most fearsome time for the folk of the world. The specter of darkness, depression, threat of freezing or starvation, and dragging days of endless loneliness used to haunt the winter. But who can be overcome by darkness and fear when thoughts of Saint Nicholas fill their heads?

"Even as a worldly symbol of commercial avarice, still I am given power over the wintry demons of despair that would consume the happiness of people's lives.

"So then, I am both ensnared and empowered by the Christmas spirit."

"Can you ever escape?" Tammy asked in wonder.

"Someday, if all humanity forgets and takes no more time for Christmas, then the power that fills this cup will wane and I will be free to travel onward.

"Until then, I drive off the wintry demons and fill the minds of humanity with brighter thoughts, even when they are hemmed in by the bleakest time of the year."

"Then I'm—I'm—" Tammy tried but she couldn't finish the statement.

"Yes, child," Saint Nicholas told her. "You have not been healed. You have transcended the lower world of humanity. You are upon the journey home."

Chapter Four

The Sword-Saint

"I don't feel—dead." Tammy patted herself seeking to find some sort of injury or weakness. "I feel—"

"Whole," Nicholas finished for her.

"Yes."

"Perfectly whole. No injuries, no scars, no weakness," he brushed a hand across her cheek and continued.

"Why, yes." She felt for the scars of the operations she'd had over the years and found none.

"Physical injuries cause no scars to the spirit," he told her.

"But, I'm not scared," she told him with a scowl. "That doesn't seem right."

"Inside, in the very fiber of your being, you know that you're going home," he told her with a laugh. "Only debased and degraded spirits quail at that journey.

"Those close to you have shown a great deal of care and attention to you or you would not even have been held to this plane for as long as you have. Soon, the thoughts of most people will turn away from you; your cup will run low, and you will be prepared to take up the next leg of your journey.

"Until then, you may bide with me here as I work about my appointed task."

"Your appointed task?" she repeated.

"Of course, Christmas is coming. I have work to do!"

"You're not going to try and tell me that you go around delivering toys?" Tammy raised a skeptical eyebrow.

He bellowed with laughter at the suggestion until there were tears in his eyes. "No. No toys, I'm afraid. But I have much traveling and work to do none the less."

He broke a twig of holly off one of the many wreaths that hung about the hall and gave it a shake. As his hand swept down the twig expanded and lengthened into a stout stick more than a yard long. Its tip sprouted with a small clutch of leaves garnished with clusters of crimson berries.

"Now you take this," he told her. "We shall travel through many fearsome places and you might need it."

For himself, he belted on a great, black sword belt that shone with metallic emblems of stars and trees of great variety. When he had secured the golden buckles, Tammy realized that his clothing had somehow shifted from its former forest green, to brilliant crimson.

"In many ways it is best to appease people's expectations," he told her as he ran a hand down the traditional red sleeve trimmed with ermine. But then he took up his long sword and winked at her saying, "Yet we all have our preferences. Sixteen hundred years and I've never given up this old spatha." He slid the sword into its sheath and took up his shield.

"Here now, speaking of expectations. You cannot accompany me dressed like that! What would people say? That they had dreams of a little girl in jeans and an old coat?" He took the wand of holly from her hand and waved it down across in front of her.

Tammy found herself dressed in thick robes of ermine-trimmed scarlet and sable-lined black boots that rose up to her knees.

"That's better. Now we're ready to travel."

Chapter Five
A Wild Ride

He tossed her the staff, which she caught in something of a daze of wonder. Then he took down a large, empty sack and threw into it his shield, his great cup, and her cup also. When full, the sack looked no bigger than it had when empty.

The little men suddenly went wild. They scurried madly about grabbing up reindeer hides and leather harness straps lined with bells. For a moment, Nicolas and Tammy were waste-deep in a sea of wildly bustling little men and then the whole crew of them ran out the front door leaving Tammy to stare after them somewhat breathlessly.

"Off we go." Her host took the sack in his left hand and offered her his right.

She took the staff and held onto his arm. He led her out the front door to where a sleigh was waiting, complete with eight reindeer. "I rode in a chariot in the beginning," he told her. "But a sleigh is traditional now."

They entered the vehicle and Nicholas cracked a whip in the air to order the start of their journey. They lunged and the sleigh jolted. Within a few lurching paces the whole vehicle, reindeer and all, had taken to the sky.

It was a very strange feeling for Tammy. Stranger than the time she'd been flown to the hospital in a helicopter. The whole world just dropped out from underneath them with. There was no feeling of support only a great tugging from the front. They whipped through the sky wildly like the tail of a kite. Speed itself seemed to be the only thing that kept them in the air.

And then, suddenly, they were on the ground and the runners of the sleigh bit into the snow to hold them upon their course.

The land about them was locked in an eerie twilight. Scattered people bustled through the streets and the headlights of cars seared the road with the brilliance of their beams.

Tammy gasped as the reindeer pulled them right onto a busy street and proceeded to drive against traffic! But the on-coming cars passed through them without effect. She didn't even feel the breeze of their passing.

"This is very weird!" she called to the driver. "They're like ghosts!"

"It is strange, isn't it!" he said with a laugh. "You see, we're in a different world than they are. The weight of the material plane has no hold upon us. They can't even see us in waking life. Although, sometimes in dream-time, or when they're half awake they can catch a glimpse."

"If they're in the material plane," Tammy asked. "Where are we?"

"We've traveled down to the second plane, down to the plane of ghosts. This is an embattled region where those in the spirit world can influence those of the material world."

Tammy grabbed his arm suddenly as a shining figure flashed past them. "Was that—" She watched as the figure disappeared behind them. "Was that an angel?"

"Yes, of course," he told her. "I told you, this is the plane that intersects that of the material world. All those creatures who wish to affect the world of humanity travel here. It becomes very crowded at times, what with battles and mobs of spirits. But at this time of year, I'm able to keep the streets cleaner than they used to be."

"What do you mean?" She asked.

"Look to the shadows and alleyways child." He pointed with his whip.

As Tammy looked out past the lighted streets, she caught glimpses of ugly movement in the shadows. There were things hiding throughout the city, dim, misshapen things lurking in dark corners waiting for victims.

"What are they?" she asked, pressing closer to him.

"Nightmares and the spirits of the fearful dead. Skulkers and night-gaunts summoned up from other realms by the whims and greed and long-ings of humanity. Those are the inner and outer demons of mankind. They are lurking, waiting for people they can attach themselves to."

"Can't you drive them away?"

"Not all the Christmas spirit of all humanity can completely drive them away," Nicholas told her. "For their legions are without number. But our presence forces them into the shadows, see. And we shall do what we can this night. Come, I will show you." He pulled up the reins and the sleigh came to a skidding halt upon a street corner.

Nicholas took his sack and jumped out of the sleigh, waving for her to follow. They proceeded through the front door of an apartment complex and up stairs.

Melting right through the closed door, they entered an apartment that was sparsely decorated with a school-made paper chain and a small fake Christmas tree that had been shoved into a corner.

"Here, see," Nicholas waved a hand at the room. "We have little enough to work with. Yet it shall suffice. Come." He led her down a hallway to a child's bedroom. When they entered, something rank and repugnant skittered away from the child's bed and hid in the darkened regions of the closet. The child moaned and tossed under his covers as though assaulted by bad dreams.

"This family has little faith in anything, much less the spirit of Christmas. Yet there is some comfort for them still."

He opened his bag to uncover his mug. He dipped a finger into the mug and then gently dripped a drop onto the sleeping child's forehead. The little boy relaxed at that. His features softened and he smiled and drifted into a peaceful sleep.

The creature in the closet gave off a hiss of rage and disappointment, and Saint Nicholas laughed at it.

"There's a withered soul that will go hungry for a while. This lad will have no nightmares for the rest of the season."

He waved for her to follow and proceeded to another room where a woman slept alone. Arrayed about her was a medley of ghastly figures that cringed and hissed at their entrance, but did not flee. They were attached to the woman with long, slavering mouths or sucking tentacles. Though she slept, the woman's face wore an expression of concern and unrest.

"Ah, this one is deeply ensnared in the problems of the world. See how the unquiet spirits feed off her pain and despair? They will not give up their feast so easily I think."

He pulled his shield from the sack and drew his sword. Tammy wondered what he would do against such a disgusting group of creatures. But the Saint never hesitated. He drove forward into them. Flailing tentacles and slashing claws thumped against the shield and his long sword flashed and wheeled. As he fought, the Saint began to glow with a fiery light that burned the demons and made them flinch from him. In only a few moments he had slashed the demons into skulking slips of twitching shadows or driven them away to cower, hissing in the corners of the room.

Nicolas then took an invigorating draught from his cup, dipped his fingertip into it, and touched it upon the woman's sleeping brow.

"Sleep in peace," he whispered before they left. Tammy looked back as they left the room and saw that the demons were collecting about the woman once again, but they were held at bay by a barrier of thin, radiant light that surrounded her.

"See there," Nicolas whispered. "The hope and cheer of the season can affect even non-believers."

Nicholas led Tammy through the wall to another apartment. This one was decorated with garlands of evergreen and holly. It had a Christmas tree displayed proudly near to the window where its twinkling lights could be seen by passers-by. There were Christmas cards standing up upon the counter top and paper snowflakes taped up upon the walls. Upon a coffee table in a corner, was a Nativity scene.

"Ah, now here we have something to work with!" Nicholas laughed. He took his cup and sprinkled drops upon the door frame. When he entered the small room where two children slept there were no specters visible although Tammy heard an eerie, scuffling movement under the bed. Saint Nicholas dipped his fingers into his cup and sprinkled drops onto the sleeping children who merely stretched languidly and snuggled deeper into their pillows and dreams of Christmas.

Then he led Tammy to their parents' room and did the same for the couple sleeping in each other's arms. Here too Tammy could hear the churning and shuffling of fears and nightmares from the shadows. But when they were sprinkled by Saint Nicholas, the couple glowed with a brilliant light that filled the room around them and drove the lurking creatures off into the cold night.

"As you give, so shall you receive," Nicholas said in blessing and then moved on.

And so it went throughout the night. Dwelling after dwelling they visited spreading peace and cheer to those who lived there. Some homes though, were so embroiled in the demons of fear and care that the Saint merely shook his head sadly at the churning bulwark of spirits and passed on.

"Those who have faith in nothing," he told Tammy. "Will be comforted by nothing."

Other times Nicholas raised his shield and fought his way through mobs of nightmares and unquiet spirits to get to a house. Once within, even a touch of Christmas cheer was enough to drive off hordes of spectral tormenters.

The ghostly plane was a place without time. Tammy didn't know if their trip would've taken years, or decades, or even centuries in the physical world. In that trip she never grew older, but she grew infinitely wiser. She witnessed flaming sky battles between angels and demons. Time and again she saw smoky legions of tormenting spirits driven back into the shadows. She saw the hordes of hollow-eyed, earthbound spirits who languished upon the ghostly plane—errant sinners in life, too fearful to move on in death. Spiritually starving, they floated throughout the world seeking vainly to feed off the warmth and energy of the living.

When they came to the houses of her friends, she helped Saint Nicholas cleanse them of care and bless them. She, herself got to drive off clinging spirits with sharp blows from her holly staff.

When they arrived at her parents' home though, she was shocked at its condition. There were no decorations. No signs of cheer. Everything was still boxed up in the attic from the year before. Worse still, the entire house was churning with dark, crawling demons of despondency and despair. The foul reek of demon-spawn clung about like sewer stink. A legion of fearsome creatures laughed and wallowed in the oppressive sorrow of the occupants.

Tammy vaulted off the sleigh in a towering rage. "Get out!" she screamed at them and swung her staff with both hands. Dark, wispy demons shredded at her strokes, others scattered shrieking before her wrath. But as she entered the house itself, she ran into huge, black creatures that her staff rebounded from. The creatures laughed at her impotent attack.

Nicolas was there behind her though. His shield wrapped around to protect her and his shining sword slashed them cunningly, searing claw and tentacle with its touch. The demons roared in frantic pain and endless hunger, and pressed in against them, trampling across their own fallen.

Tammy lashed out with her staff over and over but against these creatures it had little effect. Nicolas became grim and dealt ferocious strokes, but even he could not conquer the huge host of dark, shrieking evil that lashed about them.

Not all the Christmas spirit could drive the demons of despair from her parent's home.

Chapter Six

Bears and Angels

Tammy fought with all her might and the dark demons flinched at the power of her strokes, but she could not drive them off. No matter how she pummeled, no matter how many cringed from her blows, there were always more to take their place.

She fought on hopelessly. Yet a great anger arose in her against the creatures that tormented her parents in their time of grief, multiplying her mother and father's pain to feed off their despair. She would not give up. She would not leave her mother and father to the bitter mercy of their unseen tormenters.

Even as the battling pair were leagued about by the mass of crushing evil, a horrible scream resounded through the house. It was not a scream of the endless starvation of the demon's void, nor a shriek of frantic anger. There was pain and terror in the voice and others took up the piercing cry as a new force entered the battle.

Tammy saw a flittering form of searing brilliance flash through the dark horde. It moved like a fiery hummingbird, darting back and forth, and where it passed demons screamed, smoked, and burned.

Clouds of dark figures boiled out of the house, through the walls and into the cloaking darkness of the freezing winter night. Tammy found herself standing alone in the room with Nicolas and the shining form.

As she stared, the being's wings vanished and the searing fire of its wrath faded to a clear white, like the shine of a meadow of new-fallen snow on a sunny morning.

She could see that the figure was like that of a perfectly formed human, but its flowing robes gave a mystery as to whether it was a tall woman or a slim man. The shining aura that surrounded it made the features indistinct and she blinked her eyes, trying to focus upon it.

It brushed an open hand fondly across her head as it floated past, sending a thrill through her that gave her goose bumps all up her back. With a wave to Nicolas it faded through the wall and was gone.

"I—do angels do that?" Tammy stuttered. "I mean, can they really help people?"

"You saw the wings," Nicolas said as he sheathed his sword. "A winged angel means that it has been 'sent'. Demons dare not stand before an angel sent forth upon the word of God. As you saw, when its task is completed, the wings fade.

"It was sent for you, Tammy. You have been blessed again this night. Although your parents' hope and faith have been crushed, yours called out and was answered."

"But what were those horrible things?" she asked.

"There are many demons upon the plane of ghosts. Those were spirits of anger," the Saint told her. "As you found out, you cannot defeat anger with anger. No, anger must be fought with discipline, steadfast courage, and love."

"Oh." She couldn't think of anything else to say. She was embarrassed that she had failed.

"You did well," he encouraged her. "Come now, let's see to your parents."

He took her to their room and walked round the bed. Shaking his head, he looked at the troubled couple. They slept uneasily, their brows creased with the weight of her death and the sorrow of a first Christmas with her newly gone from their lives.

Saint Nicolas sprinkled them with drops from his cup and blessed them, and they relaxed somewhat. Tammy stood looking down at their troubled sleep and had an inspiration. She broke a twig from the tip of her staff and focused all her concentration upon it. The twig grew and sprouted and curled a little but then ceased. She looked upon it in frustration.

"That was a very good beginning," Nicholas commended. He reached around and placed his hand upon hers saying, "Try again."

She focused again and the holly grew thick and intertwined itself into a wreath. Saint Nicholas took the wreath and placed it above the headboard of the bed where it hung in the air.

The girl leaned close over her parents sleeping forms and whispered, "I'm all right. Mom, Dad, everything's just fine." She took her own cup from Nicholas' bag and sprinkled them saying, "As you give, so shall you receive," as she had seen him do many times.

Her parents shifted and settled into a calm slumber.

"Is that all I can do?" she asked.

"That is all," Saint Nicholas told her. "In this form we can have a strong effect upon the spirits haunting the material world, but we cannot touch those within it physically. The pleasure and pain of the lowest realm is beyond us now. We are no more than a whisper, a feeling, an impulse to those who will listen."

"Will they be all right now?" She reached out but found that her hand would not make contact with her mother's furrowed brow.

"They will be different," Nicolas told her. "As all who suffer loss are changed. But they will heal now that their minds are not being poisoned by the endless, raging, anger that was goading their every living moment. In ridding them of that, we have been of some service.

"And, after all, that is what Christmas is about, an intangible feeling reminding us that, even in the darkest time of the year, there is still hope in this old world."

Tammy saw her mother's arm reach out and rest across her father's chest. His hand rose up and cradled it against him.

Nicolas smiled and beckoned to Tammy. They climbed into the sleigh and Nicolas gave the reigns a shake to send them off into the night once more.

By the time they had past across the face of the world, Tammy felt exhausted. Draughts from her cup invigorated her but even that was not enough to keep her awake. When the sleigh bumped down before Nicolas's hall, she realized that she had been sound asleep.

She entered the great hall amid the scurrying pack of little men who were dragging reindeer hides and jingling harnesses along behind them. They trotted off to stow their gear and Tammy looked for somewhere to lie down. She was so sleepy her knees felt wobbly.

"Here, child," Nicolas rolled out a thick, white bearskin that was longer than she was tall. The little men returned with bearskins of their own. As each one wrapped himself in a hide, he would drop to hands and knees and give himself a quick shake. In a moment, Tammy was surrounded by a room full of grumbling, sleepy-eyed bear cubs.

"Sleep in peace," Nicolas said in a hushed voice. The lights in the hall snuffed out one-by-one, and she was left with only the roaring of the merry fire for light. Nicolas eased down into his great chair and rested the tip of his sword by one tall boot. All was just as it had been when she had first arrived.

Tammy stretched out upon the thick, soft bearskin and several of the cubs snuggled in around her to sleep. She pressed her back against one warm furry body, and rested her head upon another. In a few moments she drifted off into an untroubled slumber.

***

Tammy awoke in the dim hall to the sound of stirring and clomping boots. More than simply rested, she felt completely stripped of all cares and worries.

"You rested well, I see," Nicolas greeted her with a bright eye. "And you're ready to leave us now, it would seem."

"Am I?" Tammy blinked and looked around.

"Certainly. Don't you feel the change?"

"I feel—light. It's as though a puff of breeze would blow me away."

"Light, yes," Nicholas said with a nod. "The lingering preoccupation of your loved ones has faded in your long slumber. You have been freed of the weight of their clinging thoughts. In our travels you helped heal their spiritual wounds and, in turn, they have released you."

"They've forgotten me?"

"Not forgotten, no, yet the bitterness of your loss has faded somewhat. The wounds have healed. They remember but they do not pine or wallow. It has been many months as they measure time in the world of men."

"It was only one night—"

"A night or a year, there is always the time to accomplish what needs to be done in this realm. You have rested. Your spirit has healed. You are prepared to take the next leg of your journey."

"And what is that?"

"Upon your journey home, each step is a mystery. You can look back to see where you have been, but not where you are going. That is a mystery which is only resolved through your travels."

"Thank you, Nicholas. Thank you for everything." Tammy hugged him.

"Do you wish to eat before you go?" he asked, patting her back.

"I—no. I'm not hungry," Tammy replied with a note of curiosity in her voice.

"Ah, see, you've transcended even that. Nothing holds you here now." He walked with her to the door of his great hall and outside.

Tammy found that the sun was shining and the fog had cleared. It was a glorious day and a clear path wound away through the forest before her.

"Is it spring already?" she asked. "Where did all the fog and snow go?"

"You have moved beyond them, child." Nicholas explained. "To others they are still here, but not to you. You are ready to leave."

Tammy picked up her holly wand from against the wall where she'd left it and gave it a sharp shake. The slim stick swept out into the size and thickness of a pilgrim's staff at the motion. Nicolas laughed and nodded.

"Thank you for everything!" she said again. "Thank you all." She waved goodbye to the group of little men who crowded upon the porch dragging their bearskins behind them. They smiled and waved in return, only elbowing and kicking each other a little while they did.

Tammy set out upon the road. The flowers poking their heads up through the forest litter were newly in bloom and birds were singing brightly in the trees. Springtime was her favorite season.

She turned back just before she was out of sight and waved back at the watching group. Then she walked on down the winding path toward—home.

☠❉☠❉☠❉

About Robert Mancebo:

Rob is a former army scout and infantryman, classified courier, locksmith, alarm/video technician, X-ray /medical technician, and security guard.

He's had numerous spec-fiction, historical fiction, western, fantasy, and SciFi stories published in: Amazing Journeys, Electronic Tales, Cyberpulp, AlienSkin, Abandoned Towers, Flashing Swords, Heroic Fantasy Quarterly, Raygun Revival, and Spacewesterns magazines, as well as pieces in Rage of the Behemoth, Fist Full of Hollers, Ghosts of Taux, A Knight at the Silk Purse, and Clash of Steel anthologies. He's also spent some time as a slush reader for Flashing Swords magazine and edited for Cyberwizard Productions.

Books by Robert Mancebo

Born to Trouble
The Stars Like Candles Proudly Shown
With a Company of Rogues

Vaults of the Dark Burgeoning God

by Joel Jenkins

With thanks to Josh Reynolds for letting me borrow Charles St. Cyprian and Ebe Gallowglass for a few thousand words!

Charles St. Cyprian halted his upward hike over the jumble of snow-covered boulders which made up the central island of Minquiers, his labored breath pluming out in frosty billows, as one Ebe Gallowglass paused on the boulder above him.

"Winded already, what? We've scarcely gone a quarter kilometer." Gallowglass cut a cinematic figure standing on that boulder, dressed with the practicality of a street urchin yet with the flair of a Parisian street apache, a flat cap upon her head, and sharp, dark features which grinned in amusement.

"But most of that's been up," complained St. Cyprian. He scrambled up alongside of his companion and then took the opportunity to resume his rest, by surveying the chaotic jumble of jutting stone that thrust itself out of the English channel about nine miles south of Jersey.

"Not exactly what I had in mind for the morning celebration of Christ's birth. A warm fire, a Christmas tree, and a leisurely breakfast would be more to my liking."

"And mine," admitted St. Cyprian, "but the duty of the Royal Occultist transcends holidays and holy days, alike. Besides, today isn't really the birth of Christ."

"Bollox!" exclaimed Gallowglass. "Are you saying that He never existed?"

"Nothing of the sort, Gallowglass. It's just that reliable texts indicate he was more likely born in April than December."

This was the Maitresse, the central island, but there were a number of smaller islands and rocks that were considered to be part of the Minkies, as locals referred to it, but many of these were currently subsumed beneath the high tides. At low tides the area of the Minquiers was greater than Jersey itself, at high tides it practically disappeared.

"Well, let's get to higher ground and see what we've got," said St. Cyprian.

Gallowglass nodded toward the motor launch that bobbed at the island's edge, and the amazonian red-head, a member of the Yorkshire Archaeological Society—her hair lit up like a furnace in the cold morning sun—who tended to it. "Perhaps I should call Miss Jobson to carry you the rest of the way. She seems sturdy enough for the work, and I'm sure she's more than a little sweet on you. It's darling the way she fawns on you since that whole Deo Virido fiasco."

Beneath his outer jacket, St. Cyprian was dressed as an advertisement for Gieves & Hawkes, Savile Rowe. Still, his polished tie-pin was put to shame by the polish of his old Etonian intonations. He shot a severe glance at Gallowglass. "It's quite a change of pace from the brusque rudeness to which I've become accustomed."

"Someone's got to keep you humble, Mr. St. Cyprian."

"And you've elected yourself, Miss Gallowglass."

"I do believe it's in the job description of the assistant to Great Britain's Royal Occultist."

"Apprentice," corrected St. Cyprian. "You're my apprentice."

Gallowglass did not blink. "No, I'm quite sure that it is Assistant. My contract specifically says that I am called upon to 'assist the appointed Royal Occultist in all efforts to suppress, banish, and eradicate all That Man Was Not Meant to Know, including but not limited to vampires, ghosts, werewolves, ogres, goblins, hobgoblins, bogles, barguests, boojums and other assorted and unclassified ent …'"

"I doubt that John Dee ever had to deal with such pretensions in his apprentice," interrupted St. Cyprian.

"So why did you feed Miss Jobson that balderdash about checking out the lay of the land before calling for her?'"

"There's no point in exposing her to unnecessary danger." St. Cyprian unconsciously tapped at the trio of rings that adorned his right hand, each inscribed with inscrutable glyphs, and each an inheritance of his office as Royal Occultist to the throne. "Once we determine that the environs are safe we'll bring her up and she can make a scientific investigation of any archaeological features we might discover."

They continued to pick their way up the slope and came upon a cluster of ten abandoned fishermen's huts at the top of the stony island. These were generally used seasonally, when runs of pike and mackerel invaded the English Channel, but appeared to be quite empty now.

"I don't think that these huts are quite old enough to pique Miss Jobson's professional interest," said Gallowglass. "Perhaps you expected to find something else?"

"We have a dozens of reports of odd and supernatural aquatic disturbances and mutations all located in the vicinity of the Minkies," replied St. Cyprian. "This seems like the natural place to begin our investigation."

"If you count bulbous-eyed fish with beaks and spiked tentacles attacking hapless fishermen, I'd agree that it qualifies as odd, but I'm not sure it warrants the investigation of the Royal Occultist and his assistant."

"Apprentice…" said St. Cyprian. "And there are supernatural forces at work within the sea as well as upon dry land, Miss Gallowglass."

"So what do you think has stirred up the prehistoric bottom feeders and brought them to the surface, Mr. St. Cyprian?"

"Do you recall your lessons in summoning preterrestrial entities?"

"Not that I've had much call for it," said Gallowglass, "but now that you mention it, these huts are laid out in a similar formation to the summoners decagram, and there even appears to have once been a structure at the center."

"Very good, Miss Gallowglass." St. Cyprian strode to the center of the formation of huts and began to stoke through the rubble of a former hut with his walking stick. "I'm glad to see that my instructive efforts have not been wasted." St. Cyprian hesitated. "Hmm…"

"What is it?" asked Gallowglass. "Something have you rattled?"

St. Cyprian used the tip of his walking stick to push away a platform of rotting planks which might have once served as the floor of the hut, revealing a shaft which had been carved directly into the stone heart of the island centuries earlier. "We may have discovered something of archaeological significance that may interest Miss Jobson…"

"Besides yourself?" smirked Gallowglass.

"I'm only a handful of years older than you," St. Cyprian reminded her. "At any rate, based on the translations I made from the Demons des Mer scroll fragments this was what I expected to find. What I didn't expect to find were very recent footprints."

Gallowglass wandered over to the far edge of the fishermen's village and peered along the jagged and rocky edges of the island. "There's a blue boat pulled up behind that snow-covered cluster of rocks on the east side of the island. It's meant to be hidden, but you can see a touch of the prow if you're standing in the right spot."

A man wearing a brilliant red cravat, which was pinned with a gold pentacle, emerged from behind one of the huts, holding a Galand double-action revolver, with an ebony grip, which he trained on Gallowglass and St. Cyprian. "Toujour en retard a la fete, St. Cyprian. It seems to be a pattern with you."

"A party?" retorted Gallowglass as she reached for her Webley-Fosberry revolver. "Where's the booze and hor d'ouvres?"

"Ah, ah," came a feminine voice from not far behind her. "Touch that revolver and this double-barreled shotgun is sure to turn you into mincemeat."

When Gallowglass shot a glance over her shoulder, she saw a very young buxom blonde woman with hooked nose, but not unattractive features, training a Lefaucheux double-barreled shotgun in her direction and decided, after all, against drawing her pistol. Beneath the collar of the woman's quilted jacket, she saw a necklace that was thick with warding amulets of various schools of sorcery and necromancy. "Who are you, anyhow?"

St. Cyprian's brow furrowed and for a moment his lips compressed. "Allow me to introduce Monsieur Francois Gravelle, Head officer of the French Directory in charge of Les Affaire D'occulte. I had the displeasure of crossing paths with him in France during the Great War."

"Oh, I am hurt to the heart," said Monsieur Gravelle. "You haven't yet forgiven me for our little misunderstanding?"

"You were bringing English soldiers up from the dead for questioning, and trapping their souls within their decaying bodies for eternity," snapped St. Cyprian as Monsieur Gravelle relieved him of his Webley Bulldog. "There was nothing to misunderstand."

"They had information that was critical to the allies," snapped Monsieur Gravelle. "Unlike some royally appointed occultists I have the intestinal fortitude to make the hard decisions, so that results can be had."

Gallowglass scowled as the French blonde plucked her Webley-Fosberry out of her holster, even while pressing the barrels of the shotgun against her back. "Watch it, luv. The slightest pull of that trigger and my insides'll be decorating Monsieur Gravelle."

Monsieur Gravelle gave the slightest grin, which might have been construed as malicious. "That's my assistant, Brigitte Malin. She's quite handy with the charms and sorceries, and she knows well enough how to pull the trigger of a shotgun."

"That's what's got me tetchy," said Gallowglass.

St. Cyprian straightened his cuffs. "Mademoiselle Malin can't scarcely be out of Upper Sixth. Have you been robbing schoolyards for your assistants, Gravelle?"

"At least he admits that they are assistants," groused Gallowglass, "not apprentices."

Monsieur Gravelle smiled. "Do I detect some discord in your happy home, Charlie?"

"You may call me, Mister St. Cyprian. Who was your assistant during the Great War? I seem to recall a fellow named Angevine. Whatever happened to him? Oh yes, I remember, he was devoured by one of those monstrosities you brought up from the dead. And what of that Scottish lass, Mademoiselle Mitchell that assisted you when we last encountered each other in Paris?"

Gravelle's smile disappeared. "She left for other employ."

St. Cyprian raised an eyebrow. "Do tell? That's not what I heard. I heard that she was torn apart by a common graveyard ghoul, something about being distracted by the lecherous adva …"

Gravelle thrust his pistol forward, so that it wavered just an inch from St. Cyprian's face. "That's enough from you, Charlie! I demand to know why you and Mademoiselle Gallowglass have set foot on French soil!"

"French soil?" scoffed Gallowglass. "The Minkies have belonged to Britain since the Treaty of Bretigny."

"They are the Minquiers Islands and this particular island is the Maitresse Isle," replied Gravelle. "Even those possessing the limited intellect of Englishmen should recognize that those are French names—and therefore French territories."

"You have a talent for reducing arguments to the least common denominator," replied St. Cyprian, "but rather than argue over the semantics of sovereignties let me cut to the chase. I suspect we are here for the same precise reasons that you are: reports of strange aquatic creatures endangering fishermen and coastal citizenry—reports that smack of the supernatural."

"C'est vrai," murmured Brigitte Malin. "My own frere lost his arm when a giant fish, with bulging eyes and a beak like two knives, lunged from the sea as he drew in his nets."

"Your brother is a fisherman?" questioned Gallowglass. "Are you the only one of your family with occult skills?"

"My grandmother was a soothsayer," said Malin. "She could call up the voices of the dead and draw out their secrets."

"A talent which ma petite Brigitte, also possesses," said Gravelle, his lips stretched thin. "And, yes, we have come to put a halt to these supernatural manifestations, which emanate from the Isle of Maitresse."

"Since you have claimed the Island as French Territory," goaded Gallowglass, "I presume that the French government will be taking full responsibility, and reimbursing all parties with injury or grievance."

"Nothing of the sort will happen," replied Gravelle. "As is standard practice in situations of this persuasion, the event will be explained away, buried and forgotten."

"And have you determined just what it is we are dealing with?" asked St. Cyprian.

"Mais oui," replied Gravelle. "In fact, we have apprehended a number of cultists who were holding summoning rites upon this very island. We've spent some time questioning them, and they will receive swift trial by the secret courts of the Directory, and meet their deserved doom on the teeth of the guillotine."

"If the French have managed to accomplish such a feat under our very noses, it seems that our Ministry of Esoteric Observations has been lax in their efforts."

Gravelle was pleased to hear such an admission from Cyprian. "The problem with your Ministry of Esoteric Observations is that they do exactly that…they observe, and little else."

"That, sadly, is often the truth," said St. Cyprian. "So tell me what dread deity of darkness have the cultists dredged up from the depths of the channel?"

Gravelle motioned toward the shaft with his Galand revolver. "Since you are here you may as well see for yourself."

"Do we have any choice?" asked Gallowglass.

"Non," replied Gravelle. "No, you don't."

Hand and footholds were chiseled into the stone of the shaft and, at the urging of Gravelle's pistol, St. Cyprian was the first to descend into the dank depths of the Maitresse Island. Gallowglass went next, prompted by the gaping double barrels of Brigitte Malin's shotgun.

"You know," said Gallowglass. "I would feel a lot more comfortable with this arrangement, if someone were to lend me my Webley-Fosberry for the duration of our spelunking endeavors."

Malin rested her shotgun on her hip while she examined Gallowglass's pistol. "What is this rune upon the grip?"

"That's the seal of Solomon," replied Gallowglass. "Hasn't Monsieur Gravelle bothered to teach you anything?"

Gravelle clenched his teeth. "Mademoiselle Malin has only been my assistant for a short time. Now, down the pipe, Miss Gallowglass or I'll speed your descent with a bullet between the eyes."

Gallowglass reluctantly thrust her hand into a mossy crevice and began her descent. "You are a dodgy ponce, aren't you?"

"Is it a useful ward?" Malin called as Gallowglass disappeared into the darkness.

"In this case it's less a ward and instead a blessing upon the lead that it throws, giving it some power against creatures that usually wouldn't be harmed by a bullet."

Malin turned to Gravelle. "Your pistol has a rune on the grips. How come my shotgun doesn't have any magic?"

Gravelle's response was spat between his lips. "You don't need magic against St. Cyprian and Gallowglass. Ordinary lead shot will do just fine! Now keep an eye on them or I'll be forced to find an assistant who'll keep her mouth shut and do as I bid!"

The French occultist's voice echoing down the shaft, St. Cyprian paused to ignite his electric torch, and he shone it downward, illuminating lichen-covered walls that dropped another thirty feet until it reached a small grotto. Gripping the torch between his teeth he continued his descent at an unhurried pace, so that he didn't slip and fall. When finally he set his foot in the damp grotto below, he could hear the splash of waves resounding through tunnels leading up to the grotto. The scent of saltwater and something worse was strong in his nostrils.

Gallowglass joined him and wrinkled her nose. "It smells like death down here."

"Let's hope that it's not human remains we find." St. Cyprian cleared away the moss from the wall, revealing a number of runic symbols and pictographs etched into the stone. He shone his light upon these, examining them with great concentration. "Very interesting. What we have here is an antediluvian temple hewn out of living rock by the worshipers of the god of the dark, burgeoning depths."

Gallowglass cast a sidelong glance at Brigitte Malin as she descended the shaft, shotgun slung over her shoulder, wondering if she shouldn't rush the French ingenue just before she set foot in the grotto. "I don't believe I'm familiar with that particular god."

"He's called by any number of names over the epochs: Poisedon, Neptune, Yothsoqua, Bringer of the Drowning Death, and …"

"I got it sussed," interrupted Gallowglass and she hurled herself at Malin before she could even put her first foot onto the mossy floor. She upended the blonde occultist in a jangle of pendants and wards and when Malin fell the shotgun on her back blew both barrels, throwing up clots of moss and a cloud of grit. Gallowglass was on top of Malin, however, riding her like an American cowboy might ride a wild bronco, and thrusting her hand into Malin's belt in search of her Webley-Fosberry. Malin fought like a wild-cat, clawing Gallowglass across the face, but Gallowglass delivered an elbow to Malin's jaw and just about had her hand on the Webley-Fosberry, when a shot rang out from above, clipping Gallowglass's flat cap, so that it turned on her head.

Gravelle's voice called out from above. "Miss Gallowglass! Kindly unhand Mademoiselle Malin. We shall need her assistance later."

"And if I don't?" retorted Gallowglass.

"My next shot shall go through your head. Ask Charlie St. Cyprian if I can make good on my threat."

St. Cyprian nodded, wiping away the grit which had been thrown into his eyes by the shotgun blast. "Gravelle demonstrated quite a natural talent with the pistol in the Great War—abetted by several charms which aided his accuracy."

Gallowglass hoisted herself from Malin's recumbent form and stepped away as Gravelle dropped to the grotto, gun still trained on her.

"You have a rather feisty assistant," commented Gravelle.

"It's one of her charms," replied St. Cyprian.

Using the wall as a support, Malin—rubbing at her jaw—rose to her feet and gave Gallowglass a murderous stare.

Gallowglass shrugged. "Don't look so glum, sunshine. You've got to expect a bit of a scrum if you go around pointing shotguns at people."

Malin broke open the breach of the shotgun and pried out the spent cartridges, replacing them with fresh ones. "Francois told me that the British appoint murderers and criminals as their Royal Occultists. I guess I should have expected some treachery."

Cyprian cleared the last of the grit from his eyes, brought a bit of it to his lips to taste, and shone his electric torch down the descending corridor which hung thick with pale bryophite and was clustered with sea mussels. "I say, is that what you really have been telling Mademoiselle Malin? I believe they call that propaganda."

"I call a spade a spade," said Gravelle. "I expect the ritual chamber is down the corridor. Lead the way, Charlie."

"Just how was the God of the Dark Burgeoning Depths called forth?" asked St. Cyprian as he led the way into the tunnel.

"How should I know?" asked Gravelle, who took up the rear of the procession, following Gallowglass and Malin, who kept her shotgun aimed precisely in the center of Gallowglass's back.

St. Cyprian followed the tunnel around a low turn where he had to duck to pass. The roar of the ocean grew louder and he could feel a mist upon his skin. "Because you interrogated the cultists that you captured and because knowing how they summoned the Bringer of Drowning is critical in knowing how to close the gate that they opened. You are a reckless and ruthless chap, Gravelle, but not ignorant. I find it highly unlikely that you are unaware of any of this."

"The cultists have a propensity for killing themselves before all my questions are answered," said Gravelle.

St. Cyprian furrowed his brow in the shadows of the temple. "Really? Because you led me to believe that they would be undergoing trial by the Directory and then execution by guillotine. Which is it, Gravelle? I'm sensing some divergence in your stories. Perhaps you are having some trouble keeping your lies straight?"

"No lies," snapped Gravelle. "We interrogated a number of cultists. Some committed suicide and others are still being held for trial and execution. There's no divergence to that."

Gallowglass cast a glance over her shoulder to see that Malin was still keeping her under close surveillance with that shotgun, but her shadowed features were clouded, as though she were troubled by something.

They entered a large hollow in the center of the island. The sea rushed in through a subterranean channel on the left hand, ebbing and rising with the waves and the tide. Amidst this churning cacophony was a rock that rose up from the water. A stone bridge crossed to this central island within an island and upon it was an altar, where were chained the gnawed and flayed bones of a human.

"I was afraid of this," said St. Cyprian. "If the God of the Dark Burgeoning Depths had been called forth by Sumerian chants, ritual cuttings, or even animal sacrifice we could use like magic to close the portal and send it back, but shutting a portal opened by human sacrifice is a far more difficult thing."

"Not so difficult," said Gravelle. "It just requires someone who can make the hard choices in order to keep France…and even Britain safe." He lifted his Galand revolver to the back of Brigitte Malin's head. "It's fortunate that I've brought a sacrifice so that we can close the gate. Mademoiselle Malin, drop your shotgun, or I shall be forced to kill you now and use one of these British occultists. Please do cooperate, though. Being a virgin, your blood is preferential—more powerful for drawing out the magical energies required to do the job at hand."

Malin's jaw dropped. "You recruited me as your apprentice because you wanted to use me as a sacrifice?"

"It was a simple matter, considering you have some modest magical abilities and you were eager to help since your brother had lost an arm to one of the unnatural denizens that are infecting the Channel," gloated Gravelle. "Left unchecked, the supernatural disturbances that are plaguing the channel will become greater and greater, spreading like a cancer into all seven seas. Now drop that shotgun."

Malin considered this. "What if decide to take my chances? I'm betting that I can turn and around and put both barrels into your belly before I die from your gunshot."

"The cartridges in your shotgun are filled with rock salt," said St. Cyprian. "I tasted salt earlier when the debris of your shotgun blast sprayed me in the face. Gravelle wasn't going to give his prized sacrifice the means to escape her fate. Gravelle is notorious for using up and expending his assistants, so I wasn't surprised when I put the pieces together."

Malin laid her shotgun on the ground. "I can't believe that you would do this to me, Francois."

"It's nothing personal," replied Gravelle. He lifted up her jacket and pulled Gallowglass's Webley-Fosberry from her belt. "You are just a means to an end. You can die knowing that your sacrifice has freed France from a great scourge!"

"Is there no other way?" asked Malin.

"None," said Gravelle.

"That's not entirely true," corrected St. Cyprian. "Professor Moriarty Moreau is said to have possession of a fragment of the Pnakotic manuscript which contains directions for sealing portals without the use of human blood."

"Even if there were any truth to the rumor, Moreau is a possessive lunatic with a squad of Prussian mercenaries at his beck and call. Trust me, it's just a rumor—and a suicidal one, if anyone should be so foolish as to knock on his door asking for it."

"I can't think of a single reason why anyone should trust you," said Gallowglass. "Look where it's gotten poor Brigitte! I almost feel bad for chinning her."

"Gallowglass, Charlie," ordered Gravelle. "Accompany Mademoiselle Malin to the altar and chain her in place so I can begin the necessary incantations."

St. Cyprian hesitated for just a moment. "Are you going to be using a Pnakotic or a Lemurian incantation?"

"Leave that to me," snarled Gravelle. "Now get moving or I'll shoot you and let your assistant chain up Mademoiselle Malin."

"See," sniffed Gallowglass, "he called me your assistant."

"Yes," agreed St. Cyprian, "but given the fact he's about to sacrifice his own assistant on the altar of the God of the Dark Burgeoning Depths, I wouldn't take too much solace in your promotion."

They started across the slippery causeway, the frigid waters spraying them as they carefully picked their way across. Malin cast unbelieving glances back at her mentor, as though perhaps she were just imagining the dire turn of events which had cast her in the role of a martyr and sacrifice. She muttered something in French about Gravelle being both a cretin and a monster.

"I couldn't agree more," said St. Cyprian as they reached the grisly remains on the altar at the center."

"Not exactly how I was planning to spend Christmas—a gift to a dark god of the sea," said Malin.

Gallowglass touched her face where it had been gouged by Malin's nails. "We'll toast over a mug of nog once this is all over."

Malin's face brightened. "You think there's a way out of this?"

Gallowglass cast a look at Gravelle and his revolver. "I haven't come up with any bright ideas, yet. What about you, Mister St. Cyprian?"

St. Cyprian examined the stone altar, which was carved with depictions of various monsters and behemoths of the sea, and one radiating bulbous eye which was stained with crusted brown blood. He spoke beneath the roar of the ocean, so as not to be overheard by Gravelle. "Keep your head down once the excitement starts. It's going to be nip and tuck."

"What are you waiting for?" called Gravelle, as he began to sprinkle out a protective chalk line on the stone. He still clutched his Galand revolver in his right hand. "Chain Mademoiselle Malin onto the altar."

"You may not have noticed," replied St. Cyprian, "but the altar is already occupied, and I don't have the keys to unlock the manacles."

"You'll find the key among the charms that Mademoiselle Malin wears on her neck. I found it in the possession of one of the apprehended cultists."

Brigitte Malin unclasped a cankered iron key from among her various wards and charms and brandished it toward Gravelle. "You told me that this was the key of Skelos and that it would protect against Sumerian death curses!"

"Would you have worn it if I told you it was the key to the manacles which would hold you fast when the God of the Dark Burgeoning Depths came to devour you? Non? I did not think so."

St. Cyprian took the pitted and cankered key and undid the shackles which still tightly bound the bones of the woman who had been sacrificed on that altar. Though the bones had been stripped clean there were still gruesome scraps of flesh clinging to the wrists and ankles beneath the manacles. To avoid arousing the ire of the woman's shade, St. Cyprian gently removed the remains and placed them at the base of the altar.

Malin stood at the edge of the altar's island, contemplating throwing herself into the freezing waters, but they rushed through the subterranean channel with such force that she feared being dashed to pieces against the rocky bridge.

"Lie on the altar," directed St. Cyprian.

Malin wrung her hands. "Are you going to force me to do this?"

Again, St. Cyprian spoke beneath the rumble and crash of the waves. "Play along, Brigitte. We have to make this look good."

Malin scooted onto the blood-crusted altar and gingerly lay down, where St. Cyprian manacled her limbs one by one. Gravelle was splitting his attention between St. Cyprian's efforts and his own mystic markings, which were necessary to complete his protective circle. "Very good, St. Cyprian. Now cast that key into the sea. We shall not be needing it again."

St. Cyprian made a show of throwing the key into the churning waters, where it was immediately swallowed up. "Now where do you want us?"

"You and Mademoiselle Gallowglass sit tight. You're going to have a front row seat for the banishment of the God of the Dark Burgeoning Depths. I will summon him forth with the lure of a fair virgin, and once Mademoiselle Malin's blood is spilt I will use the blood magic to seal the portal and cast him out. If you sit quietly enough, you might even survive the experience."

"Perhaps you'd like some help with the incantations on your side of the bridge?" suggested Gallowglass.

Gravelle's response was a harsh bark of a laugh. "Set one foot on the bridge and I will shoot you."

Now, Gravelle began to chant and the shadows thickened at the corners of the cavern, pushing inward upon the light of St. Cyprian's electric torch, so that it dimmed and sputtered, sometimes strobing as the waves began to lift in obscene shapes, curls of strange vapor forming piscine figures of hideous form. The sea began to moan and gurgle, speaking in a language that was ancient when Atlantis was seized by the caliginous depths of the forsaken ocean bottoms.

"Curious," said St. Cyprian as he huddled beside Gallowglass behind the altar where Brigitte Malin was bound. "He's using a Sumerian summoning ritual, but some of the incantation forms are altered with Pnakotic verb shadings. Really it's quite brilliant…"

Gallowglass shielded her face from the chill shards of sea spray. "If only I was near enough I'd cut his scrawny neck and bleed some of that brilliance out of him." She reached into her jacket and flipped open a butterfly knife, the blade of which was marked with odd glyphs.

Gravelle's words impacted in their brains like the footprints of a trampling behemoth and Brigitte Malin screamed out in horror as a monstrous shape rose from the raging waters. It leaped from the foamy spume, with great razored fins, squamous body, and with monstrous, milky eyes that peered through realms unseen to human vision. In the fix of that unfathomable stare lay madness, and shrieking in fear, Malin threw a protective arm across her face and rolled from the blood-stained altar, the manacles—which St. Cyprian had intentionally failed to lock—rattling open as she escaped their confines.

No sooner had her body left the altar when one of the numerous tentacles, which were joined to the piscine incarnation of the God of the Dark Burgeoning Depths lashed out, scoring the stone of the altar with the steel-hard spikes that ridged it. The tip of the tentacle cracked like a whip, and Malin could feel the wind of its passing, the sound ringing in her ears as she scrambled back to join St. Cyprian and Gallowglass.

"Sacre' bleu!" gasped Malin. "It nearly took off my head!"

Gravelle continued his chant and now his words sliced like knives, piercing the meat of their brains. Those bulbous fishy eyes darted back and became aware of the man who had summoned him forth from his Ithyphallic propagations with the limicolous devils dwelling in the trenches at the bottom of the channel. Perturbed by this disruption, the God of the Dark Burgeoning Depths lashed out with a pair of tentacles, but when they reached the protective circle that surrounded Gravelle they could not penetrate, and a flash of mystical energy lit up the cavern as the two opposing forces met.

The piscine god squalled out in anger at being foiled in its sinister intentions, for it was not accustomed to being denied its whims or desires.

"We've got to get behind that protective circle," said St. Cyprian.

"And just how do you intend to accomplish that?" questioned Gallowglass. "We've got a slippery bridge and angry sea god between us—and if for some reason the octo-fish doesn't get us, Gravelle will surely shoot us before we can reach him."

St. Cyprian ripped open the collar of Brigitte Malin's jacket and thrust his hand into her bosom, fingering through the mass of pendants. "I think I saw something here that may help us."

Malin gasped, discomfitted by St. Cyprian's sudden forwardness until she realized his intentions were not lecherous. "The pendants didn't help me a moment ago when I was nearly impaled by a spiked tentacle!"

"Many of these wards are not useful unless you know the proper incantations that go along with them. That's the trouble with only a fledgling grasp of the arcane; it's far too easy to mistakenly put your trust in some useless sign or sigil." St. Cyprian plucked loose a cankered copper pendant that formed the shape of a trident, intersected with crossing arrows. The other pendants scattered around the base of the altar. "This is Rasputin's ward against the evils of the sea. I believe I know the incantation that goes along with it."

"You 'believe' you know it?" questioned Gallowglass. "That doesn't inspire much confidence."

"If you've got any better ideas, I'm all ears."

"This incantation will send octo-fish packing?"

"Hardly," said St. Cyprian. "It's merely a ward to keep him from devouring us while we get into the protective safety of Gravelle's circle."

"And how are we going to keep Gravelle from shooting us?"

"That's your job, Miss Gallowglass. All my attentions will be taken in keeping the God of the Dark Burgeoning Depths from making a meal of us!"

A tentacle whipped out and took a chunk off the corner of the altar, even while another slithered along the stone, feeling for one of the trio of hapless occultists hiding behind it. Gallowglass stabbed hard with her butterfly knife. Only the glyphs carved into the blade allowed the point of it to punch through the rubbery flesh, and she bisected the tentacle as the God of the Dark Burgeoning Depths opened up its great beak and hissed in displeasure, pulling back its probing tentacle.

"It didn't like that!" gloated Gallowglass. It was a tiny victory in the face of inevitable defeat, so she didn't pass up the opportunity to enjoy it.

Chanting a Russian incantation, St. Cyprian rose out of hiding and eased toward the sea-slicked bridge. He held out Rasputin's ward as he walked, as though it were a shield. The God of the Dark Burgeoning Depths rose higher from the waters on a quartet of its tentacles, its beak singing out mind-rattling notes of a demonic music which human ear was never meant to hear. For a moment, it appeared as though it would swallow up St. Cyprian before he had a chance to even step onto that stone bridge, but the Russian incantation, coupled with the warding symbol plucked from Brigitte Malin's neck, had power in it. Though the God of the Dark Burgeoning Depths did not shrink away from St. Cyprian, it did not lean forward and slay the British occultist, either.

"Blimey, It's working!" exclaimed Gallowglass to Malin. "Quick, get next to St. Cyprian. We're not going to be safe for much longer, crouching here behind the altar."

With quick steps, Malin and Gallowglass scuttled from hiding. Gallowglass actually was the first to step onto the bridge, butterfly knife in hand. Butterfly knives weren't intended for throwing, but maybe she could distract Gravelle long enough to keep him from shooting them.

Gravelle spat out a curse when he saw the three of them advancing along the bridge, St. Cyprian repeating the incantation over and over again, keeping the God of the Dark Burgeoning Depths at bay. "One of you has to die! I need your blood to push the fiend back through the portal and seal it shut!" He lifted his Galand revolver and fired. His first shot took the pendant right out of St. Cyprian's grasp, so that the British occultist jerked his hand away, his fingers stinging, as the copper pendant clattered against the stone bridge and then rebounded into the boiling sea water.

The God of the Dark Burgeoning Depths shrilled a ululating victory cry and lurched forward to claim its reluctant prey. Gallowglass finished her throw and the butterfly knife went whirling toward Gravelle in a clatter of handles and blade. Gravelle flinched and his second shot went awry, splitting the shoulder seam of Gallowglass's jacket, but leaving her unharmed.

One of the split handles of the butterfly knife, rapped Gravelle hard on the knuckles and the blade rotated, pushing through the sleeve of the Frenchman's jacket and drawing blood before whirling away. Spitting another curse, Gravelle raised his pistol for another shot, even as the God of the Dark Burgeoning Depths lunged forward with gaping beak, intent on gobbling up what it viewed as the source its discomfiture—Charles St. Cyprian.

Feet slipping out from underneath him, St. Cyprian managed to avoid the snapping beak, even as he felt a wave of pestilent breath sweep across him, peeling his jacket and causing the outer layer of skin upon his hands to wither and shed as he plunged backward into the turmoil of the cold sea, and became subsumed in the surf. As he struggled to the surface, all the while being dashed violently against the rock bridge, St. Cyprian wondered what foul spawn of the God of the Dark Burgeoning Depths might be lurking beneath the surface with him.

Gallowglass was already beating a hasty retreat across the bridge, right into the teeth of Gravelle's gunfire, and this time there was no knife for Gallowglass to throw, and nothing to distract Gravelle from his normally impeccable aim—except for perhaps the flailing tentacles that lashed the air and bridge behind her, grabbing up the unfortunate Brigitte Malin, and whipping her around with such strength that it threatened to break her neck.

Gravelle watched as Gallowglass skipped over a thrashing tentacle and he was about to put a bullet through her chest when a figure of Amazonian proportions and fiery red hair loomed up in the lantern light behind him. It seemed that Miss Bella Mae Jobson had not been content to wait in the boat, and though she could not comprehend the unfathomable scene that was playing out before her astounded eyes, she correctly ascertained that Francois Gravelle was up to no good. Gravelle was a wiry and thin man and dwarfed a full three inches by Jobson, who was as robust a specimen of hearty Scottish and Saxon pulchritude that one might find in all of Europe.

In one frantic movement she jerked Gravelle clean off his feet, so that the bullet from his pistol blunted itself on the stone bridge and ricocheted into the spume-blown atmosphere of the temple-cavern. Then she braced her hips and hurled Gravelle outside the protection of the mystic circle and its wards.

The God of the Dark Burgeoning Depths immediately scented the spilled blood where Gallowglass's knife had punctured his flesh. It brought down one of its large tentacles with such force that it impaled Gravelle through the back and then dragged the deserving French Occultist into its gaping maw, where it tore him asunder.

Gallowglass rolled into the protection of the circle, snatching up Gravelle's fallen pistol. "Nice work, Miss Jobson! I might learn to like you, yet!"

"Where's Mister St. Cyprian?" demanded Jobson, her eyes wide and uncomprehending as her mind attempted to process the deviation of nature that lashed the shifting spume.

There were three bullets left in Gravelle's revolver which was marked with seals and wards unfamiliar to Gallowglass, and she sent this trio of eleven-millimeter bullets speeding toward the piscine abomination which was so busy devouring Gravelle that it had not yet taken a bite of his apprentice.

This was about to change, however, for the last bloody gobbets of Gravelle were disappearing down that beaked maw, and the stunned and shaken Brigitte Malin was in no condition to put up any sort of resistance. In most conditions bullets from a pistol, even of such a healthy caliber, would be utterly insignificant to a malign manifestation of such unearthly power, but the symbols scrawled into the hilt of the pistol lent it some power, so that the bullets spattering against the beak stung the God of the Dark Burgeoning Depths. The third bullet plunged into the flesh of one bulbous eye, and pus gushed out like a lanced boil.

The God of the Dark Burgeoning Depths screamed, shaking the very foundation of the Maitresse Isle. Stone and rubble dropped into the churning surf as a battered and bruised Charles St. Cyprian crawled out at the foot of the bridge, struggling to escape the sucking waves. He found himself suddenly lurching out of the water when Bella Mae Jobson clamped one hand around his right wrist and hauled him, bodily, from the churning seas.

"Back to the safety of the circle!" gasped St. Cyprian.

Brigitte Malin's body tumbled over their heads, hurled by the anguished god of the dark burgeoning depths and struck the wall of the cavern as St. Cyprian and Jobson scrambled back to the relative safety of the chalked circle.

"This protective circle won't do us much bloody good if the entire island comes down around our ears!" exclaimed Gallowglass as the foundations of the island continued to tremble.

"Agreed," said St. Cyprian, his teeth chattering from his frigid dip into the Channel's waters. "You check on Miss Malin and escort her and Miss Jobson out of the temple."

"But what of you?" questioned Miss Jobson. "I didn't crawl all the way into this reeking hole just to leave you behind."

"Blood has been spilt and we've got the necessary juice to power an incantation. Someone's got to perform the ritual to send this devil back to the outer voids whence he came, and unless Miss Gallowglass has been doing her homework, I suspect I'm the only one who knows the incantation."

Gallowglass scowled at him, but did not dispute the fact that she did not know the necessary spell to banish the devil deity from the earthly plane. "But it was Gravelle's blood that was spilled…not the blood of a virgin."

"Contrary to popular belief, there are only a few malign entities that make the distinction. The God of the Dark Burgeoning Depths is not one of those entities. In other words, though Gravelle's sacrifice is not the preferred variety it will suffice."

Gravelle had already accomplished the sorcery necessary to draw forth the God of the Dark Burgeoning Depths from his unholy miscegenation in the fuliginous depths of the Channel, so now it fell to St. Cyprian to perform the incantations that would banish it from the earthly plane. He began to recite the words, emphasizing second and fifth syllabic intonations, for this was as critical to the spell as saying the proper words in the correct order.

Gallowglass bent over Brigitte Malin, who was conscious but still very much stunned. Her quilted jacket was torn in numerous places where the spikes of the tentacle had torn through them, but she was only bleeding in a couple of spots. "Can you walk?"

In response, Malin staggered to her feet and reeled across the chamber as though she were a drunken sailor on a three day bender. Miss Jobson caught her and propped her up. "Come with me, darling."

"I'll be okay in a minute," insisted Malin. "I feel as though I've been on a merry-go-round—an evil, loathsome merry-go-round."

"Get cracking," urged Gallowglass. "We don't want to be here when the roof comes down."

"What of Mister St. Cyprian?" protested Miss Jobson.

"He'll be along shortly," reassured Gallowglass. She cast a glance over her shoulder and saw the god of the dark burgeoning seas writhing as it was transfixed by the power of the blood sacrifice and St. Cyprian's incantations. Behind it the very fabric of reality began to waver and split, revealing a howling void that opened to devour the malign deity as surely as it had devoured the French occultist Francois Gravelle.

***

Not far from the Jersey coast, in front of a warming fire and beneath cheery electric light, four companions shared mugs of Christmas nog inside the stone walls of the Flapping Mermaid, a ramshackle tavern with uneven floorboards.

"When I heard the sound of a gunshot, I couldn't sit still in the boat any longer," explained Bella Mae Jobson.

"Just as well," commented Gallowglass. "Besides saving our skins you saved your own. There was nothing left of that boat but kindling when we got above ground."

St. Cyprian nodded. "Gravelle made several errors in intonation and instead of calling forth solely the God of the Dark Burgeoning Depths he called forth its dark spawn as well. If it wasn't for Gravelle's boat being pulled up in the rocks away from the water, we would still be stuck in the Minkies."

Gallowglass raised her mug to the blond French occultist who sat across the table from her. "Thanks to Mademoiselle Malin for the use of her boat."

"It's the least I could do after you saved me from being a sacrifice." She raised her mug. "Here's to being illegally on British soil!"

"Here's to sharing a nog with the handsomest Royal Occultist in all of the British empire," said Bella Mae Jobson.

Charles St. Cyprian raised his mug as well. "That's a very limited pool of folks, but I'll drink to that. Merry Christmas!"

☠❄☠❄☠❄

About Joel Jenkins:

Joel Jenkins lives in the heron-haunted shadows of the Rainier Mountains, and finds the perpetual twilight conducive to writing. He is the former front-man for several obscure rock bands and once impersonated a ghost. Visit his blog at JoelJenkins.net and sign up for free stuff.

Books by Joel Jenkins

Dire Planet Series:
Dire Planet
Exiles of the Dire Planet
Into the Dire Planet
Strange Gods of the Dire Planet
Lost Tribes of the Dire Planet

Tales from the City of Bathos Series:
Escape from Devil's Head
Through the Groaning Earth

The Gantlet Brother Series:
The Nuclear Suitcase
The Gantlet Brothers Greatest Hits
The Gantlet Brothers: Sold Out

Damage Incorporated Series:
The Sea Witch
The Sun Stealer

Denbrook Supernatural:
Devil Take the Hindmost

Children's Books:
The Pirates of Mirror Land

Arthurian Fantasy:
Island of Lost Souls

Collections:
Weird Worlds of Joel Jenkins
Weird Worlds of Joel Jenkins 2

Biography:
One Foot in My Grave

Lone Crow:
The Coming of Crow

The Greattrix Chronicles:
Skull Crusher

THE TEETH OF WINTER

By Josh Reynolds

With thanks to Joel Jenkins, Algernon Blackwood,
Manly Wade Wellman and August Derleth

The winter wind moaned through the trees, setting the aspens to quaking. There were no leaves to rustle, but the branches squealed and popped, setting Charles St. Cyprian's teeth on edge as he climbed down out of the saddle. New fallen snow crunched beneath his boots, and icy flakes stung his face.

His breath frosted the air as he stroked his horse's neck. The animal was restive. It whickered softly beneath its breath, and stamped nervously. He murmured quietly, trying to calm it, but to no avail. He looked back at his companion, who was awkwardly clambering off of her own agitated mount. "We'll have to leave them here. All for the best, in any event, given our quarry's predilection for horse-flesh. Tie them, but loosely. No sense in preventing them from finding their way home if worse comes to worst."

"Cheerful," Ebe Gallowglass said. Her horse nipped her and she squawked.

"Practical," St. Cyprian countered. He shook his head as his assistant whirled and punched her stroppy steed in the snout. "And please don't fight the animals. They're rentals." They'd borrowed the animals from a rancher named Annandale, just outside of Fort Kent. Annandale had been only too happy to let the beasts go, given that it was at his behest that St. Cyprian and Gallowglass had come to northern Alberta, and on Christmas, no less. Or close enough to it to count. Though if there were anywhere less Christmas-y than the spot where they were currently standing, amidst aspens shorn of all greenery and buffeted by moaning winds, with snow steadily spiralling down, on the trail of a man-eating wendigo, he was hard-pressed to think of it.

St. Cyprian and Gallowglass were a study in contrasts. Gallowglass was short and dark, with black hair cut in a razor-edged bob, and a battered flat cap resting high on her head. She was dressed with louche practicality, in a man's clothes, tailored for a woman of her small stature, beneath a heavy convoy coat, sturdy boots and thick gloves. She carried an MP18 submachine gun in her hands and undoubtedly had more weapons stashed about her person, including her ever-present Webley-Fosbery revolver.

St. Cyprian, on the other hand, was tall and rangy. He had an olive cast to his features and hair a touch too long to be properly fashionable. All of this, combined with the hunter's tweeds he wore under his battered army greatcoat, made for a dashing, if trifle exotic, presentation. He carried no weapons save for the stubby Webley Bulldog revolver, resting in the pocket of his coat. It was loaded with bullets made from melted down church bells. He'd carried the pistol from the Somme to Ypres, and then back to Blighty, and it hadn't let him down yet.

He hoped today would not be the day it chose to do so. But if it did, he had plenty of other tricks. He patted his pocket, taking comfort from the pistol's weight, and said, "The trading post should be just up ahead, through these trees."

Something howled, out in the snow. For a moment, as the quavering echo of the sound hung on the frosty air, the snow began to swirl as if in agitation. It was impossible to tell where the noise had originated from, as it sprang from tree to tree and whipped through the air. The horses shrieked in fear and pulled themselves loose from their tethers. A moment later, they were galloping back the way they'd come, followed by Gallowglass' curses. As the sound faded, St. Cyprian made the third Hloh gesture, tracing it in the air with two fingers, and murmured a prayer of protection.

"Think it was...?" Gallowglass began, as she hefted her MP18.

"Maybe. Or maybe it was a decidedly large, and lonely, timber wolf," St. Cyprian said. "Whatever it was, I think it's best to go on, eyes open." He gestured towards the fleeing horses. "Not like we can leave, even if we wanted to."

"Why are we even out here?" Gallowglass said, pulling her coat tighter about her. She cast a last, lingering glare in the direction the horses had gone, then she sniffed and hurried after St. Cyprian.

"Mutilated horses, missing citizens, strange noises in the night... sounds like our sort of job, I'd say," St. Cyprian said. The rancher, Annandale, had lost a corral full of prized horses. The people of Fort Kent had lost a good deal more—sons, daughters, wives, husbands, a dozen or more people, snatched up in the night and only stains of sticky red splashed across white snow left to mark their passing. Out here, it seemed, the winter had teeth. And it wasn't shy about using them.

"No, I mean we're out of our territory, aren't we?" Gallowglass gestured at the close-set poplar trees around them with the MP18. "This ain't exactly the Peak District."

"While Canada and its provinces are not strictly within our purview, this vast trackless wilderness is still technically a territorial possession of His Royal Majesty. And this job is all about technicalities. Besides which, it's not like you're missing anything back in Blighty. Unless you've developed an appreciation for figgy pudding and mistletoe that I'm unaware of?" He glanced at her. "And weren't you the one who remarked just the other day that we never go anywhere interesting?"

Gallowglass glared at him, but didn't reply. St. Cyprian smiled, satisfied. The duties of the Royal Occultist were not easy ones, and the sooner his assistant learned that, the better. The duties in question included the investigation, organization and occasional suppression of That Which Man Was Not Meant to Know—including ghosts, werewolves, ogres, fairies, boggarts and the occasional worm of unusual size.

All such oddities fell under the purview of the Royal Occultist, by order of the King (or Queen), for the good of the British Empire. Formed during the reign of Elizabeth the First, the office of Royal Occultist (or the Queen's Conjurer, as it had been known) had started with the diligent amateur Dr. John Dee, and passed through a succession of hands since. The list was a long one, weaving in and out of the margins of British history, and culminating, for the moment, in the Year of Our Lord 1921, in one Charles St. Cyprian and his erstwhile assistant-cum-apprentice, Ebe Gallowglass.

Snow fell from the trees, filling the air with sudden sounds which served to punctuate the dull, arrhythmic crunch of their boots on the ground. St. Cyprian could feel something watching them, though whether it was their quarry, or frightened wildlife, or something else entirely, he couldn't say. Between the trees, and the snow, his eyes were playing tricks on him, making him glimpse things that weren't there. He wondered if it were toying with them...from what he'd read, that wouldn't be out of bounds for the beast. Wendigos weren't something he had a lot of experience with, however.

As they walked, St. Cyprian kept an eye on the sun. It would be dark soon. So far, their quarry had only struck in darkness, but that didn't lessen his anxiety over walking right into its lair. Or what their guide had assured him was its lair. Speaking of which, he thought, as he scanned the trees. *I wonder where the old devil is. He was supposed to meet us—*

His thoughts were interrupted by the sound of a revolver being cocked, startlingly close to his ear. He froze. Gallowglass cursed and lifted her gun, and he hastily waved her back. He turned slightly, and caught sight of a stocky shape, standing still and silent between two trees, a Peacemaker .45 clutched in its hand.

Past the silvery barrel of the pistol, iron-gray braids framed a weathered, seamed face beneath a broad, flat brimmed hat. The hat, like its wearer, had seen better years, as had the plain brown coat he wore. He was broadly built, and slightly stooped by age. But his hand didn't tremble, and his eyes were clear, cool and calculating.

"What ho, Lone Crow?" St. Cyprian asked placidly, as he used a forefinger to nudge the barrel of the revolver away from his cheek. "I was wondering where you had gone. I rather thought you were going to meet us back there."

"You shouldn't make so much noise," the old man said, softly. He lifted the revolver, lowered the hammer and slid it back into its holster. "It could hear you, if you keep it up."

"It's there, then?"

Lone Crow shrugged. "As likely a place as any. You heard that howl?"

"We did. Did it come from...?"

"I didn't go in, if that's what you're asking." Lone Crow scratched his chin. "But there were none of the usual signs. Beasts like this aren't clever, or careful. They don't hide their presence. If old Ukaleq hadn't been the one to put me on its trail, I'd suspect this witiko was more moonshine than monster."

St. Cyprian frowned at the mention of Ukaleq. He wished the old Inuit angakkuq were here now, with them. He'd first met Ukaleq in London, before the War. St. Cyprian had been an assistant to Thomas Carnacki, the then-Royal Occultist at the time. Ukaleq had come to London on the trail of a tupilaq—a murderous, avenging spirit—that had its sights set on the wife of a former missionary. Between them, Carnacki and Ukaleq had defeated the creature, and sent it ravening after the un-lucky man who'd created it.

It had been Ukaleq who had advised the rancher, Annandale, to seek out the Royal Occultist, and Ukaleq who had warned Lone Crow of its depredations. He was a shaman without peer, and had battled spirits more ancient and terrible than any English bogey. If he'd had his dru-thers, St. Cyprian would have happily left the hunting of this particular cannibal-spirit to Ukaleq. Unfortunately, the old angakkuq had his own difficulties to deal with, according to Lone Crow. So he'd sent others in his stead, to do what must be done, for the good of all.

Ours is not to question why, ours is but to do and hopefully not die, he thought. While Canada was still part of the empire, it was his to defend from the grotesque and ghastly alike. Both terms were applicable, in this case. The wendigo, or windigo, or witigo, witiko or one of a dozen variations, was as foul a beast as any Cornish giant or Dartmoor ogre. It had come with the winter, and made Fort Kent and the surrounding area its hunting ground. "No sign of it at all, then?"

"Not even a foot print." Lone Crow crouched down with a grunt, his old frame creaking slightly. "Then, it's said they can walk through the air as easily as they can cross the ground." He was older than St. Cyprian by at least three decades, possibly more, the last survivor of an extinguished tribe, who had lived hard for most of his life. That life had been filled with unnatural occurrences and escapades that would have put the liter-ary exploits of Haggard and Burroughs to shame. He'd fought all manner of nastiness in his time, both on behalf of others and for his own reasons. He was a shaman, of sorts, and deadly with a gun, even now, in his twi-light years.

It was for those reasons, St. Cyprian thought, that Ukaleq had asked Lone Crow to investigate. St. Cyprian had recognized the power in the old man the moment they'd met in Edmonton. There was a strange sort of grace to him, an air of holiness, wholly at odds with his battered appearance. Whatever it was, it could only be helpful against a monstrosity like the wendigo. And he had a feeling they were going to need every advantage they could get.

When they'd reached Annandale's ranch, Lone Crow had gone ahead, to scout out the area. There were only a few places where a beast like their quarry might hide, and only one close to hand—the remains of a trading post, close to a tributary of the Peace River. St. Cyprian had singled it out immediately as the most likely spot. Such monsters had remarkably similar tastes in lairs, whatever their place of origin.

Using a twig, Lone Crow sketched out a map of the trading post in the snow. "Not big, but most trading posts weren't. A palisade, around a few buildings; there was a fire, at some point. The buildings are gutted, but still standing. Fresh snow this morning probably explains the lack of footprints, and there's more snow coming in, on the wind." He looked up. "The beast will be abroad tonight, if it's not already." He peered about. "I can feel something watching us, at any rate. Maybe not the beast...but something."

"Yes, I felt it as well. I had rather hoped that it was you," St. Cyprian said, shivering slightly. He cast a quick glance around, and reached up to clasp the tiny charm bag dangling from his neck. Ukaleq had made them, and given them to Lone Crow, to give to he and Gallowglass. Supposedly, the charm bags would protect them from their quarry, hiding them from it, until it was time to strike. That was the theory at any rate.

"Witiko move with the winds, and the snows, prowling where the storm takes them," Lone Crow said. "Makes them hard to predict. Harder to spot."

"Silence said as much, yes," St. Cyprian murmured.

"Dr. Silence is a smart man," Lone Crow said. St. Cyprian wasn't surprised that the other man had recognized the name. "Extraordinary physician. Too sensitive, though."

"Be that as it may, he knows his Canadian cannibal-spirits," St.

Cyprian said. He peered up at the lead gray sky. Snow drifted down through the trees. "We need to get in there and find the creature. Before it kills anyone else."

"If it's even there," Gallowglass said.

"It will be. There's nowhere else within miles, and that trading post has a bad reputation. Just the sort of place our beastly quarry would be drawn to. Wendigos are as much evil spirits as they are monsters, and like all evil spirits, they flock to places of pain and suffering like pigeons to Nelson's column," St. Cyprian said, with a confidence he did not entirely feel. What he knew about wendigos could fill a matchbook.

He'd dug into the folklore of the region, as well as the Royal Canadian Mounted Police reports of the Fort Kent disappearances, on the trip over, sitting in his cabin aboard a steamer bound for Thunder Bay, and then later, as they took the Canadian Northern Railway to Edmonton. Even with what he'd learned from Silence's monograph on the subject, and what Ukaleq had shared with Lone Crow, he still wondered about the nature of the beast. It was quite unlike any bogey he and Gallowglass had tangled with before, and unfamiliarity led to uncertainty. Would any of his tools prove useful?

At the thought, he touched his other pocket, opposite the one that held his pistol, and felt the warm, flat shape of the Monas Glyph. Made from blackened silver, stiffened with copper wire, the glyph was roughly the size of a ritual dagger, and was shaped like a composite of various astrological and religious symbols, combining ankh, cruciform and crescent into a single device. Supposedly it had been crafted by the hands of Dr. John Dee himself, and it was a potent artefact, one that had been known to send unruly spirits fleeing. And one which could very easily kill the wielder, if used improperly.

Indeed, even using it properly was inordinately taxing. It often left him wrung out and shivering when he employed it, which was rarely. It was like a tuning fork for the psychical, and it made his soul shiver in him. Hopefully, it would be of some use.

"So what happened here, then?" Gallowglass asked, as Lone Crow led them through the trees. "Why the bad reputation? Another wendigo?"

"Werewolves," Lone Crow said. "Lots of them."

"Lovely," Gallowglass muttered.

"Could be worse," St. Cyprian said cheerfully. "Could be vampires. Or extradimensional fungi."

Gallowglass snorted, but said nothing. They moved quickly through the trees, and soon, the tumble-down remains of the once-imposing palisade came into view. Where there had once been a gate, there was now only a ragged hole, clustered with snow-capped trees. The fort looked as if it had been swallowed by the forest.

It had never had a chance to flourish, not truly. The trading post, and all its people had vanished from the history books, like so many others. Just one more lost colony, one more spooky story to tell around a camp fire. Whether it had been werewolves, as Lone Crow said, or something more banal, the end result was the same—a brooding ruin of fire-marked wood and rusty cooking pots.

True to Lone Crow's observations, it wasn't big. Once past the rotting, snow-covered palisade, St. Cyprian took in his surroundings—several buildings, some larger than others, their purpose lost to fire and nature; shattered drying racks, where furs would have once been stretched; the tumble-down remains of a well and what might have once been a smithy, before its roof had collapsed beneath the weight of a fallen section of the palisade. And amongst it all, the trees. There was no bird song. There was no sound at all, save the creaking of loose wood in the wind, and the soft susurrus of falling snow.

The sun was a strip of fire across the top of the palisade. St. Cyprian pulled the collar of his coat up and said, "Well then. Time isn't on our side. Where do we start looking?" he asked. He looked at Lone Crow.

"You know magic. I was hoping you could locate it," Lone Crow said, not looking at him. "That was why Ukaleq told me he sent for you."

"I know some, but tracking a spirit-beast...that's not exactly my bailiwick. I might be able to do it, but I'd need certain things."

"Like what?"

"The teeth of some of its victims, perhaps," St. Cyprian said. Lone Crow grimaced, but St. Cyprian pressed on. "That'd work for starters. Failing that, a bit of blood or hair or..."

"How about all three?" Gallowglass asked. She was standing near one of the outbuildings, peering in through the sagging, rotted deerskin that had acted as its door, once upon a time. "Blood on the deerskin," she said, holding up two fingers, "Fresh, too."

"Annandale's missing horses," St. Cyprian said, knowing even as he said it that he was wrong. He could smell a familiar stink on the air. He knew that smell. It had taken up permanent residence in his nostrils for the entirety of the War.

"Only if they wear trousers," Gallowglass said, peering into the shack. She grimaced and turned away. "Figgy pudding is starting to sound real good, right about now."

Lone Crow stepped past her, and peered into the gloom of the building. He turned away after a moment, face set. "It's a larder," he said.

St. Cyprian caught sight of what the other two had seen—bits of bodies, stacked like cordwood, purple with frost and blood. The smell of it, even weak as it was in the cold, reached out for him, and for a moment, he was back in the trenches. He closed his eyes and shook his head. "How long?" he asked, quietly.

"A day, maybe more," Lone Crow grunted as his eyes swept the outpost. He drew his pistol. "I've got that feeling again. Like an itch between my shoulder blades."

Gallowglass stepped back, away from the shack. "Snow's picking up," she said.

St. Cyprian turned. He could sense it now, just as Lone Crow could. A vile sort of miasma, like a whiff of something foul, caught just as you turned your head, or the pressure of unseen eyes on your back. "I wonder...did we wake it up, or has it been watching us, this entire time?" he asked, softly.

"Does it matter?" Gallowglass snapped.

"No," Lone Crow said.

Something howled. The sound stretched out over the trading post, covering it like a shroud. St. Cyprian's skin crawled as the sound settled on him, and he looked at Lone Crow, who grimaced. "It's here," he said.

"I don't think it ever left," Lone Crow said.

The snow was falling faster now, making it hard to see. The shattered roofs of the outbuildings creaked as the aspens groaned. Metal rattled, as if something had kicked it aside in haste. There was a soft sound, as snow tumbled from the edge of the palisade behind them. They turned, and saw something crouched on the palisade wall. St. Cyprian had the impression of an emaciated frame and a complexion the color of death, like a skeleton only recently disinterred from a grave. The stench he'd caught a whiff of earlier returned, stronger than before, and he gagged, choking on the foulness of it. Lone Crow raised his weapon to fire, but the shape was already gone.

"Fast, innit," Gallowglass murmured.

"Too fast," St. Cyprian said.

Roofs moaned beneath the weight of something as it loped across them, unseen in the falling snow. It moved quicker than a living thing ought, and as if it were flying, rather than running. The thing was at once something ghostly and yet solid, as if drawing strength from the winter storm. Its lean, starved shape bled into view for a moment, and then vanished in a swirl of snow in the next. A hungry panting noise echoed all about them, pressing close through the dull groan of the storm.

Lone Crow cocked his revolver and glanced at St. Cyprian. "Now's the time for magic," the old man rasped, as he turned away, staring into the snow.

"Quite right," St. Cyprian said. He extended the Monas Glyph. "Cover me, if you would." Lone Crow opened his mouth as if to reply, but instead, whirled, pistol aimed at a point halfway between St. Cyprian and Gallowglass.

Gallowglass spun as the wendigo exploded from out of the storm behind them. The MP 18 stuttered, and the creature shrieked as it crashed down. Snow sprayed into the air as it thrashed its way back to its feet and Lone Crow stepped back, coolly firing his pistol. Gallowglass continued to fire as well, emptying the MP 18's clip into the filthy white hide of the beast. Even starved and stretched thin to the point of emaciation, it was larger than any of them. It was a giant, capable of scooping a man up and eating him like a pastry.

St. Cyprian scrambled back while his companions kept the beast occupied. He still held the Monas Glyph in one hand, and its warmth was a comfort in the bitter cold. The wendigo didn't seem too bothered by the bullets, blessed or otherwise, hammering into it. Then, he supposed it wouldn't be. What little was known of such creatures made them out to be as much things of spirit as flesh. Half-ghost, half-beast, as Silence was fond of saying. That meant where the physical failed, more eldritch means might succeed.

He clasped the Monas Glyph and held it up, as he closed his eyes. Even as he did so, his psychical senses stirred. He traced the sacred shape of the Voorish Sign in the air with a finger and let his inner eye flicker open. The spirit-eye, Carnacki had called it, though St. Cyprian's acquaintances in the Society for Psychical Research insisted that it was merely a very focused form of extrasensory perception. Whatever it was, it had taken him several years to learn how to utilize it safely, and it was still a chancy thing at best. But necessary, he thought, especially if his theory was correct.

When he opened his eyes, the world faded and stretched, becoming distorted. It became soft at the edges, and yet somehow more vibrant. He could hear the thunder of his heart, as loud as if he were in a bell tower at vespers, and he could hear the rumbling shriek of the wendigo, like snow falling from a glacial shelf. Its aura was like frost on glass, or ice cracking underfoot. He saw the auras of his companions, as well. Gallowglass burned like an open flame, leaping and biting at the shape of the wendigo. Lone Crow, by contrast, was a simmering campfire, steadily burning in the dark.

He focused on the beast. The wendigo was two souls in one, and he could see both as clear as day with his inner eye. The first, and brightest, was a man, his features distorted by madness, fear and hunger. The second, larger than the first, loomed over the first, holding onto his skinny shoulders, as if simultaneously pushing him forward and guiding him. It was a nightmare thing, with wide antlers which seemed to scrape the sky, and features that were obscured by the swirling snow. Its belly bulged with wailing wraiths—the souls of all those it had eaten. It swelled with the storm, billowing like a cloak, drawing strength from the man whose soul it clutched in its icy talons. The latter was in torment, driven into a bestial frenzy by the psychical parasite which clung to him, and St.

Cyprian felt his heart give a lurch of pity.

He took hold of the Monas Glyph with both hands and focused on the places where the two souls connected. If he could sever those bonds, however briefly, the others might be able to put paid to the beast. He began to speak the words of the second ritual of Hloh, for the casting out of burdensome spirits. The wendigo-spirit whipsawed around at the moment the first syllable left his lips, and fixed its hell-spark eyes on him. He forced himself to continue speaking, despite the chill that enveloped him.

The brute lunged towards him, jaws wide. This close, he could not help but smell the raw, abattoir stink of it, and he nearly choked on his own words. Lone Crow threw himself forward, using his body to tangle its feet. The wendigo shrieked and fell, just short of St. Cyprian, its claws gouging the earth. Gallowglass was on it a moment later, the MP18 chattering. The wendigo screamed and bucked, flinging her off. It clawed at her as she fell, and she only just barely interposed the length of her gun between its talons and her face. She was hurled backwards by the force of the blow, accompanied by the shattered remains of her weapon.

Lone Crow, on his back in the snow, raised his pistol and fired, drawing the creature's attentions back to himself. It lunged for him, its great hands seizing his shoulders and slamming him back against the ground, as its jaws opened wider than ought to have been possible. Still chanting, St. Cyprian stepped forward, spitting the last words of the Hloh chant like bullets from a gun, and a cleansing light speared forth from the Monas Glyph to strike the wendigo.

For a moment, the beast was limned by a corona of colourless light, and the shadow shape of the wendigo-spirit heaved and thrashed as its physical body began to smoke and steam. Its shape grew tattered, and wraiths fled, wafting away on the wind, rising or falling as the weight of their sins decreed, free from the belly of the beast. St. Cyprian felt the wendigo's rage like a physical blow, and staggered. The great antlered skull of the spirit dipped towards him, stretching away from its host to reach for him with talons of ice and old blood. Out of the corner of his eye, he saw Lone Crow drag a tomahawk out from within his coat, and bring it around to chop deep into the neck of the wendigo's physical body. The spirit's jaws gaped, as if to swallow him whole, but the light of the Monas Glyph held it at bay. But only just.

The wendigo's host staggered, and clawed at Lone Crow, who hung on grimly, hacking at it with his tomahawk. Gallowglass joined him, a bruise purpling on her cheek and the broken stock of her MP18 in her hands. She smashed it against the pale, thin body of the beast like a club, trying to bring it to its knees. St. Cyprian felt his will begin to erode as the wendigo-spirit sought to envelop him. It was as if all of the dark and cold of a northern winter were crashing down on him, all at once, and his mind shuddered beneath the terrible weight of it. But he refused to give in. He spat banishing spells and incantations as quickly as he could call them to mind.

The Monas Glyph was hot in his hands. He could feel it through his gloves, and as the wendigo-spirit pressed down on its light, the heat became painful. He tried to ignore the pain, but smoke was curling from his palms. The wendigo-spirit was all around him now, like a sentient storm, pulling him into its chill embrace. He heard the clash of great teeth, and the slobbering groan of something whose hunger was never sated. He had freed the souls in its belly, and now it wanted his to replace them. Even as his hands burned, he could feel icy talons tearing at his spirit, and he cried out in pain.

Then, a new sound pierced the cacophony. A low, calm sound, the sound of a voice singing in a language he only dimly recognized. The wendigo-spirit stiffened. Its host screamed and turned, as if seeking the source of the noise. Blood like ice water poured down its hide from the wounds Lone Crow and Gallowglass had inflicted. He realized that his chanting, and that of the mysterious voice, had had some effect—the creature was growing weaker, as the spirit's hold on its host grew more tenuous. St. Cyprian saw it stumble, long arms sweeping out desperately to drive its attackers back. It presented its back to him.

He seized the moment and drew his Webley with one hand. He took aim, whispered a prayer, and fired. The wendigo pitched forward as the blessed bullet smacked into its skull. It fell onto all fours with a wail. Lone Crow had recovered his own revolver, and he fired as well, face tight with disgust. The spirit writhed, as if it were trying to pull itself free of its host. The song continued, the voice rising and falling with the wind. Gallowglass joined them, her Webley-Fosbery in her hand. She emptied the cylinder of the pistol into the thrashing body. By the light of the Monas

Glyph, St. Cyprian could see that the creature was shrinking, and steam rose from it.

He looked up, as the spirit at last tore its way free of the body, and clutching its head in ethereal talons, staggered off, climbing upwards through the sky with great strides. The singing grew louder and louder as the wendigo-spirit grew smaller, as it moved, until it was only a blotch on the darkness.

And then, with a final, despairing scream, it was gone.

The singing faded, and St. Cyprian looked around, seeking its source. "Ukaleq," Lone Crow said, and laughed. St. Cyprian turned, and saw a familiar, squat figure, wrapped in furs, trudge out of the darkness, staff in hand. Lone Crow was right. It was Ukaleq. St. Cyprian shook his head as he looked back and forth between the Inuit and Lone Crow.

"Am I missing something?" He looked at the new arrival. Ukaleq looked much as St. Cyprian remembered—short and thickset, with wide, beaming features, and dark eyes that gleamed merrily. It was impossible to say how old the angakkuq was, but he moved with the grace of youth, whatever his years. "Ukaleq, what are you doing here?"

"Singing," Ukaleq said.

"More than that, I think," Lone Crow said, holstering his pistol. He kept his tomahawk to hand, however, and cast a wary eye towards the body.

"Oh no, just singing. And badly at that," Ukaleq said dismissively. "It was you who fought it." Ukaleq smiled and tapped Lone Crow in the chest with his staff. He did the same to St. Cyprian. "I couldn't have done it. But you two...ah. Mighty hunters, you two."

"Three," Gallowglass said.

Ukaleq smiled and nudged her shoulder with the staff. "I am old and forgetful. Three," he said, chuckling. He moved past them and sank down beside the body of the wendigo. Or, rather, what had been the wendigo— now, it was nothing more than the body of a naked man. He had been young, St. Cyprian saw, and his hands and feet were black with frostbite.

"Who was he?" Gallowglass asked, looking down at the dead man.

"Just a man," Ukaleq said. He reached out and closed the staring eyes of the corpse. "Like any of us. Once, before the witiko got into him, and made him something else." He sat back on his haunches with a sigh. "And now it has left him, and he is nothing. That is the way of it." He looked up. "It is gone now. But it will return, like a winter storm. And that too is the way of it. He always comes back, that old witiko."

"Why are you here, Ukaleq?" St. Cyprian said. He tossed the Monas Glyph from hand to hand, as it cooled. The palms of his gloved were scorched black, and he knew, without a doubt, that the skin beneath would be red. "I thought..."

"It was smart, that witiko," Ukaleq said. "Smarter than me. I have been hunting it for some time, following it down from the far north. But whenever it felt me get close, it slipped away." He smiled and looked at them. "But you caught it, and I helped sing it away, back to the black places where its kind roam, away from the haunts of men."

"You mean, you caught it while we distracted it," Lone Crow said, bluntly.

"I told you, it was smart," Ukaleq said.

"So you set a trap," St. Cyprian said, smiling slightly. He was beginning to get the picture, despite Ukaleq's reticence. The old man was clever. He'd used them as stalking horses, in order to lull his prey into revealing itself. He'd wondered why Ukaleq had asked them to come, earlier, and now he knew. "And you say you're no hunter, Ukaleq..."

"Me? No. Not a hunter," Ukaleq said, smiling again, and shrugged. " I am but a humble angakkuq."

About Josh Reynolds:

Josh Reynolds is a professional freelance writer of moderate skill and exceptional confidence. He is not, however, an influential 18th Century English painter. He hopes that, given time, you will get over that disappointing fact. Visit his eminently interesting Royal Occultist blog at Royaloccultist. wordpress.com.

Books by Josh Reynolds:

Dracula Lives!
Gotrek & Felix: Road of Skulls
Neferata
Master of Death
Knights of the Blazing Sun

The New Adventures of Jim Anthony Super Detective: The Death's Head Cloud
Jim Anthony, Super Detective: The Mark of Terror
Jim Anthony & Dillon: The Vril Agenda

The Royal Occultist: The Whitechapel Demon
The Royal Occultist: The Jade Suit of Death

Dillon and the Night of the Krampus

By Derrick Ferguson

1.

The gigantic black and green truck with BIG PIG! written on the driver's side door in bright, arcing blood red letters with a jagged lightning bolt for an exclamation point, barreled down the narrow, winding mountain road like a runaway boulder. Despite the thick ice and snow lying more than two feet deep on the ground, the truck managed to keep to the road, thanks to the numerous ice studs protruding from the tires, activated at the touch of a button on the dashboard. The owner and driver of Big Pig sat behind the mahogany steering wheel, golden eyes blazing with excitement as he expertly maneuvered his vehicle, keeping it firmly in the center of the road.

The main complication at the moment was not the ice and snow on the road, although they certainly did not help. It was the three eight-wheeled German made Blizzard class armored combat vehicles chasing Big Pig. The lead vehicle came equipped with a twin .50 caliber machine gun mounted on the roof. This weapon was currently being fired at the truck. Thankfully, the gunner had more enthusiasm than skill in using the weapon, as most of the bullets went wild. And those that did hit Big Pig were blunted by the truck's own armor. Thankfully, the narrowness of the road prevented the vehicles from following in anything other than single file and so the rear vehicles weren't able to use their weapons. But pretty soon somebody would get the bright idea to lob a grenade or use a missile launcher and then things were going to get interesting.

Inside the cab of the truck, the driver had his hands busy steering but also dealing with his two passengers, both of whom had definitely not expected to be shot at by a small force of mercenaries, and let the driver know so in most descriptive and—for one of them—highly obscene language. But then again, considering that the driver was Dillon and his passengers were Reynard Hansen and Wyatt Hyatt, both of whom had been on several past adventures with Dillon, they shouldn't have been surprised at all.

"I don't wanna die!" Reynard howled, clutching the dashboard as if drawing hope and strength from it. "And especially not on Christmas Eve! Dammit, Dillon!"

"You're being awfully babyish about this," Dillon replied in a calm voice. "One would think you'd never been shot at before." He never took his eyes off the road, following the twisty trail with easy, smooth manipulation of the steering wheel.

"Not on Christmas Eve! I've never been shot at on Christmas Eve! Have you?"

The third man in the cab spoke in a voice pitched somewhere between Reynard's hysterical shrieking and Dillon's near inhuman calm. "Don't distract him, Reynard! If we go off the road—"

"Go off the road? Go off the road where?" Reynard howled back.

Reynard did have a point. Sheer vertical gray cliffs of ragged stone were on both sides of the hideously twisty road. There was no danger of going off the road but there also was no chance of getting up enough speed to outrun the vehicles behind them. A fresh barrage of .50 slugs resumed beating a lively tune on the rear of Big Pig.

"Come take a quick trip to Alaska, you said! In and out, you said! To visit an old friend, you said!"

Dillon yanked at the wheel, slammed through gears as he took a sharp right turn, the tires throwing up arcing plumes of snow fifteen feet high into the air. They showered down on the gunner of the lead Blizzard, blinding him. "You act like I planned on this," he grunted as Reynard and Wyatt slid into him. "And didn't I tell you two to put on your seat belts? Do it now!"

"Why? To hold us in place so the bullets won't miss when they hit us?" Reynard snapped back, but he did as he was told.

A mournful wailing emerged from the rear of the cab. Wyatt turned his head. "Aw. The poor little guy. Dillon, can't I take him out and—"

"No! last thing we need is him jumping around up here! He's better off where he is!" Dillon's gloved hands blurred as he turned the wheel to navigate a tight left turn, again throwing up plumes of snow to further disorient their pursuers, forcing them to slow up some.

"I'd be better off back there with him!" Reynard grumbled.

"I'd be better off with you back there too, you sissy," Dillon muttered. The sounds of the .50 caliber bullets hitting the back of Big Pig increased in volume and rapidity. "We've got to come up with something quick to get 'em off our tail."

"Grenades?" Wyatt said hopefully. "Surely you have some in here?"

"Sure I do. But—" Dillon broke off as he saw something ahead of them. His face brightened as his familiar Cheshire Cat grin spread wide. "Ah HA! Boys, we got our out!" He pointed.

Wyatt and Reynard looked at where he was pointing and the only thing they could see was the road widening as the pass abruptly ended. The road straightened out as it continued on down to a frozen lake.

"Are you crazy?" Reynard yelped. "We can't take this beast on a frozen lake! We'll fall in!"

"Look! Look! There's a road across the ice! That means it's used regularly for transport on a daily basis. It'll hold long enough for me to get our pals back there off our asses. Wyatt, slide on over here!"

There was much grunting, muttering and mild cursing as Wyatt unbelted himself and climbed over Reynard. Considering that Wyatt had a build like a defensive tackle while Reynard was considerably more slender and lighter it was a maneuver not achieved without much profanity unleashed by Reynard. Dillon merely climbed over the back of the driver's seat as Wyatt slid in. The truck slowed down slightly as the transfer was made. Wyatt tromped on the gas and Big Pig lurched forward again.

"Floor it until you hit the ice road then slow 'er down to around forty or fifty, hear?" Dillon said as he opened a weapons locker in the rear. In response to the pitiful whining coming from his left, he turned briefly and whispered, "It'll be okay, boy. I promise. We'll be rid of them soon. There's a brave boy." Dillon turned back to the weapons locker and took out a pair of grenades which he thrust into the pockets of his bronze-colored shearling jacket. "Wyatt, you take it easy on the ice road but when I yell at you to punch it—you go, son and I do mean go! You got it?"

"I got it, I got it!" Wyatt's grin was that of a big kid having the time of his life. "Can I honk the horn?"

Reynard goggled at Wyatt in total astonishment. "You really think this thing can go across that frozen lake?"

"Sure. Don't you ever watch 'Ice Road Truckers'?" replied Wyatt. "Hey, Dillon, what about the horn?"

Dillon didn't answer. He was too busy climbing out of the hatch in the roof he'd opened. Only his kicking legs were visible to Reynard, who turned around in his seat to see what Dillon was doing. "Hey! Where the hell you goin'?" Reynard shrieked.

Dillon didn't answer, as he clambered onto the roof. He left the hatch open and hung onto the edge as he braced against the howling wind battering his back.

He could see the three armored vehicles right behind them, cascading quite the wake of ice and snow, themselves, as they came after Big Pig. It looked to Dillon as if the gunner of the lead vehicle were reloading his guns. It wasn't easy, as the vehicle weaved from side to side, throwing off his balance. The driver wasn't used to these conditions or their vehicles didn't have ice studs on the tires. Which was just sloppy and careless on their part. Dillon smiled grimly. If there were two things that would kill you faster than a bullet in this business it was sloppiness and panic. His pursuers had supplied one and Dillon was about to provide the other.

"This is crazy! We're gonna crash through the ice and die!" Reynard howled. He pounded on Wyatt's muscular right arm. "Look, let's stop and take our chances with those jimokes! We can shoot it out with 'em!"

"I suggest you brace yourself," Wyatt replied with a healthy chuckle as he slammed his foot down on the gas. Big Pig leaped forward as if kicked in the rear, vaulting the few feet separating solid ground from solid ice, landing on the frozen lake with a hideously loud and terrifying cracking of ice. The huge wheels spun briefly until the ice studs dug in and caught traction. Big Pig surged onto the ice road across the lake, gaining distance from the pursuing enemy.

The impact of landing flipped Dillon off of the roof and into the air where he let loose with a weird yodeling yell as he pinwheeled wildly to land with bone jangling impact in Big Pig's dump bed. He took about ten seconds to shout out some interjections then scrambled to his knees and take stock of their situation.

They were on the ice road, doing about fifty and the three Blizzards were just coming onto the ice road themselves. "Gotta give it to them," Dillon thought. "Those guys are determined." He reached inside his right jacket pocket and pulled out the grenades. He shouted as loud as he could, "Wyatt! Slow down some!"

Inside the cab of Big Pig, Wyatt yelled, "What did he say? What did he say?"

Reynard pounded on Wyatt's shoulder as he yelled back. "Slow down! Slow down! Slow down!"

Indeed, due to Big Pig's speed, the ice studs were losing their firm grip on the ice and slowly, the huge truck slewed to the right, since the rear of the vehicle was lighter and so the ice studs weren't able to keep their traction.

Dillon yanked the pin on the grenades with his thumbs and flung them out. He wasn't aiming for anything in particular. As long as they hit the ice it was good.

The grenades arced over the lead Blizzard. The gunner opened up with his twin .50 calibers again and Dillon ducked for cover as a vertical storm of bullets slammed into the dump bed which, thankfully, was also armored. Dillon snarled in anger and from his cross draw holster yanked out his Jericho 941 and fired back from behind the cover of the tail gate. He knew his bullets couldn't penetrate the armored hide of the Blizzard, but it made him feel better to shoot back and not just slide around in the dump bed while they took shots at his truck.

Wyatt and Reynard were, meanwhile, engaged in a furious slap fight inside the cab of Big Pig for control of the steering wheel as the truck continued its slow but determined slide, turning completely around in a 180 degree spin so that the front of Big Pig was now facing the Blizzard. Wyatt manipulated the gearshift, putting Big Pig into reverse. The huge truck was now racing away from the Blizzards backwards, still sliding from right to left on the ice road.

"Leggo the wheel, Rey!"

"No! You don't know what you're doin'!"

"Stop! Dillon told me I could drive!"

"Dillon ain't here!"

"Unhand that wheel!"

"Poindexter!"

"Thief!"

"Momma's boy!"

"Carpetbagger!"

The grenades exploded on the surface of the ice lake. A geyser of freezing water gushed some twenty feet into the air. The results were immediate as the ice had already been weakened by the vibrations of the heavy vehicles roaring across the surface of the lake. The ice splintered, broke apart into giant chunks. Appallingly large zigzagging cracks raced out in all directions from the shimmering, foaming fountain.

Reynard and Wyatt stopped their fighting, gawping in astonishment as they watched water exploding upwards from the cracks that rapidly widened. Slivers and lumps and nuggets of ice flew into the air, sparkling and glistening like diamonds.

The rearmost Blizzard dropped into a crack so quickly it might just as well been yanked in by a tow chain. Great gouts of escaping air bubbled in the spot where it went down. The two remaining Blizzards speeded up, trying to outrun the ruptures and crevices that, now, were also moving faster as the structural integrity of the ice road was going all to hell.

Dillon banged on the rear of the cab. "What the hell are you idiots doing in there? Turn this thing around and get us pointed in the right direction!"

Wyatt shoved Reynard away and laid his big hands on the wheel, pumping the brakes steadily but firmly, trying to regain traction and he gently steered into the turn. Dillon tried to maintain his balance as Big Pig gradually began to swing around in the right direction.

The second Blizzard went down into the lake with no one even noticing. The lead Blizzard outpaced the other two, rapidly gaining on Big Pig. The gunner opened the hatch and laid gloved hands on the triggers of the

.50 caliber, aimed it in the direction of Big Pig.

Wyatt worked the wheel like a pro, maintaining a steady course in one direction, ignoring the ice flying all around them as it collapsed into the lake. The crunching and grinding of huge slabs of ice destroying themselves filled the air, drowning out the sounds of Big Pig's engine.

"That's it!" Dillon yelled. "Keep her steady! Don't fight her! Work with her!"

Reynard couldn't watch. He covered his eyes, mumbling over and over and over again; "HolyMaryMotherofGodprayforussinnersnowandatthehourofourdeathAmen.HolyMaryMotherofGodprayforussinnersnowandatthehourofourdeathAmen.HolyMaryMotherofGodprayforussinnersnowandatthehourofourdeathAmen."

Big Pig skidded to the right, the ice studs sending a fine shower of ice crystals flying. But Wyatt eased her back into her proper course, turning gently into the skid and thereby maintaining more control over the huge vehicle.

The gunner on the Blizzard opened up again with the .50 caliber, forcing Dillon to duck down so that he was low enough in the dump bed that the bullets couldn't reach him. He once again took out his Jericho. "Enough of this shit," he muttered to himself.

The gunner, not seeing Dillon anymore, stopped firing. He had to wipe the lenses of his goggles clean anyway. Dillon took the opportunity to sit up straight and fired four times. The first three taking the gunner right in the chest and the fourth went through the left lens of his goggles. Which only meant that he died about a minute before the driver and whoever else was in the Blizzard, because down it went into the lake.

Icy water splashed against the rear tires of Big Pig. "Wyatt!" Dillon bellowed. "Punch it, man! Give it everything she's got!"

Wyatt obliged and put his right size-14 all the way down. Big Pig's front tires came a couple of feet up off the ground as the monster truck roared across the final few feet of crumbling ice, frosty water splashing on both side of the truck as it gained ground. The front tires came down, bit into solid earth and in a spray of water and glittering ice, Big Pig cleared the lake and roared onto safe, dry land.

Wyatt hit the brakes. Big Pig shuddered to a grumbling stop. He shut down the engine and opened the driver's door. He jumped down and ran around to the dump bed where Dillon lay, grinning as if all this was just another day's work for him. "Dillon, you okay?"

Dillon extended a hand so that Wyatt could help him out. "Better now. Wyatt, if I paid you a salary I'd give you a raise. That was some kinda driving."

Wyatt grinned back. "Thanks. Just glad we were able to get out of this one without getting shot or drowned. Look at that lake, would you?"

Dillon and Wyatt stood side by side and watched the churning, frothing lake as the waters consumed the last of the ice. "What gave you that idea to blow the ice?" Wyatt asked.

"Desperation. Where's Rey?"

They found Reynard on his knees next to Big Pig, salaaming furiously, repeating over and over; "ThankyouJesusThankyouJesusThankyouJesus."

"Oh, get up, you." Dillon yanked the smaller man to his feet. "Never thought I'd see the day when Reynard Hansen loses his nerve. What's wrong with you?"

"What's wrong with me? First of all, I didn't ask to come up here to cold-as-hell Alaska! You said you were coming up here to see a friend and pick up something and you wanted company! What is it, I ask. It's a surprise, you say. Nobody told me I was going to be shot at by—" Reynard stopped his ranting as a new thought struck him. "Say...who were those guys anyway? Who's trying to kill you now?"

Dillon shrugged. "I'd say they were Germans. The man I went to see is still wanted by the German government. From time to time they send assassins after him."

"So what were they doing chasing you, then?"

Dillon sighed. "I don't know and unless you've got a Ouija board so we can talk to the dead, we'll never find out. And besides, it's more important that we figure out a way to get back to Archie. Wyatt?"

"Way ahead of you." Wyatt climbed back into Big Pig so that he could use the truck's onboard computer and GPS to find out where they were.

"We need a way back to the airfield. We definitely can't go back across the lake and those mercs blew up the bridge to Hoover's cabin." Dillon said. He climbed up into the truck as well and unlatched the door of a cage. "Come on out, boy!" Dillon hopped back out of Big Pig and held out his arms. An Alaskan Husky puppy leaped out of the truck into Dillon's arms, wriggling ecstatically and enthusiastically licking Dillon's face. Dillon laughed as he hugged the puppy to his chest.

"And that's another thing. Just who is that guy Hoover anyway? He looks like Jed Clampett's mean-ass grandpa."

Dillon placed the puppy on the ground and the puppy immediately began dashing around Dillon's legs, barking and panting, delighted at having been let out the cage at last.

"Hoover's a guy I met years ago. He keeps a lot of dogs, as you saw. I wanted one, so I called him up and said I would come and pick it up. And here he is." Dillon hunkered down. The puppy placed his paws on Dillon's knees and looked up in Dillon's face, tongue lolling. "I'm gonna call you Festus. How's that?"

Festus answered with a bark that plainly indicated that he liked it just fine.

"Festus? Sounds like a sore," Reynard said, as usual giving his opinion even when it wasn't asked for.

"Well, Festus was Marshall Dillon's deputy on that TV show, y'know. And when I tell people my name is Dillon they always ask me—"

Reynard waved his hands. "I get it. I get it. You mean that folks still ain't tired of that old gag?"

"Guess not." Dillon scratched Festus behind his ears which Festus seemed to enjoy greatly.

"But there was another deputy Marshall Dillon had. Why don't you call the dog Chester?"

"Oh, that was the name of my first dog."

"Your first dog?" Wyatt joined in the conversation, leaning half out of the door. "How many dogs have you had?"

Dillon looked up at Wyatt and Reynard, frowning in honest confusion. "Just two. Chester died two years ago but I've just been too busy to get up here and get me another dog. What the hell is wrong with you two?"

"What's wrong with us?" Reynard snapped. "In all the time I've known you you've never mentioned that you had a dog! Or showed me a picture of a dog!" Reynard whirled around and glared at Wyatt. "Did you know he had a dog?"

"First I'm hearing of this myself. We've never seen you with a dog, Dillon. Where did you keep him? In a kennel?"

The confusion on Dillon's face increased. "Well…no. I kept him at my house. That's where he stayed."

"Your HOUSE?" Both Reynard and Wyatt shouted.

"The both of you are acting really silly about all this. What, you didn't think I had a house?"

Wyatt cocked his head in puzzlement. "Dillon, in all the time I've known you, you've lived out of hotels and temporary safehouses. I thought that was your chosen method of living since you never so much as hinted that you had a permanent residence somewhere. Now you just casually throw out that you not only had a dog, you never thought to mention to us, but a house as well."

"Actually, two houses. I acquired another one when we did that Judas Chalice job."

"Ain't this 'bout a bitch!" Reynard howled. "Wassmatta, man? You didn't trust two of your so called friends with the information of where you lived? I betcha Eli Creed knows where you live."

"Uh, in fact he doesn't."

"You gotta be kiddin' me." Reynard placed his fists on his hips, the steam of his breath seeming to explode from his mouth as he spoke. "Me an' the poindexter risk our lives for you because we trust you with them and you don't even see fit to trust us with knowing where you live or that you had a dog? What, you maybe got a wife and kids that we don't know about?"

"Reynard is right, Dillon." Wyatt said in a quiet, hurt voice. "I thought we were friends. But it's obvious that there's a lot of things about your life that you keep hidden from us. Even after we've made you privy to many private details about our lives. That's simply not fair."

"Yeah! For once the poindexter is talkin' like he got good sense! That guy Hoover, you never mentioned him before. Your house, your dog. Is Dillon even your real name?"

Dillon held up his hands in surrender. "Look, I see your point. But I swear to you that I never kept any of this from you because I didn't trust you. I've trusted my life with you just as much as you've trusted me with yours. Isn't that so?"

"Yeah, that's so," Reynard grumbled. "But still, I thought we were partners and friends. Now, I owe you more than I'll ever be able to repay in this lifetime. You know that. So far as I'm concerned, you're entitled to your privacy if that's the way you want it. But I, for one, don't like to think you don't trust me. Or Wyatt. Not after all we been through."

"It's not that, really. It's—" Dillon sighed. "It's complicated."

"That's not all that's complicated," Wyatt said. "According to the GPS we've got eight hours of driving ahead of us to get to a main road that'll take us back to the airfield."

"Is there any place we can stop and get something to eat?" Dillon asked.

Wyatt consulted the GPS again. "Town—name of Reynolds. A three hour drive from here."

"Okay. Let's get there, chow down and then get back on the road. If we push it maybe I can have you guys back to your homes for Christmas."

The three men climbed back into Big Pig—Dillon once more behind the wheel, Wyatt next to him with Festus in his lap and Reynard on the end. Dillon cranked up the truck and tromped down on the gas.

"And while we're on the way you can start clearing up a few things," Reynard said. "Like where you know that guy Hoover from."

Dillon sighed. "That's a long story, boys."

Wyatt elbowed him. "We've got nothing but time."

Dillon put them on the road and stepped up Big Pig to a satisfying sixty miles an hour. "To tell you how I met Alaska Jim Hoover I'd have to start with another story first. A story about a man I was looking for in New York that had specialized knowledge I wanted to learn. That man's name was Jim Anthony…"

2.

"You simply have got to be kidding me."

Characteristically it was Reynard who had the first opinion of the town of Reynolds. Big Pig rolled into the town, passing a number, of what appeared to be, residential buildings. They were on what had to be the main road since it also was the only road. It was wide and well plowed, free of snow and ice, and Dillon slowed Big Pig down so that they could look it over.

"Doesn't look like a bustling metropolis, does it?" Dillon offered. Festus barked his agreement.

Wyatt pulled up the town specifications on his phone. "Reynolds, Alaska…town population two hundred and seventy-four, believe it or not. There's only fifty-two families residing here."

"What in the hell do people want to live so far away from anything for?" Reynard said in amazement. "Betcha there isn't a decent club or restaurant within a thousand miles of this hood."

"That's the whole point, Rey," Dillon said. "Some people like living far away from anything."

"You oughta know," Reynard said. "What else that thing tell you about this town, poindexter? I bet there ain't no brothers or sisters living up in here."

"Racial makeup of Reynolds is sixty-one percent white, eleven percent Native American and the rest is Latino, Asian and African-American."

"You're making that up!"

Wyatt silently handed over his phone so that Reynard could see for himself.

"I still don't believe it until I see me some brothers for myself," Reynard said firmly as he handed back the phone. "Looks like the place is deserted. There ain't nobody outside at all."

"It's thirty degrees outside, Rey. Nobody's going to be outside on a casual stroll," Wyatt said while stroking the puppy's neck.

"Maybe so but something still isn't right," Dillon said. "It's Christmas Eve. Even in a small town like this, that you could put in your hip pocket and walk away with it, there would still be Christmas decorations somewhere: strings of lights on the houses, animatronic reindeer on the lawn, inflatable Santas on the roof. Stuff like that. But there's absolutely nothing."

"Maybe everybody in town is a Muslim," Reynard said with a braying laugh.

"You got nothing but jokes today, don't you?" Dillon replied. He pointed at a church on their right. "Look. Even the church has nothing out front—like a manger scene. Can't tell me that isn't strange."

"Maybe it's the Church of Satan. Look, ain't we gonna find someplace to get our grub on? My stomach thinks my throat's been cut."

Dillon had to admit he was hungry as well but he couldn't shake the feeling he now had that something wasn't right here. He hadn't lived as long as he had, in this business, by ignoring his instincts. Spying a small restaurant that boasted the somewhat grandiose name of "Empire Café", he pulled into what would have been one parking space for a regular size truck, but for Big Pig that meant it took up two. Dillon shut down the engine, put on the brake and opened his door. Festus leaped out and immediately began to look for someplace to take care of his business. Dillon climbed down, shut the door.

He looked up and down the street. Days in this region of Alaska at this time of year, generally got about six hours of sunlight and there were maybe two left for this day to go. But the long street was as deserted and devoid of people as if it were midnight. The bracing wind whined between the buildings and light poles. A fine mist of snow swirled in the air. The buildings lining both sides of the street were dark. No lights at all burned in any of the windows. To Dillon, it felt more like Halloween than Christmas Eve in this lonely and remote town.

Reynard and Wyatt stood in the doorway of the restaurant. "Hey, you comin' or what?" Reynard yelled.

"You boys go on in. I want to look around some. Come on, Festus."

Festus barked his agreement and trotted at Dillon's side as they went in the direction of the church.

Wyatt watched him go. "Maybe we ought to go with him?"

"You do what you want. Me, I'm for eats." Reynard opened the door and went inside. Wyatt reluctantly followed him. The two men stood just inside the restaurant, letting the door bang shut behind him. They removed their gloves, and unbuttoned their coats as they surveyed the restaurant. They were the only two in there. Tables were covered with traditional red and white tablecloths and booths contained condiments and silverware wrapped neatly in napkins and in their proper places next to plates laid out as if it were expected that people would be coming in to eat. But the grill and stove were both cold.

Reynard stuffed his gloves into the pockets of his parka. "What the hell?" he looked up at his bigger companion who looked back at him, equally mystified. "Isn't this how horror movies usually start?"

"Don't be silly. Probably just closed up early. It is Christmas Eve." Wyatt raised his already considerably loud voice; "Hey! You open? You've a pair of hungry customers here!"

Silence answered him.

Reynard took it upon himself to walk around the counter, through the batwing doors into the kitchen proper. While he did that, Wyatt checked the restrooms. They rejoined with even more mystified expressions. "Not a livin' soul in the joint, man."

Wyatt nodded. "Nobody in the restrooms, either."

"Maybe you're right. Maybe we're makin' more of this than it really is. Could be the owner is getting' ready to lock up for the night and went out for a bit. Small ass town like this, everybody knows and trusts each other. He probably lives right next door and went to his house for something."

"So what do we do?"

"You do what you want. Me, I'm hongry. I'm gonna fix me something to eat. You down?"

"Absolutely." Wyatt knew that Reynard was just as good a cook as he was a thief. "We can just leave money for whatever we eat."

"If I'm cookin', you're payin'. Let's keep it simple. Steak and eggs okay by you?"

"Fine. While you get that going, I'll organize a pot of coffee."

It didn't take long before the interior of the restaurant filled with the mouth-watering delicious smell of three sirloin steaks being grilled. Reynard had his jacket off and now wore an apron. Wyatt sat at the counter, a mug of piping hot coffee in his big hands. Reynard seasoned the meat as he said, "So what do you think about that story Dillon told us?"

"It was some story. And it made me think there's a lot about Dillon we still don't know. Made me think there's a lot about him that we've both taken on trust."

"Yeah." Reynard cracked eggs into a bowl. "How many you want?"

"Four. Sunny side up."

"You'll eat 'em scrambled or you don't eat 'em at all. But you know something that I noticed he managed to leave out?"

"That he never mentioned where he was or what he was doing before he went to New York to look for Jim Anthony?"

Reynard half turned to grin at his friend. "Good to see you use that big brain a'yourn for something more than crunchin' numbers."

"Do you think that it's important?"

"I think that—" The banging open of the restaurant door interrupted Reynard as four men stormed into the restaurant. Big men. Hard men used to living in a hard country most of their lives. All of them had hunting rifles they pointed at Wyatt and Reynard. Wyatt slid off his stool, reached around to the small of his back and drew his Single Army Action revolver. At the same time Reynard smoothly drew his H&K P30 from its shoulder holster.

The cold air whistled through the restaurant as the four men took up positions where they could fire at Wyatt and Reynard without hitting each other. Wyatt and Reynard said nothing, just picked their targets and waited for the four men to make their move.

"Somebody better do something real quick," Reynard suggested. "'Cause if'n my dinner burns I'm really gonna take it personal, you can b'live that."

And now a woman walked into the room. A woman wearing a white ankle length parka. She threw back the hood and regarded Wyatt and Reynard with an almost queenly manner. She possessed aristocratic, striking molded features and moved with athletic grace. Her eyes and hair were almost the same shade of chestnut, her eyes being two or three shades darker than her hair. "Well, the quicker you put your guns down, gentlemen, the quicker you can eat your meal and then we can take you into our custody."

"We weren't going to steal the food," Wyatt replied earnestly. "We were going to pay for it. We're no thieves. Uh…well…to be honest, he is—" Wyatt jerked his head at Reynard. "But I'm not and—"

"Shut up, poindexter. I'm handlin' this. And this is what's going to happen, lady. Tell your boys to put their guns down. Then we'll talk."

The woman's voice didn't raise in volume but it filled the entire restaurant as she slowly and softly closed the door to cut off the wind. "You're outgunned. Seems to me it's stupid to die over a steak."

"Even stupider to die over a simple misunderstanding." The new voice came from the door leading to the storage room. Dillon stood there, brushing snow off the shoulders of his jacket. Having spied the woman and her men going in through the front from across the street, Dillon thought it more prudent to go into the restaurant via the rear service door. Festus stood just a bit behind him, growling slightly. "Hush, Festus. Let's all be nice." Dillon unbuckled the high collar of his shearling jacket as he said, "So what's all this then?"

"The poindexter and I came in, found nobody here, man. Place was empty as Al Capone's Vault. We were just fixin' eats is all. We was gonna leave money to pay for what we et."

"Seems a little excessive for you to want to gun them down for that now doesn't it?" Dillon said to the woman, slowly unzipping his jacket.

"We have a situation in this town. Strangers aren't exactly expected or welcome."

"On Christmas Eve? Now what kind of hospitality is that?"

The woman sized Dillon up with what might have been approval in her eyes. "As I said, we have a situation."

"Maybe we can help. My friends and I are somewhat expert at resolving situations. We'd be happy to offer our services."

"And exactly who are you and your friends?"

"The big one over there is Dr. Wyatt Hyatt. Smartest guy I know.

What he doesn't know about technology isn't worth knowing. The smaller guy is Mr. Reynard Hansen, the world's greatest thief. And you couldn't ask for better if you need somebody to watch your back who can think fast and move even faster."

"And who are you?"

Copper eyes sparkled and a grin as wide as the Cheshire Cat's spread across his face. "My name is Dillon."

"And what do you do?"

"Like that song says, I'm your boogie man. I'm here to do whatever I can."

Despite herself, the woman couldn't help but giggle. "I see. Not the most impressive of resumes…but amusing."

"My steaks is burnin'!" Reynard yelped. "We gonna start shootin' or what?"

"Put away your guns, boys. It's cool." Dillon said.

"I'm afraid we're going to have to ask you to surrender them," the woman said firmly.

And even more firmly, Dillon said, "That's just not going to happen. My friends and I have a strict policy of not giving up our weapons for anybody. But we'll put them away as a show of good faith. Put 'em away, fellas."

Wyatt and Reynard holstered their weapons. Reynard immediately turned back to the grill, cursing and muttering, trying to save the steaks.

Dillon stood with his hands on his hips, jacket pushed back to show his own holstered gun. "Well?"

The woman motioned for her men to lower their rifles. She walked over to where Dillon stood. "You've got nerve. I like that. Maybe you can help us."

"We'll do our best, miss…?"

"It's Professor actually. Professor Ursula Van Houghton."

"A pleasure to meet you, Professor. Reynard, why don't you whip up some more steak and eggs for everybody. And Wyatt, that coffee sure smells good. Can you help us out with a couple of cups over here? As for us,

Professor, why don't we sit over here in this booth, have our coffee and get acquainted. And then you can tell me about this situation you're so wound up about."

3.

"She checks out, Dillon," Wyatt said, looking at the information on the screen of his phone. "Ursula Van Houghton teaches at Grand Lakes University. She's a tenured, highly respected professor there. And get this: she's got advanced degrees in and teaches Occult History, Folklore and Mythology."

"You're makin' that up! Gimme!" Reynard snatched the phone out of Wyatt's hand and read the information for himself. He grunted and gave it back to Wyatt. "That's why I love white folks. They can make a livin' doing just about anythin' they want to." He leaned forward slightly to look around Wyatt's chest to speak directly to Dillon. "We really gonna help these people out, man? Don't we have enough problems of our own? Supposing those Germans we dropped in the lake have friends who come looking for them?"

Dillon replied, not taking his eyes from the road. Big Pig followed a Ford pickup truck driven by one of the armed men who comprised Ursula's escort. Big Pig's powerful halogen lights were only at half strength so that they wouldn't blind the driver or his passengers. "It's Christmas Eve, Rey. What better time to extend the helping hand of brotherhood?"

"Especially when the brother is a smokin' hot chick. Can't say as how I blame you, though. Woman that fine could get me to follow her anywhere, anytime. Damn shame she gotta be a poindexter."

Wyatt spoke up. "Did she say anything at all about what this trouble is supposed to be?"

Dillon shook his head in a negative. "Said she could fully explain with the town's pastor and the mayor. That's where we're going now. She said the entire populace of the town is in the school. It's the only building large enough to hold everybody. Plus it's got more than enough bathroom facilities and a kitchen."

"What could the entire town be doing in there?" Wyatt said wonderingly. "You mean the whole town is there?"

"That's what Professor Van Houghton said."

"See? I todja horror movies start out like this," Reynard grumbled.

"Oh, be quiet, will you?" Wyatt said in mild annoyance. "If you're not going to contribute anything constructive then just don't say anything."

From his spot on the seat between Dillon and Wyatt, Festus barked as if agreeing with Wyatt.

"Hey, just don't come cryin' to me when The Thing With Forty Eyes bites your head off is all I'm sayin'."

Seeing as how he'd once come thisclose to having his own head bitten off by The Thing With Forty Eyes, Dillon didn't find that statement the least bit amusing but he ignored Reynard and followed the pickup into the parking lot of the two story schoolhouse. Ursula had explained that all the town's children attended and were taught in the same school. One wing of the first floor was given over to pre-K and kindergarten while the other wing devoted to elementary school and junior high school. High schoolers were taught on the second floor. They drove around to the back of the school and the pickup truck stopped. Dillon halted Big Pig and disembarked, along with his friends. Festus scampered around, glad for the chance to stretch his legs.

Two men stood at the rear entrance, both of them armed with automatic weapons and dressed warmly against the biting cold. They regarded Dillon and his friends with open surprise and some suspicion but a word from the leader of Ursula's escort put them at ease and they opened up the doors for them to enter.

The spacious gym was full of heat and noise. The heat came from a dozen industrial strength space heaters up against the walls, separated evenly so as to provide the maximum coverage for the entire gym. The noise was provided by children laughing and playing on one side of the gym which had been cleared for that purpose. Rows and rows of cots occupied the rest of the floor area.

Ursula and her men shed their outerwear and so did Dillon, Wyatt and Reynard. It was downright toasty inside the gym. Ursula motioned they they should follow her. They did so. The children kept on with their playing but the adults sitting on the cots or at folding card tables having coffee, talking and playing cards stopped what they were doing to regard the strangers. Most looked amazed but a significant amount of others looked upset or angry.

Ursula led them to an office where she politely knocked on the door. "Come on in, Professor!" a male voice inside responded. She opened the door and went in. This obviously was a coach's office, going by the awards on a shelf against the far wall and pictures of football players hung on the wall behind a desk—the desk behind which a solemn looking man with almond-shaped brown eyes, a long beard and thin mustache stood up to shake hands. "I'm Byron Perkins, mayor of Reynolds. This here's our community spiritual leader, Pastor Russell Kirby."

Pastor Kirby stood up to shake hands. A black man of medium height, Dillon was impressed by the strength of the pastor's grip. It was difficult to gauge his age. He could have been anywhere from forty to sixty.

"My name—" Dillon began but Mayor Perkins held up a hand to pause him. He gestured over his shoulder at a CB radio on a small table of its own behind him.

"Professor Van Houghton took the liberty of filling us in while you drove over. Please, sit down."

"I'd rather get down to what's going on around here, if you don't mind." Dillon said. "Professor Van Houghton said she'd rather wait until we got here to explain."

"Speaking of explanations, son, would you mind explaining exactly what you're doing in this part of the world?" Pastor Kirby asked. "As you can imagine, we don't get many strangers here. And especially not during the wintertime."

"I went to visit a friend of mine who lives over near Belcher's Gulch to get myself a dog." He pointed at Festus, in the the process of busying himself investigating the office, carefully sniffing everything.

"You came all the way up here for a dog?" Pastor Kirby shook his head. "That's awfully hard to believe, son."

"It's a special dog, okay? My friends and I got lost on our way back to our plane and ended up in your town."

"Still doesn't explain why you'd want to concern yourself with our business," Mayor Perkins insisted.

It was Ursula who spoke next. "But the fact of the matter is that they are here. And from what I've seen of them in just the short time I've known them, I would say that Dillon and his partners are men who have been in some hairy situations before. It could be that with their help we can put an end to this once and for all."

"Is somebody ever going to get around to telling me exactly what this is all about?" Dillon's store of patience just about used up.

"It started three years ago," Mayor Perkins said, resuming his seat. "Christmas Eve just like this one. Just one difference. During the night twelve children were abducted. Taken right out of their homes."

"What did the authorities say?"

Perkins sighed. "I don't think you quite understand our situation up here. As you can see for yourself we're at least four hundred miles from any civilization at all. And during the winter we're pretty much isolated. Our nearest neighbors is a mining camp about twenty miles from Lake Hancock."

"We used the ice road on the lake to get here. I wondered why there was one all the way out here. But where was the mining camp?"

"The signs that direct you there must have blown down. It happens a couple of times during the winter. If you had seen them you'd have been there instead of here. And when winter hits, up here, it hits hard. The nearest law is four hundred miles away. And half the time they can't fly in due to the storms. Storms tend to sneak up on us in these parts. You get caught in one and there's a good chance you're going down way faster than you'd like."

"So you're telling me that three years ago you had twelve of your children kidnapped and you did nothing about it?"

"Oh, we tried to do something about it," Pastor Kirby said. "You see, we knew what it was that took our young'uns. We lost five of our men trying to get them back."

"We lost another four men the next year when we lost another twelve children," Perkins said unhappily.

"Waitamminit…you sayin' this happened two years in a row and you still didn't call the cops?" Reynard demanded. "I think I see the problem here, Dillon. These folks is crazy."

"Last year we hired half a dozen mercenaries to stop the child thief. They went out looking for it. They never came back." Kirby gestured in Ursula's direction. "This year we hired Professor Van Houghton to help us. We did our research, found out she's an expert on stuff like this. Thought that maybe what we needed was an expert with her knowledge and not just guns."

"You're telling me that for three years you've had children kidnapped on Christmas Eve and didn't tell anyone in authority about it? You could have had the FBI and The National Guard up here. What kind of people are you?" Dillon demanded. He turned to Ursula. "Talk plain, Professor. Why are you here?"

She folded her arms under her breasts and sighed. "Have you ever heard of the Krampus?"

"Sure. It's a creature based in Germanic folklore although legends of the Krampus have spread throughout Europe where it's known by several names—but Krampus is the most popular. To put it in simple terms, the Krampus is the Anti-Santa Claus. Where Santa Claus rewards good little boys and girls by giving them presents, the Krampus punishes bad children by stuffing them in his sack and carrying them away to his lair to toil away digging coal forever. There's a lot more to it but that's the basics."

Ursula blinked in surprise. "May I ask how you come to know that so readily?"

"I took some courses in archaeology and cultural anthropology at the University of Northeastern California."

"Ah!" Understanding lit up Ursula's face. "Let me guess…you studied under Professor Sydney Fox?"

"Sure did. You know her?"

"She's an old friend. And yes, substantially everything you said is right on the money."

"Waitamminit, waitaminnit," Reynard interrupted, waving his hands above his head. "What's all this got to do with these kids bein' took?"

Ursula said calmly and seriously. "That's what has been taking twelve children every Christmas Eve from this town for the past three years. The Krampus."

Dillon looked at Reynard. Reynard looked at Dillon. Reynard and Dillon looked at Wyatt. Wyatt looked at Dillon and Reynard.

All three men burst out in uncontrollable, raucous laughter. Ursula, Perkins and Kirby seemed to have expected this reaction as they said nothing, merely waited until the hilarity died down. Festus, who had been trying to catch a quick nap in a corner jumped immediately to his feet. Seeing that it was just humans being silly, he curled back up in his corner. Reynard flopped into a chair, arms wrapped around his lower torso. "My sides is hurtin' over here!"

Dillon wiped his streaming eyes with the backs of his hands as he finally got control of himself. "If you people are working on an insanity plea at your trial, it's a good one. No wonder you haven't gone to the police if that's the best you can come up with."

"Everybody in this town will swear that they have seen the Krampus at least once, Dillon," Ursula said. "I assure you, I wouldn't have come up here on my own if I didn't think there was something real here. Look." Ursula handed over her phone and Dillon looked at the picture she had pulled up on the screen.

He stopped laughing.

He looked up at Ursula, back down to the screen. "You've got more photos like this?"

She shook her head. "Just that one. It was taken last year. That's the one Mayor Perkins sent me to get me interested."

"I don't understand why you just didn't take this picture to the authorities."

"You know what they'll say, Dillon," Wyatt interjected, stepping forward, handing out his hand for the phone. "They'll say it's some knuckle dragger fooling around with Photoshop. Let me see it."

Dillon gave him the phone. Wyatt took out his own phone and went over into his own corner.

"What's he going to do?" Ursula wanted to know.

"He's going to verify that picture wasn't altered in any way."

Kirby looked skeptical. "He can do that with just his phone?"

Dillon grinned. "You're lucky he doesn't have his laptop with him. And yes, he can do that with his phone. Trust me when I say there's very little he can't do with that phone. But let's get back to the topic at hand. Professor, you can't honestly think there's a Krampus targeting this town every Christmas? And why only twelve children at a time? And why this particular town?"

Ursula shrugged. "You haven't asked any questions I haven't asked the mayor and the pastor since I arrived a day ago." Ursula gave Dillon a strange smile. "That's why, when I encountered you and your friends, I thought you could have better luck getting a story out of them."

And then Dillon understood the smile. Ursula, herself, smelled a rat. A big dead rat that stunk up this whole town. The mayor and the pastor knew more than they were telling. She couldn't make them talk but she was placing all her chips down on the table that Dillon could.

"It's genuine," Wyatt said, returning Ursula's phone to her. "The picture hasn't been tampered with."

"You gonna let me see what it is?" Reynard demanded. Wyatt handed him his phone as he now had a duplicate digital image on his device.

The door to the office slammed open. Several of the townspeople stood in the doorway, plainly upset. Their leader, a tall and gangly woman with oil dark eyes, half-shouted in a shrill voice. "What's going on in here?"

Perkins stood up, frowning. "Mrs. Gibson, I'll thank you to knock on my door like you got some good sense and wait to be invited in."

Mrs. Gibson ignored that and continued on; "Who are these men? What are they doing here? Where did they come from? We got a right to know!" From behind Mrs. Gibson came grumblings and mutterings of assent from the men and women backing her up.

"They're strangers here. Got lost is all. They ended up in Reynolds and—"

"They got guns!" Mrs. Gibson shouted. "Frank and the others who picked 'em up with that professor lady said all three of 'em got guns! Why they got guns?"

Reynard laid his hand on his gun. "You want me to show you why I got a gun, sweetheart?"

"Why don't we all just calm down," Pastor Kirby advised, stepping in front of Mrs. Gibson. "I assure you that these men are simply lost strangers."

"Then why do they have guns? You hired them, didn't you? You and that lyin' ass partner of yours!"

And now Pastor Kirby moved forward with purpose and gripped Mrs. Gibson by her upper left arm. He firmly shoved her backwards, out the office door. The rest of the townspeople backed up as well. "I think this is a conversation we should best have outside." Kirby closed the office door behind him.

Dillon turned back to Perkins. "You want to explain what that was all about, Mr. Mayor?"

Perkins resumed his seat, cleared his throat. "I think that you can appreciate that Christmas Eve is supposed to be a time of joyous rejoicing. Instead we find ourselves living under a cloud of terror. Such a strain on the emotions makes folks behave strangely."

"Why did they think that you and Pastor Kirby hired us?"

"I told you that we hired men last year to catch or kill the Krampus. Naturally, Mrs. Gibson and the others thought that you were more men we hired."

"They didn't look particularly happy about that at all," Wyatt said.

Dillon said nothing, stood with his arms folded, sizing Perkins up with sparkling copper eyes for a bit before turning around. He motioned to Wyatt and Reynard to follow and said to Ursula, "Would you mind joining us, Professor?"

"Not at all."

Dillon let out with a short whistle and Festus bounded to his feet. Dillon led the way out, shoving past the crowd that still stood outside the office. The men and women glared hostilely but none dared put their hand on Dillon and his little band as they walked across the gym to a staircase. They pulled the door shut behind them. They could still look out and keep an eye on the crowd, but they could talk in private.

Dillon turned to Ursula. "Professor—"

"Ursula, please. This is no time for formality."

"Ursula, exactly what is going on around here?"

She shook her head. "I'll be damned if I know. I came up here strictly to help in any way I could and to satisfy my own curiosity. Those men that came with me to the restaurant? I get the distinct impression they were just as much my captors as they were protectors."

"Well, we're your bodyguards now, Professor," Wyatt said. "Right, Dillon?"

"Right. From now on you stick with us, Ursula. Reynard, where are you going?"

Reynard had his hand on the door. "Saw a liquor store aways up the street. I'm gonna get my Christmas cheer on."

"Reynard—"

"Hey, hey, hey! Look, you wanna buy some cockamamie story about some kinda monster snatchin' kids and whatnot, that's you. All I know is it's Christmas Eve and I'm way the hell up here freezin' my tailbone off in Alaska when I should be back in Brooklyn at Scatta's, enjoyin' her hospitality. Only party she throws bigger than her Christmas Eve one is her New Year's Eve and I sure as hell ain't gonna miss that one. But if I gotta miss this one, I'm gonna do it drunk!" The door opened and boomed shut behind Reynard.

"You want me to go shake some sense into him?" Wyatt asked.

"No. He's got a right to be mad. This wasn't supposed to be a job." Dillon sighed. "He's not on the clock. Leave him be."

"What do you need me to do?"

"You think that using the satellite link-up systems in Big Pig you can get us some eyes overhead?"

Wyatt grinned. "I can certainly take a crack at it. There's a number of meteorological satellites I'm sure I can hook up with. I'll get right on it. What are you going to be doing?"

"Ursula and I will have another go at the mayor and the pastor. And look here, Wyatt…get out one of the big duffle bags and load it up with some extra ordinance. Whatever you think we might need."

"You think there's really a monster, Dillon?"

"I don't know about a monster but I do know there's an angry mob out there and the only thing that's going to impress them is superior firepower."

Wyatt nodded and left the staircase.

Festus rubbed up against Dillon's leg. Dillon smiled and sat down on a step, scratched the dog behind his ears.

"How long have you had him?" Ursula asked.

"Oh, just got him today. Earlier this morning."

"He seems to have taken to you quite well."

"My friend Eli says that I'm a dog person. He says he doesn't trust a man who doesn't like dogs or that dogs don't like."

"My father used to say the same thing."

Dillon looked her straight in the eyes. "Ursula, why did you come here? Really?"

Ursula sighed, came over to sit down next to Dillon on the step. She finger combed her hair, as if straightening out her hair would straighten out her thoughts. "I'd like to tell to you. I think that you're a man that people trust. But I don't want you to think I'm crazy."

Dillon smiled gently. "Don't worry about that. I've got some stories of my own that can out-crazy anything you would come up with. Go ahead. Spill."

Ursula took in a deep breath. "Okay. I came up here because when I was a kid, I saw the Krampus take my cousin Tessa." She peered at Dillon closely. She fully expected him to laugh or tell her she was making it up or she was dreaming. Dillon did neither. He simply nodded.

"You believe me?" Ursula asked.

"I do. How did it happen?"

"My mother and father were academics whose work took them all over the world. They would sometimes leave me at Uncle Walter's house. He was my father's brother. Tessa was their daughter and she delighted in being an obnoxious brat. It's not that she was a bad seed or anything. Tessa just honestly liked getting into trouble. She just didn't care. Uncle Walter and Aunt Gert told her that the Krampus would come get her if she kept misbehaving. Tessa just laughed and kept on being a bad little girl.

"My parents had to go to South America one year during the month of December and they made plans to leave me with Uncle Walt and Aunt Gert to would and spend Christmas with them. I didn't mind. Uncle Walter and Aunt Gert were very good to me—treated me as if I were their own daughter. And when Tessa wanted to, she could be a friend.

"Well, two weeks before Christmas, Tessa pulled the worst stunt she had ever pulled. She tied firecrackers to the tail of one of Aunt Gert's cats and lit them. The poor little thing was so terrified it ran across the yard and out into the street where it got hit by a car and was killed. My Aunt Gert was so angry that she screamed that she wished the Krampus would come and take Tessa. Uncle Walt spanked her and Tessa did what she usually did. She shrugged and started planning her next act of mayhem. But I talked to her and told her that she shouldn't push her luck, that she probably wasn't going to get any presents because of this.

"Tessa was a devil. She took me to the basement and showed me where our Christmas presents were hidden. She giggled and called me stupid for believing in Santa Claus. She said she'd known for a couple of years that it really was her parents who bought the presents and that they never returned them, no matter how she acted up. Still, she behaved herself but I was crushed. I was so depressed that Uncle Walt wanted to take me to the hospital, but I snapped out of it. I didn't want Uncle Walt and Aunt Gert to know that I knew there was no Santa Claus, you see. Even at that young age I figured out that it would hurt them just as much, if not more, than it hurt me.

"Christmas Eve came. Tessa and I were put to bed early but we stayed awake for another couple of hours, giggling and talking about the toys we were going to play with. And then, sometime after midnight we finally fell asleep.

"I don't know exactly what time it was when I woke up, but I do remember that the night outside the window looked blacker than any night I could ever remember before in my life. And the room was cold, even though Uncle Walt had turned up the heat as he usually did when before we went to bed. I could see my breath steaming. I heard a noise coming from Tessa's side of the room and I turned to look. What I saw terrified me so much that I couldn't speak. Couldn't move.

"It was the Krampus. His horns scraped the roof of our room. A long forked tongue lashed the air. The Krampus was covered in black fur and its eyes were like two great big orange headlights. I couldn't scream and neither could Tessa. Me, because terror locked my throat. The Krampus had one huge hand over Tessa's mouth. All I could see were her eyes bulging out at me. She kicked and thrashed around, trying to get free, but the Krampus ignored her. He thrust her into a large sack it held in its other hand. Then it turned to me and grinned with overlapping, pointed yellow teeth. I fainted."

"Damn. What happened after that?"

"The next morning Uncle Walt and Aunt Gert searched the house for Tessa, assuming she was pulling another one of their pranks. I told them that the Krampus took Tessa away. They gave each other an odd look and finally called the police. There was an investigation. Of course, Tessa was never found."

"Even after you told the police what you saw?"

"You honestly think they took me seriously? They said I must have had a nightmare or saw a man kidnapping Tessa and my imagination blew him up into a monster. They closed the case as a kidnapping, saying that a man must have gotten into the house somehow and taken Tessa. This was despite no evidence that the house had been broken into or any signs of a burglar or prowler."

"How did your uncle and aunt take it?"

"Oh, they were appropriately grief-stricken. But I couldn't help but notice that they seemed to be drinking an awful lot of champagne. Along with a lot of smiling and laughing. You see, they had Tessa late in their married life and she would have been a handful for a young couple. I'm not saying they weren't sorry about what happened to Tessa-"

"They just weren't that sorry. I get it. So since then you've been looking for the Krampus?"

"Whenever I get word of a Krampus sighting I try to get there and talk to the people involved. This is the closest I've ever come. Because this is the only place the Krampus has been sighted more than once. Why does he return here? I think that if I can solve that mystery then maybe, just maybe I can find out what happened to Tessa."

Dillon abruptly stood up and held out his hand to help her up. "In that case, let's go look for some answers."

4.

Reynard pulled up the hood of his parka as he left the gym. The armed guards at the door eyed him but wisely made the decision to leave him be. He crossed the school courtyard and made his way toward the liquor store. A nice good shot of something was just what he needed now and he intended to get it. He crossed the windy street, bracing himself against the sharp, biting wind. Back in Brooklyn they had a name for a wind like this. They called it 'The Hawk' due to the screeching sound such a wind made, much like the cry of that bird of prey. Reynard privately thought it was an acronym for "Howling Ass Wind Kills" but that was just him.

Reynard ran the last few feet to the front door of the liquor store and tried the knob. Locked. Figures. The door of the restaurant was left unlocked and wide open but the liquor store was locked up tight. Still, that wasn't much of a problem for him. Reynard reached to his belt and unclipped an oblong pouch. He opened it, revealing his set of lockpicks. In fifteen seconds he was inside the store.

Reynard turned on the lights and took off his gloves. He rubbed his hands together and hunted up a cardboard box to put his booze in. Four bottles of Moet Champagne. Two bottles of Remy Martin. Three bottles of Gray Goose Vodka. Couple bottles of over proof rum. Reynard surveyed his haul. He figured that should be enough for a proper party. He reached for his wallet and took out enough money to cover his purchases. Professional thief he was, and proud of it, but he was an honest professional thief. He put the money on the counter and picked up the box. He headed for the door and stopped dead in his tracks.

The thing that looked at him through the large picture window of the liquor store was a demon out of a nightmare. Covered in matted black fur with blazing, baleful orange eyes that, right then, looked to Reynard to be as large as soccer balls. A face of hideous ugliness. A dripping, scaly tongue hung out of its mouth, lashing this way and that. Huge horns curled up and back down like a ram's. Massive clawed hands pressed up against the glass, smearing it.

The Krampus roared.

Reynard screamed.

The Krampus kept on roaring.

Reynard kept on screaming.

He dropped the cardboard box and the bottles within shattered, filling the inside of the liquor store with heady smells. Reynard clawed at his coat, trying to get at his gun. By the time he got to it and got it out, the Krampus was gone.

Reynard burst out of the liquor store, gun extended, looking wildly this way and that. But it was gone. How in the hell had something that big—

Another hideous roar filled the night. Reynard whipped around, looked up, and spied the Krampus standing on the roof of the store. Those fiery eyes seemed to throw off such a radiance that Reynard felt as if he were caught in a spotlight.

Reynard abandoned all thoughts of shooting the Krampus and instead took off at top speed for the gym, head thrown back, arms and legs pumping. In five seconds flat he was moving at a speed that would have wrung tears of envy from Usain Bolt, had he been there to see.

***

Dillon leaned on the desk and put just the slightest bit of threat into his voice as he said, "You'd be wise to come clean with me right now before my friends and I put our lives on the line for you and your town. Because if my friends get hurt I'm not going to like it."

Mayor Perkins looked unruffled. This was a man who'd been under pressure a time or two and didn't bluff easy. "Look, if you want to take your friends and go, that's fine by me. I welcome your help but I won't be threatened—"

The door to the office opened and Wyatt Hyatt stepped inside, holding his phone in one hand. "Okay, Dillon, I managed to hook up to a meteorological satellite. It's not in geosynchronous orbit, which means it'll pass out of range in a couple of hours but—"

Reynard Hansen burst into the office, gibbering wordlessly and leaped on Wyatt's back, wrapping his legs around Wyatt's waist, and arms around the bigger man's neck and face, blinding him.

"What the hell?! Is that REYNARD?! Have you gone insane? Get OFF of me!" Wyatt shouted. He spun around in a circle, arms waving. "Dillon, get him OFF!"

"K-K-K-K-K-K-K-!" Reynard squawked.

Perkins looked as if he didn't know whether to burst out laughing or throw them all out of his office. Ursula merely stood out of the way, looking quizzically at Dillon. Festus barked at Reynard and Wyatt, trying to do his best to get them to stop.

From the outside, the townspeople, alerted and alarmed by the yelling and shouting, not to mention seeing Reynard run into the gym as if he were being chased by hungry hounds, approached the office.

Pastor Kelly shoved in front of them, got inside the office first and shouted at the townspeople, "Get on back and see to your children! I'll deal with this!" He slammed the door shut, locked it and turned around, bellowing, "What foolishness is going on in here?"

"Soon as I figure it out, I'll let you know," Dillon snarled. He laid hold of Reynard, tried to pry him free from Wyatt's back. "Rey! Let go!"

"K-K-K-K-K-K-K-!" Reynard stammered, eyes rolling wildly. Dillon yanked him free and set him on his feet. Wyatt stumbled clear, coughing as he got air back into his lungs.

"Have you gone completely crazy?" Dillon demanded. "What the hell is wrong with you?"

"K-K-K-K-K-K-K-K-K—" Reynard gestured wildly with his arms, moving them so rapidly that they left behind after images as he pointed in all directions. Behind him, Wyatt mimed various actions: drinking from a bottle. Snorting recreational pharmaceuticals up his nose. Smoking funny cigarettes. Popping pills. Catching Dillon's amused look, Reynard whirled around and caught Wyatt in the act. "Dammit, I ain't drunk and I ain't high! In fact I dropped a whole case of booze when I saw it!"

"Saw what, Rey?" Dillon asked.

"KRAMPUS!" Reynard howled.

The room went totally silent for about ten seconds. Dillon broke the silence, stepping in closer and said in a low, darkly serious voice; "Reynard, this is not the time to be playing around. If this is a joke—"

"Look at me, man! Look in my eyes! Do I look like I'm joking or do I look like I'm scared to death?"

Dillon looked deep in Reynard's eyes and then he whirled around to speak to Mayor Perkins. "He's not kidding. Whatever he saw, it's enough to scare him silly and that means I'm scared as well."

Perkins nodded. "So what do we do? Should we send out men to look for it?"

Dillon shook his head in a negative. "You've got the advantage in that you have what the Krampus wants right in here. Which means it has to come to you. Judging by those pictures on your wall, you're the football coach, right?"

"Correct."

"Which means you probably know this school well, correct?"

"I daresay the only one who knows it better are the custodians and the principal."

"Okay, then you're with me and Ursula. Pick three men to go along with us."

"What for?"

"We're going to go through this entire building from the top to the bottom, and check any and every possible way that the Krampus can get in here. Any weak points we find, we're going to secure."

"I assure you that we've done that already—"

"And I'm sure you did the best job you could. Indulge me, okay?"

"Why don't Rey and I go with you, Dillon?" Wyatt asked.

"Because you're going to be here securing the perimeter. You got extra guns from Big Pig?"

"Sure did."

"Give them to men and women who know how to use weapons. You two organize and supervise. I want this entire floor secure by the time I get back."

"I'd like a gun, please," Ursula said.

Dillon sized her up before asking, "You know how to use one?"

"Does eight years in the Army Reserve qualify?"

Dillon turned to Wyatt, jerked his thumb over his shoulder at Ursula. "Let her look over what we've got and pick out what she wants."

"What do you want me to do?" Pastor Kelly asked.

"Go out there and keep your people calm and quiet. And do a sweep of this floor. Bathrooms and kitchens. Get everyone not on guard duty back in this gym and keep them here. Okay, people. You're on my clock now. Go to work."

***

Dillon had to admit he was impressed with the way the building had been secured. The doors were all metal and equipped with heavy, solid bolts. The windows had steel shutters over them and were padlocked shut. The windows in the gym had bars on the outside and while Dillon wasn't entire happy with that, it would have to do.

Dillon stood just outside Mayor Perkins' office, chewing thoughtfully on a thin black unlit cigar in his mouth, arms folded across his chest. Festus sat next to him, looking around with great interest. Ursula joined him, a H&K UMP45 hanging on a strap looped over her shoulder, bumping gently on her hip. Dillon nodded with approval. "Happy now?"

"Very. You really think that the Krampus is going to come in here after the children?"

"You tell me. You're the expert. All I know about the thing is that it snatches kids, right? Well, we've got all the kids in here. You do the math."

Ursula nodded. She cocked her head to the side, half-smiling. "So exactly what is the deal with you and your friends? You drive around in a vehicle armored like a tank and carry around enough weaponry to fight a war. And your friends treat you like…well, like…this is going to sound silly… but they defer to you almost as if you were royalty. A prince or something."

Dillon chuckled around his unlit cigar. "Trust me when I say that I'm far from royalty."

"Then who are you?"

"Just a guy who hires out for pay and does jobs for people they can't do themselves, that's all. No more, no less. I go here. I go there. I go anywhere I'm asked to. People pay me a lot to help them solve their problems. Or sometimes I do it for free."

"Like now?"

"Like now."

"But why?"

Dillon turned and looked at her, copper eyes twinkling. "Because it's Christmas Eve, that's why."

Mayor Perkins came out of his office, followed by Pastor Kelly. The two of them had sequestered themselves in there for a private meeting and Dillon could guess at what the subject of that meeting had been. Perkins walked up to Dillon and said in a no nonsense tone of voice, "I don't appreciate the way you're taking over. This is my town. I'm mayor here. Any and all orders that need to be given will be given by me."

"Amen," Pastor Kelly boomed.

Dillon regarded him with amusement. He took the cigar from his mouth and used the end that had been in his mouth as a pointer he gestured at the pastor. "Bet it was you who put the steel in his spine to say that, wasn't it?" he said with a lopsided grin.

"I have no idea what you're talking about."

"Sure you do. There's something hinky about the both of you and about this whole setup. And like I said before, if one of my friends and that includes my new one—" Dillon nodded in Ursula's direction, "gets hurt because of anything you two are holding back, the both of you are going to wish you'd never laid eyes on me. And that's my gospel." Dillon replaced his cigar in his mouth.

Pastor Kelly angrily took a step forward, and that's when all the lights went out.

Screams, curses and cries of terror echoed around the gym. Dillon's clear, controlling voice cut through the din. "Stay where you are! EVERY-BODY! Stop MOVING!" Dillon reached to his Steranko belt. Made of ballistic nylon and leather, the belt was distinguished by the number of snap shut pouches of various sizes. Dillon carried a variety of devices, in those pouches, he found extremely helpful in his work—especially the powerful flashlight he now employed. Upon seeing light, the townspeople calmed down considerably. "Okay, now everybody just be cool. You've got portable battery powered lanterns here. Turn them on and stay together."

Reynard and Wyatt joined Dillon and Ursula. "You think that thing is smart enough to monkey around with the power?" Reynard asked.

"Sure seems that way, doesn't it?" Dillon replied. To Perkins he said, "Where's the main power switches?"

"Downstairs in the basement."

"Take two men and go check it out. Reynard, you go with them." Dillon headed for the doors leading out to the parking lot. Festus trotted at his heels.

"Where are you going?" Wyatt called after him.

"To Big Pig to get some hand lanterns. If Reynard can't get the power back on we'll need them."

"I'll go with you," Wyatt said, started walking with Dillon.

"No, you stay here and keep an eye on things. I need a cool head to keep them quiet." Dillon gestured at the townspeople.

Wyatt turned to Ursula. "You go with him. Watch his back."

Dillon started to protest, "Wyatt, I'm just going to the truck and back. I—"

"Either she goes or I go. You're not going out there by yourself. And I will not entertain any debate about it. Which is it going to be? Her or me?"

Dillon sighed. "C'mon, Ursula."

She fell into step with him as they walked to the doors. "I think it's sweet how he looks out for you."

"Wyatt's the youngest out of the three of us, but he's got this way sometimes of making Reynard and I feel like we're children and he's the adult. Problem is that when he puts his foot down like he did just now, he's always right. I wouldn't let him or anybody else go outside by himself and he was right to call me on it. Damn him." But the smile on his face and in his voice let Ursula know he didn't mean it. "And it makes sense to take along a pair of extra hands. This way I only have to make—"

Dillon opened the door and for one of the few times in his recent life he was taken totally by surprise. The Krampus stood just outside the door, eyes glaring with orange fury, his tongue lashing about like a whip. Massive, apish hands with clawed fingers at the end of long arms nearly touched the ground. It stood on wide, cracked cloven hooves that steamed and smoked.

The Krampus howled and a long arm went up and out. Dillon took that huge fist right in his chest. He flew backwards through the air to land on the ground some twenty feet away, the air totally knocked out of him. Festus yelped and scrambled out of the way as the Krampus stomped inside the gym, his howls turning into ugly laughter.

Ursula brought up the H&K and fired a short burst right into the face of the Krampus. Bullets shredded the already hideous visage. Instead of red blood spurting out, a thick goo the color of pus oozed out. Ursula put another burst in the thing's chest. She saw the bullets go into the heavy black fur matting the Krampus' chest but she had no idea if the actually pierced the flesh.

And then she saw stars as the Krampus swung its left arm, knocking her to the ground. the Krampus stepped into the gym on its smoking hooves and bellowed its defiance to all.

The townspeople screamed and scattered in all directions. Those with children snatched them up or dragged them after as they sought to escape from the gym. The floor shook from the thunderous impact of hooves as the Krampus waded into the hysterical mob and plucked a squealing child from the arms of her mother and popped the child into a large sack secured to the monster's waist by a chain. Festus ran around and around the monster's legs, barking for all he was worth.

Wyatt Hyatt leaped on the Krampus' back, wrapping one thickly muscled arm around the furry neck of the creature. Wyatt threw himself backwards and actually got the Krampus off balance. The Krampus yowled in frustration, its long arms reaching around and over its own shoulders to seize Wyatt. The Krampus yanked Wyatt off its back and threw him away as if he were trash. Wyatt hit a wall and collapsed to the floor, coughing and hacking.

Dillon got to one knee and carefully aimed his Jericho. He fired one shot.

The Krampus' head jerked to one side as the .40 S&W bullet slammed into it. Dillon clearly saw goo fly out of the other side of that misshapen head. The Krampus dropped to its knees, mooing softly. Dillon fired again at the Krampus and again caught it in the head. The Krampus toppled over on its side with a massive crash.

Festus stood a safe distance away, still barking. Dillon ran over to where Wyatt lay and helped him up. "You okay?" Dillon asked. "Anything broken?"

"Just my pride that I got my ass kicked so quickly," Wyatt replied. "Is it dead?"

"I sincerely hope so. Festus! Hush that noise and come away from that thing!"

Festus did so reluctantly, growling over his shoulder at the Krampus as he trotted to Dillon. Ursula also joined them. She seemed incapable of taking her eyes off the thing. She said in a small voice; "It's still holding onto the bag."

Indeed. Still clutched in one grotesquely clawed paw was the sack the Krampus had been stuffing children in. The bag bulged from the kicking of the children inside and they could hear muffled screams of terror.

"Ursula and I will keep him covered. Wyatt, get the bag." Dillon gestured with his gun, indicating the direction Ursula should take to approach the thing. Most of the townspeople had regained some sort of composure and were also inching closer to the downed Krampus. The mothers of the children in the bag were in hysterics, fighting with the men holding them back.

Festus crept close to one of the still smoking hooves, sniffed suspiciously at it. He let out with a growl and looked over at Dillon as if to say, "Be careful. I don't like how this smells."

Wyatt circled around the head and the ram's head horns making his way to the thrashing bag. He reached out one hand, his intention to try and wrest the bag free and let the children out.

With a thunderous howl, the Krampus bounded back upright on its hooves, throwing its arms wide, sending Dillon, Ursula, Wyatt and Festus flying. Those townspeople armed with guns opened fire on the Krampus, the crashing din of the shots drowning out the screaming pleas of the mothers that they stop firing lest they hit the squirming bag with the children. They were ignored. Panic took over the gym.

Reynard and Mayor Perkins entered the gym along with the two men that had went along with them to check out the power situation. "I leave for five lousy minutes and everything goes to shit," Reynard groused. Hearing the two men at his side cocking their weapons, he reached out an arm to knocked their rifle barrels down. "Don't! We've got more than enough idiots firing wild already! Just stand here and wait!"

The Krampus resumed its mission, snatching up children and tossing them into the sack. Any adults trying to hang onto their children were flicked off with no trouble at all and the child popped into the bag to join the others. The Krampus ignored the bullets smacking into its furry hide. It opened the bag and Dillon could see its lips moving as if counting silently to itself. The Krampus nodded as if satisfied and stomped towards the door, casually tossing the sack over one shoulder. Then the Krampus slipped into the chill night, and disappeared into the pressing darkness.

Reynard ran over to where Dillon, Ursula and Wyatt stood. "I guess our side didn't do so good, huh?"

Dillon replaced his Jericho in the holster. "What do you think?"

"What's our next move?" Wyatt wanted to know.

"Get your coats on. Wyatt, get us goggles from Big Pig. Check your weapons, make sure you've got plenty of ammo. We're going hunting."

"You think we can track that thing through all that snow out there?"

Dillon looked down at Festus. "Think you can find him, Festus?"

Festus barked back that he could.

Several of the townsmen stepped forward. One of them said "We're going with you."

"No, you're not. We've got to move fast and quick and we don't need to be dragging a mob after us. Stay here and take care of the rest of your kids."

"We're going along," Pastor Kelly said. Mayor Perkins stood at his side, nodding in agreement.

"Somehow I thought you might," Dillon replied. "be ready to move out in five minutes or you'll be left behind."

5.

The snow came down slow, thick and quiet. If it hadn't been for the serious work that was ahead, it would have been serene. It was the kind of snow that should be coming down on Christmas Eve. The kind of snow that made one think of peace on Earth and goodwill to all men.

Dillon climbed out of Big Pig. He had gone inside to grab himself a Remington 870 Modular Combat Shotgun. Reynard and Wyatt also now had shotguns. Ursula stayed with the H&K but also had a .44 Magnum revolver holstered at her waist.

"Man, you shot that thing twice in the head and it still got up and walked away. Not to mention I don't know how many rounds it took from everybody else blastin' away at it. You really think more firepower is gonna do any good?" Reynard asked.

"No. But I don't have any RPGs or tactical nukes in the truck so we're gonna have to make good with what we've got."

"Where's our guns?" Perkins demanded.

"You don't get any," Dillon said flatly. "I'm not sure I trust either one of you behind me with a gun in your hands."

"You don't expect us to go after that thing without being able to defend ourselves!"

"I don't expect a thing from you except that you stay out of my way. Now, you can come with us or stay here. It makes no difference to me which." Dillon turned his back on them and knelt down to the eager Festus. "You ready, boy?"

Festus barked that, "yes, he was more than ready and that they should get going."

"Okay! Go find it!"

Festus barked once more in conformation and lowered his head, sniffing loudly, his small head going back and forth.

Kelly snorted. "This is such nonsense. You can't honestly expect that silly little puppy—" he stopped, his mouth having suddenly gone dry due to the glaring molten gold look Dillon gave him.

"Don't you bad mouth my dog. Understand?"

Kelly gulped. "Ah…yes…certainly."

Festus barked for attention and started off, nose to the snow as he trotted into the middle of the street and headed north. Dillon, Reynard, Wyatt and Ursula followed. Perkins and Kelly looked at each other for a few seconds before following.

The buildings on either side were just shadowy outlines. The snow continued to come down in big fluffy flakes. The wind was practically non-existent and the only sounds that could be heard was the crunching of their boots on the snow underfoot, and the snuffling of Festus as he followed the trail. The only light they had were the tactical flashlights on their weapons

Dillon felt a wave of déjà vu as he recalled last year's Christmas Eve when he had walked through a similar snowfall on his way to an equally uncertain fate. He felt that same sense of unreality now that he had felt then. It was as if the snow were some kind of portal from one world to another—a white limbo bridging the gap between one realm of existence to the next. Dillon shrugged off that feeling. It would do nothing except distract him at this critical moment and distracted was the last thing he needed to be. He had enemies before him and behind him. And the lives of helpless children depended on him. But this time there was a difference. Dillon turned his head to look his his friends close beside him. Last Christmas he considered himself lost and alone. But he would never feel that way again. Not while he had such good friends in his life.

"You okay?" Reynard asked. "You got a goofy look on your face like you just ate a whole cheesecake."

"Fine. Just thinking."

Reynard grunted but said nothing.

They continued on through the middle of town, walking down the center of the street. Festus followed the trail, stopping every so often to look over his shoulder as if making sure the others were still with him. He then resumed his hunt, head down, intent on following the trail.

A huge square building gradually came into view through the thick flakes. Festus stopped and growled at the building. "Looks like we're here." He turned to Kelly and Perkins. "What's that up ahead?"

"Just a building used for storing old machinery and such. It's sort of a community storage," Kelly said.

"Well, Festus says that the Krampus is in there."

"I'll keep my own counsel as to what I think of your dog's ability to successfully track anything."

Dillon grunted. He turned to Reynard, Wyatt and Ursula. "Ursula, you stay with me. We're going to go right in through the front. Reynard, Wyatt…you make your way to the back, find another way in."

Reynard gestured at the pastor and the mayor. "What about Frick and Frack?"

"They'll stay with me. I'll feel better with them close by where I can keep an eye on them."

Reynard nodded. He nudged Wyatt in the ribs, "C'mon, poindexter."

"Be careful," Wyatt threw over his shoulder before jogging after Reynard. They were soon lost in the the falling snow.

Dillon said to Ursula, "Stay close. When we're inside, watch for my hand signals." He turned to Kelly and Perkins. "Hang back a bit. If the

Krampus gets us, I suggest you get back to the gym."

The sliding metal door pushed back with a tortured screech. Dillon went inside, going to the left while Ursula went to the right. Festus stayed at Dillon's side, eyes wide and bright. As Kelly had said the spacious interior of the building contained old machinery that looked as if it had just been put here and forgotten. Judging from the dirt on them, nobody had attempted to do anything with these machines in years. Old crates were stacked in a corner. In another corner battered furniture had been stacked as high as the ceiling.

But from another corner, an eerie rosy glow emanated, throwing radiance into the room. From the rear of the building, Dillon heard a low whistle. In reply he said, "Come on in, Reynard. Looks like there's nothing in here. But we've still got something."

Reynard and Wyatt joined Dillon and the others. They looked down upon a rude staircase descending through the concrete of the floor. The rosy glow originated deep below the building.

Out of the corner of his eye, Dillon caught a swift, startled look shared between Kelly and Perkins. He ignored it. He had a feeling that whatever was wrong in this town would be shortly be revealed.

Festus stood at the head of the stairs, sniffing. He turned to look at Dillon as if to say he didn't like what he was smelling one little bit.

"Something tells me we're going down there," Wyatt said, taking off his gloves and stuffing them into the pockets of his jacket. He took back his shotgun from Reynard and held his weapons while Reynard did likewise.

"Indeed we are. Let's go." Dillon brought up the barrel of of shogun, leveled it on Kelly and Perkins. "But this time I think you gentlemen should take the point."

"But we have no weapons!" Kelly protested.

"You've got more than enough guns at your back. Let's go. Time's a'wastin'"

Kelly squared his shoulders and looked Dillon definitely right in his eyes. "We refuse!"

Dillon smiled that Cheshire Cat grin of his but this time it was not one of mirth or amusement. "You sure you want to pick this moment to make a stand?"

"You'd shoot a man of the cloth?"

"No. I'd shoot you. Somehow I get the impression you haven't been a man of the cloth for some time now." Dillon's voice turned ugly. "Move. Now."

Perkins and Kelly went first down the rough hewn flight of stairs. "This wasn't here," Perkins said in a shaky, small voice. "I regularly inspect this storehouse every three or four months and this wasn't here back in September. I'm sure of it."

Dillon said nothing. He was right behind the mayor and the pastor. Festus followed him, then Ursula, Wyatt and Reynard brought up the rear.

They descended to the bottom of the staircase which opened into a ragged, circular tunnel stretching before them. They all heard faint sounds that none of them could identify. Festus growled.

"Hush," Dillon said. Festus subsided. But the angry look on his face stayed. To the others he said, "Okay, let's go. Pastor, Mayor.. you've been doing a swell job leading so far. Keep it up." Dillon gestured with his shotgun and the two men went on ahead. Illuminated by the glow ahead of them and their tactical flashlights, the group made their way through the long tunnel which looked to Dillon's eye as if it had been hewed out of solid rock. Certainly no professional digging apparatus had been used to dig this tunnel and it was not natural, either. He'd done his share of caving in Africa and Asia and knew natural caves from man-made ones.

And then the tunnel abruptly came to an end and the group looked down on a scene that most certainly was the last one they'd expected to find.

The tunnel opened up into an enormous cavern that was the central hub for a number of tunnels going off in all directions. A crude rail system linked the tunnels together. The cavern was the heart of a mine and the sounds they had been hearing were pickaxes and shoves at work excavating precious yellow metal from the earth. It was Ursula that spoke first; "The children! It's the children!"

Indeed, the children of Reynolds take had been taken for the past two years worked the mine. Dressed in ragged clothing, their faces drawn and haggard with exhaustion, they pushed iron carts filled with yellow metal and worked at digging it out and one look at the faces of Kelly and Perkins told Dillon what that yellow metal was.

"Gold. That's what this is all about, isn't it? Gold. That's what those kids are digging out for you! You knew about this all along!"

"No! No! Wait! I can explain—" Perkins began. But his explanation was cut off by Kelly leaping forward to wrap a powerful arm around Perkins' neck. Kelly produced a .45 automatic that he pointed at Ursula.

"Drop your weapons or the woman gets it!" he shouted. His response was the cocking of weapons as Dillon, Wyatt, Reynard and Ursula aimed theirs right at Kelly and Perkins.

"Can't you count, stupid?" Dillon asked. "If anybody is dropping their weapon, it's you."

Kelly pressed the barrel of the gun to Perkins' head. "Then I'll kill him! Drop your weapons, I said!"

Dillon sighed. "He's your partner, you blockhead. What do we care if you kill him?"

Kelly looked at the determined faces and at the firepower pointed at him. Disgusted, he threw down his gun. "Can't blame a guy for trying."

"See, the problem is that people see that work on TV and the movies and think that's they way it's supposed to go down. It's not."

"What would you have done?" Perkins snapped, glaring at Kelly while rubbing his bruised neck. "Shot right through me?"

"Without a bit of hesitation. Now, what's the deal here with—"

The Krampus appeared seemingly out of nowhere. So intent had Dillon and the others been on Kelly that no one had seen the Krampus scrambling up a sheer rock wall to reach them, and now it was too late. The Krampus lashed out with a solid backhand, catching Dillon in the side and throwing him into Wyatt and Reynard. All three men hit the ground hard.

Ursula fired her H&K in short, tight bursts but for all the good it did she might well have been throwing popcorn at the Krampus. It slapped her silly, spinning her around completely from the force of the slap. She hit the ground still spinning.

Festus barked like mad and the Krampus ignored the puppy as it reached out massive hands to lay hold of Perkins and Kelly. Then with one prodigious leap, it sprang off the ledge and down the rock face to land at the bottom, some sixty feet down on those smoking hooves. It ran across the floor of the cavern, children screaming as they scampered to get out of the creature's way. It held the two struggling men under its arms as easily as if they themselves were children.

"Come on!" Dillon yelled. "After it!" He reached down for Festus, tucked him inside his jacket and zipped it up to secure the puppy inside. "You be still, now," he ordered. Slinging his shotgun over his shoulders he started climbing down the rock face. Reynard and Wyatt helped Ursula to her feet and they also started to descend. Dillon reached the bottom first and was immediately mobbed by a solid wall of screaming, crying children.

"I wanna go HOME!"

"I want my mommy! I want my mommy!"

"Mister, mister! You got any food?"

"I need a bath!"

"This place SUCKS!"

Dillon gently struggled free of the children, yelling over his shoulder, "Wyatt! Reynard! Get those kids up to the tunnel best way you can! I'm going after the Krampus!"

"Not without me!" Ursula yelled, pushing her way through the distraught children and running after Dillon. Festus bounded out of Dillon's jacket and led the way, barking loud enough for a dog three times his size.

The Krampus, despite its size, could run with the swiftness of a second story man caught in the act. It ran into another tunnel, hooves striking sparks on the rocks underneath as it plunged into thick shadow. Festus, Dillon and Ursula remained hot on its heels. They came to another, smaller cavern filled with a golden glow so intense that it actually seemed to warm the room. It came from gold.

Gold in pebbles, chunks, slabs, and boulders was heaped in a pile in the center of the room which had to be at least eight feet high. Dillon and Ursula were stunned at the sight of so much gold amassed in one place. Dillon let out with a long, low whistle. Even Festus fell silent.

The Krampus dumped Kelly and Perkins on the ground and stomped over to where a stooped woman ceased her task of emptying an iron cart. Her legs were swaddled in dirty rags in lieu of proper footwear and the parka she wore looked and smelled as if she did everything while wearing it. Tied around one side of her head was a faded red bandanna. The Krampus uttered a low mooing and pointed at Perkins and Kelly.

The woman hit the Krampus in the stomach. "Fool! Oaf! Thoughtless ox! Why bring them here?"

Dillon lifted his shotgun, aimed it at the woman. "When you get a minute, would you care to explain what's going on here?"

"Just shoot her!" Kelly yelled, scrambling to his feet. "Obviously she's in league with this monster and has kidnapped the children! Shoot her!"

"If I'm going to shoot anybody, it'll be you. Now shut up and stand still. What's the deal here, lady?"

The woman cackled. "Deal? Deal? You want to know the deal? I'll tell you the deal! These crawling worms that call themselves men robbed me of the only thing I cared about in my life and so I'm robbing them of the only thing they care about!"

"The gold?" Ursula asked in wonderment. "Is that what this has been all about?"

"Yes, yes!" the woman shrieked. "The good mayor and pastor discovered the gold mine under the town three years ago! They got the townspeople in on a scheme to dig up the gold and keep it for themselves so that they wouldn't have to share it with the mining company!"

Dillon nodded. "Oh, I get it. The mining company has the rights to mine in this region. If you informed them the gold was here, they'd have a right to claim a share."

"They have no right to anything!" Perkins yelled. "The gold is under our town! Why should they be entitled to it?"

"The children!" Ursula exclaimed. "The children weren't kidnapped! You used them to dig out the gold!"

Kelly nodded in resignation. "Everything was fine until—"

"Until my boy was crushed and killed!" the woman shrieked. "My sweet little Lester! He died in this filthy hole like an animal! And it's their fault!" She pointed a shaking finger at Kelly and Perkins.

"And so you started kidnapping the children every Christmas Eve with the help of the Krampus. But how could you keep them here?"

The woman threw out her arm wide to indicate the Krampus standing at her side, glowering at all the humans as if he would like nothing better than to kill all of them. " The Krampus is my servant! He does my bidding thanks to this!" The woman tore away the bandanna to reveal that her left eye was gone. In its place, a glittering red gem had been inserted into the socket. Scar tissue held it in place. "This gem, passed down in my family for generations! From mother to daughter, from aunt to niece! Always in the hands of a woman who knew what to do with it. And yes, even the Krampus must obey its power!"

"Mrs. Camden, we told you that we'd give you an extra share of the gold—" Perkins began but was cut off by the wild shrieking of the woman.

"What good would gold do me when you have robbed me of my very flesh! And I have robbed the town of its children just as you have robbed me of mine! And here they will stay! But as for you—Krampus! Kill them!"

The Krampus roared in assent and rushed upon the humans, long arms outstretched. Dillon fired his shotgun and the Krampus halted as if startled more than anything else. Dillon continued firing, advancing on the Krampus, the impact of the shotgun blasts making the Krampus stumble backwards. "Get those two idiots out of here, Ursula! I'll hold it back!"

Ursula ignored Dillon's command and instead ran directly at Mrs. Camden, ducking under the swipe of one of the arms of the Krampus. Dillon uttered a curse under his breath and continued firing at the Krampus. It toppled over on its back, legs and arms flailing.

Dillon dug in his pocket for fresh shells to reload the shotgun but he was tackled from the side by Perkins and Kelly. Kelly vicious kicked him in the head, and ripped the shotgun from his hand while Perkins grabbed hold of his Jericho.

Kelly pointed the weapon at Dillon. "Not so much of a badass without a gun, are you? Now get up and-yowtch!" Kelly's scream came from the pain in his right bicep which appeared to have grown a six inch long kunai throwing knife.

Dillon, who had accurately thrown the knife while in a prone position and half-dazed, had another one in his hand, ready for Perkins. He didn't need it. Perkins dropped the Jericho, screaming, "I give up! I give up!"

Ursula leaped upon Mrs. Camden and the two women rolled around on the rough-hewn ground, kicking up clouds of gold dust as they did so. Mrs. Camden snapped at Ursula's neck as if she were a mad dog. Ursula looped a short right jab at her jaw.

The Krampus lurched upright on its hooves as if pulled there by invisible cables. It took several steps and reached down a hand to lay hold of Dillon by an arm and a leg. It raised him over its head, the intention plain; it intended to pull Dillon apart like a chicken wing.

Festus growled, ran and leaped. He chomped down as hard as he could on the left leg of the Krampus, just above the hoof. It was enough. The Krampus screamed like a woman, dropping Dillon. The fiend lifted the leg, shaking it furiously. Festus held on for all he was worth, biting down even harder.

Dillon hit the ground, rolled over to where Perkins had dropped his Jericho and from his lying down position placed four shots in the middle of that wide, hairy chest. The Krampus grunted, rocked back on his heels by the impact of the bullets. It continued to try and shake the tenacious Festus off its leg.

Ursula delivered another jab to Mrs. Camden's jaw and muttered, "My deepest apologies." She reached down with two fingers and deftly plucked the jewel out of the pit of scar tissue it nested in. Mrs. Camden screamed. More in fright than pain. And soon, Dillon and Ursula knew why she screamed in such terror.

As soon as Ursula fell away, the gleaming crimson jewel in her hand, the Krampus' head whipped around so quickly Dillon could have sworn it make a sound like a whip cracking. That ugly face broke into a smile, overlapping teeth dripping foul smelling saliva as the Krampus finally shook Festus free with one final side thrust of the leg. Festus yelped as he sailed through the air to be caught by Dillon, who rolled under the puppy in time to safely catch him.

"Hiya, pal," Dillon said, holding the puppy close to his chest. Festus licked Dillon's nose in response.

The Krampus reached into thin air and snatched his sack out of seemingly nowhere. It shook the sack open and with his free hand reached for

Mrs. Camden. "No! No! Noooooooo!" she hollered at a shrill, eardrum busting pitch. The Krampus ignored her, grabbed her by the head and threw her into the sack.

It then turned to the shaking and shivering Kelly and Perkins, both of who were too numb with fright to move. The Krampus stomped over to where they stood and reached out a clawed hand. First Perkins and then Kelly went into the sack. Dillon could hear the three of them in there, yelling and cursing at each other. The Krampus slung the sack over his shoulder, looked directly at Dillon and gave out with a final roar.

And then it was simply gone. The only evidence that it had ever been there at all were the smoking hoof prints that it left behind.

Ursula joined Dillon and Festus, dropping to her knees next to them. "Well, I must say that didn't work out quite as I expected."

"What did you think was going to happen?" Dillon asked with a tired grin.

"I had no idea at all. I just figured that the Krampus wouldn't be under the control of that woman and be easier to deal with. Where do you think the Krampus took them?"

Dillon shrugged. "I have no idea. You're supposed to be the expert. Where does the Krampus take the bad little boys and girls who misbehave?"

6.

"Merry Christmas, everybody!" Dillon shouted, raising his bottle of Bollinger to clink with identical bottles in the hands of Reynard, Wyatt and Ursula. Dillon poured some in a bowl for Festus before joining them in a long drink from their bottles.

After returning the children to their parents in the gym and informing the good townspeople that they should elect a new mayor and put an ad in the paper for a new pastor, the five of them had retired to the Empire Café for a champagne breakfast. So far there had been more champagne than breakfast.

"Sun's comin' up," Reynard noted. "One hell of a Christmas Eve, I'll tell you that."

"You should have seen my last one," Dillon said, taking another swig from his bottle.

"One thing still bothers me," Ursula said. "The townspeople were surely all in on this. They must have known their children were being held captive by that horrid woman and her pet Krampus. And they did nothing at all. I hate the thought of them profiting from that gold. Aren't they just going to dig it up themselves now?"

"Oh. That reminds me." Dillon took out a silver cylinder from a pocket of his jacket hanging on the back of his chair. He flipped open the top to expose a red button. He pressed it with his thumb. All five of them felt a slight vibration under their feet and dimly heard what sounded like a muffled explosion. "Remember after I dropped you guys off here I said I had something to do? I went back to the mine and dropped a couple pounds of C4 into the mine. If they want it, they're going to have to work awfully hard for it."

"And even then they'll be working for nothing," Wyatt said. "Seeing as how I've sent off an anonymous email complete with video attached to the proper authorities. I think that the good people of Reynolds will soon have a lot more to worry about than digging up gold."

"I'd say that means our work here is done," Dillon said, standing up and reaching for his jacket. "C'mon, guys, we've got a long road ahead of us."

"Are you going to be okay to drive?" Ursula asked. "You've had quite a long night."

"You'd be surprised at how many nights I've gone without sleep. I'll be good, don't worry. I'll sleep while I drive."

"Say what?" Ursula looked startled.

"Nevermind." Dillon shrugged into his jacket and helped Ursula on with her coat. "I'm just sorry that we couldn't get you any answers about the Krampus or where it took your cousin."

"I still have this." Ursula opened her hand to show the crimson jewel in her palm. "I've got some friends who may be able to tell me more about this gem and its properties and that may lead me to the Krampus that took my cousin."

"Yo. Throw me me keys so I can warm up Big Pig, man." Reynard said. Dillon tossed them to him and Reynard left the cafe with Wyatt.

"What do you mean by that?" Dillon asked. "You sound like you're trying to say that was a different Krampus we fought tonight."

"It was. Oh, it was similar in a lot of ways to the Krampus that took Tessa. But the one we fought tonight was bigger and had different horns. And my Krampus didn't leave smoking hoof prints."

"Wait just a rock pickin' minute. Are you actually trying to tell me that there's more than one Krampus?"

Ursula shrugged. "What can I say? The Krampus that I saw the night he took my cousin Tessa was definitely not the Krampus we fought last night. Related, yes. The same, no."

"What would you call more than one Krampus? Krampuses? Krampi?"

The discussion was interrupted by Reynard's bellowing; "Let's see some hustle, people!"

Dillon and Ursula ran outside. Reynard and Wyatt both had binoculars and both were looking at a snow cloud on the road they had used to come into town—a fast moving snow cloud. There were undoubtedly vehicles on the road, coming this way at top speed. Dillon took Reynard's binoculars and looked for himself.

Half a dozen Blizzard armored combat vehicles were heading right for Reynolds and would be entering the town in less than ten minutes. Dillon lowered his binoculars. "Gotta go," he gulped.

"See! See! I tolja those guys we dropped in the lake had friends!" Reynard scrambled into Big Pig, Festus beating him to it by leaping onto his back and from there, springing inside the cab. Wyatt placed his big hands on Reynard's butt and shoved him up and in. He then hauled his own big body inside.

Dillon turned to Ursula. "Sorry that we have to run out on you—" she was gone. She was also hauling herself up into Big Pig. Dillon ran over to the truck and yelled up into the cab, "Where the hell do you think you're going?"

"Well, you can't very well can't leave me here in this town after all that's happened, now can you?"

"Ursula, there's a whole lot of guys with a whole lot of guns heading our way looking to kill us!"

"And you're wasting time. Let's go!"

Dillon clambered up into the cab of Big Pig and slammed the door shut. He reached for the gearshift and was interrupted by Ursula turning his head in her direction so that she could place a quick, soft kiss on his lips.

"Merry Christmas, Dillon, " she whispered, smiling rather mischievously.

Dillon grinned back, got the huge truck in gear and soon Big Pig roared down the main street of the town of Reynolds, kicking up a respectable snow cloud of its own as it sped out of town.

About Derrick Ferguson:

Derrick Ferguson is a Brooklyn, New York Native who is infamous for his Better in the Dark movie Podcasts with co-host Thomas Deja, and as the creator of the global instigator known to many as Dillon.

Books by Derrick Ferguson:

Dillon and the Voice of Odin
Dillon and the Golden Bell
Four Bullets for Dillon
Dillon and the Pirates of Xonira
Young Dillon in the Halls of Shamballah
The Vril Agenda
Dillon and the Last Rail to Khusra

Other Books from Pulpwork Press:

PulpWork Christmas Special (2011)
PulpWork Christmas Special 2012
PulpWork Christmas Special 2013

Printed in Great Britain
by Amazon.co.uk, Ltd.,
Marston Gate.